I_

the Dress

Fits

Praise for

DAISY JAMES

'One of the finest written romances I have ever read. . .I will certainly be looking out for any future stories by this exceptionally talented author!'
— *Splashes Into Books* on *The Runaway Bridesmaid*

'In *The Runaway Bridesmaid*, Daisy James delivers a stunning debut novel, with beautifully constructed sentences, swift-flowing plotlines, oodles of love and dollops of delights that were masterfully stirred with engaging characters.'
— *The Nest of Books*

'*The Runaway Bridesmaid* is a great novel that any true romantic will love. A woman torn between two men, romance on the cards and mouth-watering food! What more could a girl ask for!'
— *By The Letter Book Reviews*

'Sweet and romantic. . .Just the thing when you want a feel-good read to leave you with a smile on your face.'
— *Portobello Book Blog* on *The Runaway Bridesmaid*

'A lovely easy story to read, perfect for a day curled up on the sofa.'
.— *Fiona's Book Reviews* on *The Runaway Bridesmaid*

'I love the British-ness of this book. . .authentic and fresh.'
— *Random Book Muses* on *The Runaway Bridesmaid*

'As amusing as its delightful cover. . .a warm and witty story.'
— *Shellyback Books* on *The Runaway Bridesmaid*

'The author writes beautiful descriptions. . .and the dialogue sparkles with perfectly judged humour.'
— *Being Anne Reading* on *The Runaway Bridesmaid*

DAISY JAMES

is a Yorkshire girl transplanted to the north-east of England. She loves writing stories with strong heroines and swift-flowing plotlines. She has written two novels, *The Runaway Bridesmaid* and *If the Dress Fits*, both contemporary romances with a dash of humour. When not scribbling away in her peppermint-and-green summerhouse (garden shed), she spends her time sifting flour and sprinkling sugar and edible glitter. She loves gossiping with friends over a glass of something pink and fizzy or indulging in a spot of afternoon tea – china plates and teacups are a must!

Daisy would love to hear from readers via her Facebook page or you can follow her on Twitter @daisyjamesbooks.

Also by

DAISY JAMES

The Runaway Bridesmaid

If
the Dress
Fits

DAISY JAMES

CARINA™

This edition is published by arrangement with Harlequin Books S.A. CARINA is a trademark of Harlequin Enterprises Limited, used under licence.

First Published in Great Britain 2016
By Carina, an imprint of HarperCollins*Publishers*
1 London Bridge Street, London, SE1 9GF

If the Dress Fits © 2016 Daisy James

ISBN 978-0-263-92734-4

98-0716

Our policy is to use papers that are natural, renewable and recyclable products and made from wood grown in sustainable forests.
The logging and manufacturing processes conform to the legal environmental regulations of the country of origin.

Printed and bound by
CPI Group (UK) Ltd, Croydon, CR0 4YY

To Mum and Dad,
for instilling in me a love of reading

PROLOGUE

Twelve years ago

'Do you think I should get my nose pierced, Callie?'

'No way! Your mum would kill you.'

'My mum is not the boss of me.'

'She is when you're fourteen years old and you have
to sit opposite her at the dinner table every night as she
tuts and rolls her eyes at you and generally despairs
about what teenagers call fashionable nowadays. Or
worse, she could bang on about all those infections
people get from body jewellery that she comes across
every day on the wards. Gross.'

'Killjoy. Hey, turn the radio up – I love this song!'

'Boring! Robbie Williams is old enough to be your
dad! What is he, like, forty?'

'Thirty. So what, if he's gorgeous?'

Callie spun from her stomach into a sitting-up
position – no mean feat when she had just finished
painting both her fingernails and toenails in a delectable
shade of fuchsia – and cast her eyes over the posters

plastered across every spare inch of Nessa's bedroom walls. She even had a Robbie Williams pillow, for God's sake. Crushfest or what?

Nessa finished her off-key rendition of 'Millennium' on a high note. With a theatrical swoon, she dropped down from her bed onto the sheepskin rug next to Callie, her bare feet swinging in the air behind her, her chin cupped in her palms as she studied Callie's pencil sketch.

'Wow, that's stunning, Callie. I'm definitely booking you to design my wedding dress.'

'For when you marry Robbie, right?'

'Yep. Look.'

Nessa reached underneath her bed and hauled out a large square box decorated with a collage of wedding scenes she'd cut from sheets of wrapping paper. On the lid, Nessa had glued a glossy photo of her idol.

'So you've relegated Seb to second place, have you?'

'Your cousin is gorgeous, Callie, but, well, this is Robbie Williams we're talking about!'

Callie giggled. These Sunday afternoons at Nessa's house were what she looked forward to all week. They'd established a routine whereby each week they'd add something new to their wedding scrap boxes. This week it was veils and headpieces and that morning she'd found a heavenly tiara in one of the Sunday supplements. She passed the cutting over for Nessa's valued opinion.

'What do you think?'

'Exquisite taste as usual, Callie-Louise, fashion designer to the stars. And I see Theo is still in residence.' Nessa pointed to the picture sellotaped to the lid of Callie's own wedding scrap box. 'There are loads of other guys to choose from, you know.'

'But I'm dating Theo. And I'm going to marry him!'

'No one meets their soulmate when they're fourteen, Callie.'

'I've known Theo since I was ten, Nessa. He's been Seb's best friend and partner in crime since the day they liberated Gordon the gerbil from his home in Miss Porter's reception class.'

'But you've got to spread your wings, try a few more before you buy.'

Callie tossed a fluffy cushion at her best friend. 'Hey, stop dissing my boyfriend. Anyhow, you're just jealous!'

'You got me there. It's true – he's hot!'

Nessa collected her imaginary microphone, flung her auburn curls over her shoulder, and struck a pose on top of her duvet, her recently applied emerald nail polish glittering in the afternoon light that bleached through her bedroom window.

Listen up, all you music fans out there! Mr Theo Dalton Drake, seventeen-year-old heartthrob and lead singer in up-and-coming teenage rock band The Razorclaws, is taken! Yes, you heard right! The hunk with hair the colour of sand washed in warm summer sunshine, the cutest chin this side of Leeds and a body to die for has fallen for his childhood sweetheart, Callie-Louise Henshaw.

'When asked to comment, Miss Henshaw clasped her chest and informed the braying paparazzi, Oh, my, I just knew we were destined to be together when – aged only ten – our eyes met across the headteacher's office after we'd been found snogging in the bushes. Stay tuned, peeps, for details of our helpline number!'

Callie rolled her eyes at her BFF, but her smile was as wide as an actress's in a toothpaste commercial.

CHAPTER ONE

'Callie? Earth to Callie?' smirked Flora, dragging a gargantuan cardboard wardrobe into the design studio, a bangle of brown tape around her wrist and a coffee cup balanced precariously in her hand. 'Are we ready to pack this glitzy creation of silk and pearls into its protective shell? The courier will be here any minute and you know what they're like – won't be kept waiting for anything. You don't want to miss the deadline, do you? Can I help?'

'No!' Callie raised her head from where she had been snoozing at her desk. An unpleasant waft of stale pizza assaulted her nostrils and a crumpled Post-it had attached itself to her cheek. She held up her palm to Flora's face. 'Step away from the dress! I mean it, Flora. If you even come one step closer with that skinny latte, I'll be forced to shoot you with my staple gun. What's possessed you to bring coffee in here, anyway?'

Her response sounded like the snap of an irate dragon, a mother protecting its young, and so it was to

Callie. The gestation of the Callie-Louise entry into the wedding gown competition of the decade had been a full nine months and was now, save for a few final tweaks, ready for its delivery into the outside world – well, to the Audley Suite at The Dorchester, where the judging would take place the next day.

'Sorry, Flora, don't take any notice of me. I'm just exhausted. Thanks, though. Only these last few seed pearls and I'm done. But you could do me a huge favour by asking Scarlet to come down here?'

'Sure.' Flora meandered from the room, humming to herself. She was not the sharpest pair of scissors in a tailor's armoury, but her sweet temperament and her willingness to skip down the street for their regular infusions of espresso, latte and cappuccino made her a popular and essential member of the Callie-Louise Bridal Couture team.

Callie rethreaded her needle, knelt down at the hem of the gown and, with her bottom pointing to the ceiling, resumed the intricate task of squinting at the exquisite ivory silk that had formed the backdrop to her dreams for the last six months. The nationwide competition to design the wedding dress the celebrity actress Lilac Verbois would wear for her forthcoming marriage to Finn Marchant at York Minster at the end of July had gripped the country. She hadn't been able to believe it when she'd been informed on the first of January that her design had been shortlisted from over two hundred and fifty entries to be made up as a sample garment. These gowns were to be presented to Lilac, who would make a final decision on the choice of her wedding dress with the assistance of her mother, her PA, Nikki Coates, and her wedding planner, Tish Marshall, at her hotel suite at The Dorchester on the last day of March, when she had a break in her filming schedule. There wasn't an academically trained fashion advisor in sight, so it was anyone's guess who would win.

Callie experienced a flash of excitement. The wedding was being billed as the celebrity event of the year. TV crews and the paparazzi would be out in force at the ceremony. The reception, to be held in a majestic stately home in North Yorkshire, would be attended by every A-lister who could wangle an invitation. The whole wedding had morphed from being just one more movie star marrying a musician into a fairy-tale romance. Lilac and Finn, whether by generosity or insanity, had opened up the celebration of their union to the whole country by creating the competition to design Lilac's wedding gown.

Callie-Louise Bridal Couture was her creation, a project she had worked ferociously and diligently on ever since leaving university three years ago. She understood what an honour it was whenever one of her designs was chosen to become the star attraction at the most important occasion in a girl's life. She had designed wedding gowns for several actresses, even a minor royal, but Lilac and Finn's wedding would be the highlight of her career. She did not intend to let anything scupper the opportunity of a lifetime to showcase her talents to a nationwide, if not international, audience. She intended to seize it with both hands, even if this had meant the exclusion of all life's other demands.

Over the last three months, her world had become a frenzy of late nights, cold pizza and too much coffee. She had existed on snatched naps at her work table. Mannequins heard her complaints, dressmakers' dummies her confessions, but there was nothing new there.

Callie checked her watch. Her initial excitement and anticipation tipped over into nausea and tendrils of fear looped around her flat abdomen. Time was running out. There was only an hour left to apply the final embellishments by hand and she could not depend on Scarlet or Flora to do it to her exacting standards. Once she had attached the final pearls, the gown had to be sealed into the custom-created cardboard wardrobe provided by Lilac's wedding planner and ready for the specially appointed courier to collect at seven o'clock that evening, before completing its fateful journey from conception in their tiny studio in South West London to its debut into the glitzy world of The Dorchester the following morning.

What if something happened to the dress en route? What if it didn't arrive? What if the courier had an accident, or stopped for a beer and overindulged, or had to deliver twins in a roadside café?

She pushed her neurotic vacillations into the crevices of her exhausted mind. Jules Gallieri, the milliner who owned the hat shop round the corner from Callie-Louise Bridal and who created exquisite wedding fascinators and tiaras for her clients, labelled her work ethic as obsessive. It was true. She'd even succumbed to regular nightmares involving Bondesque espionage by her fellow competitors. Lilac's team would not be announcing the winning designer to the general public until her wedding day – if Callie heard nothing, it meant the Callie-Louise design hadn't been selected. And who could blame Lilac for that? The media would have been camped outside the chosen studio for the next four months, hoping for a sneak preview they could splash across their pages, and what bride wanted that?

Callie trusted no one, especially in an industry where integrity fought ignorance and ambition on a daily basis. She had sworn the whole team to absolute secrecy. If even a whiff of the design were made public, the Callie-Louise Couture entry would be disqualified. All her hopes and dreams were pinned on winning this competition, which would catapult Callie-Louise Bridal Couture into the upper echelons of bridal fashion design, the pinnacle of her lifelong ambition and the fulfilment of a promise she had made to her parents when she'd used her inheritance to start her business.

'Take a break, will you, Callie? Flora tells me she found you snoring at your desk!'

Scarlet, as slender as a shop mannequin, lounged against the cutting table. She gazed intently at the deft weaving of the needle as Callie completed the final essential touches whilst she nibbled at the tips of her fingernails, painted the colour her name demanded.

'You know, I still can't grasp the reasoning behind Lilac's crazy scheme. Why splash open your marriage to one of the hunkiest men alive in a nationwide competition to design your wedding gown? I mean, she's one of the most sought-after actresses of her genre – especially since she won that BAFTA for best supporting actress last year. And Finn, well, what I wouldn't do to trade places and get my mitts on those buttocks of steel! *And* they could get hitched anywhere in the world: a yacht moored off the Cote d'Azur, a white-powdered beach in Hawaii; I'm even certain that St Paul's Cathedral would have overlooked the residence requirements. But, oh, no, Lilac Verbois wanted to get married in Yorkshire. Nothing wrong with Yorkshire per se and York Minster is the most gorgeous venue for the ceremony. But, well, you know… Yorkshire?' Scarlet wrinkled her pert, freckled nose as she twisted a glossy lock of her amber hair around her ring finger. 'Why didn't she go for The Plaza in New

York or a palazzo in Venice? There's no competition, in my humble opinion.'

'Hey, quit dissing Yorkshire! You know it's where I grew up.' Callie smiled, exaggerating her accent. 'The Verbois/Marchant wedding is going to be the glitziest, most glamorous wedding, no matter where it's held. And it's what Lilac wants, Scarlet. Don't you think a bride *should* be able to choose where she ties the knot?'

Scarlet pulled a face. 'But why the competition to design her wedding dress? You know, I wouldn't want the job of that poor wedding planner – what's her name, Tish? – for all the silk in China. I bet you she's already planning to shoot herself and the competition hasn't even been finalised yet. It's the end of March, the wedding's on the thirty-first of July; that's just four months away. I predict a confetti-infused nightmare!'

'Well, it's just as well she did, isn't it, Scarlet?' Callie smiled, tucking the sharply angled sides of her ebony bob behind her ears. She blew her fringe away from tickling at her eyelashes as she finished the last embellishment, then snipped the thread like a ceremonial ribbon.

'Why?'

Callie rolled her eyes. Scarlet was her clear-headed second-in-command, but sometimes she seemed to inhabit a galaxy far, far away. 'Because, Scarlet darling, in case you haven't noticed, Callie-Louise Bridal Couture has been shortlisted through to the final stages.'

'Oh, yes. And your design will win, Callie, I know it will. It's a heavenly creation! I'm so proud of what you've done.'

'What we've all done. This has been a real team effort. Even Flora has had an input.' Callie rubbed the heels of her hands over her eyes in an effort to squeeze one last drop of energy from her addled brain.

'Sure.' Scarlet's perfectly outlined Cupid's bow stretched to reveal her white, even teeth.

It was difficult not to adore Scarlet, with her signature red lips and nail polish chosen to clash violently with her auburn hair. She had, without a murmur of complaint, hand-sewn the tiniest of crystals onto the ivory silk until her fingers bled and she was banished from the studio for fear of jeopardising the pristine fabric. After that, she had assumed the mantle of caring friend, force-feeding Callie a diet of chocolate digestives and toast – the extent of her culinary knowledge – for which Callie had been immensely grateful. Some days it was the only sustenance to pass her lips and had kept the hunger pangs at bay.

Never one to hold back when delicacy was required, Scarlet would regularly burst forth with gems of her own brand of wisdom. 'You need to get out more' was a regular refrain delivered to Callie's ears, and the ubiquitous 'all work and no play', before she went on to dispense a dose of friendly criticism of her failure to frequent the capital's bars and restaurants. She would end with a demand that Callie join her and Flora for a night on the town when Callie could no longer focus her eyes on the wedding dress of the decade.

Callie had watched from her seat in the Grand Circle as Scarlet took her own advice and lurched from one romantic encounter to the next, leaving her heart-broken conquests littering her fragrant slipstream.

'So, what's new on the relationship front, Scarlet?'

'Well, now that I'm about to be freed from the shackles of my workaholic boss, I intend to make up for my enforced dating celibacy by hitting the bars in the West End and sampling a different cocktail in every single one, starting with your personal favourite – a vodka martini. And you will be perched on the stool next to me, Callie. You haven't had a date in months. In fact, when was the last time you agreed to go out with a guy?'

'Oh, you know me. I don't have time to date. I'm just too busy with…'

'We're all busy, Callie. But that's not it. You always seem to come up with a convenient diagnosis of a fatal flaw in every guy you date. You seem to perform the dating equivalent of an archaeological dig in order to unearth any perceived imperfection that you can hone in on as an excuse not to take things further. Remember Marcus? He was gorgeous – a model, for God's sake! He could make a bin liner look sexy. He was perfect!'

'And didn't he know it,' muttered Callie.

Scarlet ignored her. 'And Andrew? The paediatrician? The guy who sent you flowers every day for a month?'

'Too attentive, too studious, and he talked about having kids the whole time!' Callie averted her eyes from Scarlet's stony glare.

'What about Carter? He was an American footballer! What's not to like? He flew you to New York for the weekend! You stayed at the Waldorf Astoria!'

'It rained the whole time.'

'You know, Callie, I wish I'd had half your opportunities to find "the one". You've got to relax, give someone the chance to get to know you. But there's something else going on here, isn't there? Something you're not telling me. What exactly are you searching for?'

Scarlet shook her head slowly, then fixed her eyes on Callie and lowered her voice to a whisper. 'It's Theo, isn't it?'

CHAPTER TWO

Callie was too exhausted to disguise her emotions from her friend and she could feel her face colour. The look of sadness that washed across Scarlet's pretty features sent a spasm of irritation into her chest at being sussed so easily.

'I knew it. You still love Theo, don't you? After all this time?'

'No, I don't...'

'It's understandable that you still have feelings for him, Cal. You dated him right through high school and university. Hey, and wasn't he the first guy you kissed when you were, like, twelve or something? But I thought you said you'd moved on?'

'I have.'

'So why is your face the same shade as my nail polish?'

'It's not. Anyway, Scarlet...'

'And isn't Theo's band playing at Lilac and Finn's reception? It was a real coup when Finn announced he'd pulled that one off. The Razorclaws will be on tour in Germany at the end of July so they've interrupted their schedule as a special favour to Finn. Wasn't he at music school in Manchester with Theo?'

'Yes,' murmured Callie. She felt like a deer caught in the headlights of Scarlet's examination technique. She hadn't mentioned the fact that Theo and his band would be playing at the wedding to her friend for exactly this reason. Nothing got past Scarlet.

'So you'll get to see him again.'

'Only if our design wins the competition and that's by no means a given.'

Callie watched the cogs turn behind Scarlet's emerald eyes.

'So there's a lot more than I thought resting on Callie-Louise Bridal Couture winning this competition.'

'Look, Scarlet, you know I have no desire to see Theo again. I had to think long and hard about continuing with the entry when it was announced his band would be a part of the wedding arrangements. But I've worked my butt off to make it as a fashion designer and I couldn't let an old relationship stand in the way of achieving my dream. If we do win, yes, I'll need to be at the ceremony, but Theo won't be there and my services won't be required at the evening reception.'

'So you're still avoiding him?'

'No, I just…'

'Yes, you are. Which means you are *not* over him.'

'Scarlet, you know what happened. You know what he did.'

'Yes, but there are two sides to every argument.' Scarlet affected an American accent. 'I've heard *your* submission, Counsellor, now let me consider the case for the opposition.'

'Oh, no…' Callie buried her head in her hands and massaged her temples with her fingertips. She didn't want to hear this right now. She didn't have the strength to fight back.

'Let's see, these are the facts, Your Honour. A rep from a record company was attending one of The Razorclaws' gigs. It was the most important night of Theo's life and his girlfriend had promised to be there, cheering him on from the wings. Said girlfriend was, once again, so engrossed in fulfilling her own dreams that she was late to the party. The Razorclaws got the contract, the champagne flowed, and they had been celebrating for hours before Theo's neglectful girlfriend arrived to witness a drunken clinch with an anonymous girl groupie whom he said had thrown herself at him. What was Theo to do, Cal?'

Callie swallowed down her agony. Every time his name was mentioned, it surprised her that the pain was still so raw and near the surface three years later. After that fateful night, she had escaped back to London and used the money her parents had left her to set up Callie-Louise Bridal Couture. She'd refused every one of Theo's calls and made her Aunt Hannah, who had brought her up after her parents' death, and her best friend, Nessa, swear they wouldn't disclose her new address to Theo.

She had never thought she could experience such a kaleidoscope of emotions. Theo had always been there for her. He knew every detail of her history; they'd shared the same highs and lows, the same friends, the same dreams, or so she'd thought. When she was thirteen, Theo had borrowed his father's spade and dug up one of his mother's prize rose bushes. He'd raced round to collect her from her aunt's house and dragged her to the local churchyard, where he proceeded to plant the white rose bush next to the headstone of her parents' grave. When she was fourteen, Theo had kissed her under the canopy of the old oak tree in the garden behind her Aunt Hannah's haberdashery shop, Gingerberry Yarns, and then he'd carved her initials into the knobbly trunk. The entwined initials 'CLH' had, years later, become the logo for her bridal boutique. She had loved him and it still hurt a great deal that he was no longer in her life.

But he'd never understood her need to sever the rural guy ropes and branch out on her own, to forge a life for herself away from the Dales. She had been so adamant about her desire to leave Allthorpe that she had expected Theo to share her ambition, with the clamorous draw of city music venues proving too tempting to refuse. But refuse he had. He remained at home with his parents and insisted on commuting to his degree course in Manchester, crashing at his friends' digs when he had to. He had also remained loyal to their childhood friends – four of them made up his band – but whom, apart from Nessa, she'd not seen for years. Tears always gathered on her lashes whenever she recalled the nights they had spent together in Archie's parents' garage, jamming and tossing around suggestions of what to call the band. The Razorclaws had been an amalgamation of Theo's suggestion of The Northern Claws and hers of The Razors.

The three years she'd spent studying at Northumbria University's prestigious School of Fashion and Textiles had been the best years of her life. She'd loved the people, the nightlife, the restaurants, the theatres, the fashion opportunities, even the football club. She had emerged from her time in Newcastle with a first-class honours degree in Fashion Design and Textiles and won a coveted place at the Royal College of Art to study for her MA in Textiles.

Whilst in London, she had striven to put her dreams of becoming a fashion designer first and had embraced the freedom of the individual creative design philosophy her MA allowed her to explore. She had served her apprenticeship with Christianna Boulet, the well-respected doyenne of haute couture with a penchant for geometric print fabric edged with neon-woven tweeds.

At Christianna's insistence, she had learnt the more mundane aspects of the fashion business as well as the techniques required to produce a glittering showcase of catwalk-quality garments.

But it had all come at a price when, after years of religiously returning to Allthorpe to fan the flames of their courtship, she had returned that night, albeit late, to stumble upon the scene that had remained scorched on the inside of her eyelids ever since. The shock had galvanised her into taking her dreams to a new level and the eponymous Callie-Louise Couture had been born.

Every spare crumb of her love and affection had been lavished on her business. It was her baby and craved every moment of her attention. She was grateful for that as it meant she had no time to dwell on what had happened. But she had never forgotten Theo's betrayal of their relationship.

However, Scarlet was also right. What was Theo to do when girls threw themselves at him? And things could only have got worse now that The Razorclaws had topped the charts with their recent album. She just couldn't see herself as part of that itinerant lifestyle. And she definitely couldn't handle the roller coaster of emotions that went along with dating a famous rock musician.

And, anyway, wasn't Callie-Louise Henshaw about to become the most celebrated fashion designer in the country?

CHAPTER THREE

'Look, come on. The courier will be here any minute now and we can't risk him leaving empty-handed. I'm going to slide the dress into the wardrobe on the dressmaker's dummy; less opportunity for it to crease. I'll never forget that image of Princess Diana's wedding gown on the steps of St Paul's Cathedral.' Callie grimaced as she recalled the profusion of crinkles the dress had displayed to the seven hundred and fifty million people who'd been watching around the globe.

'This is, without a doubt, the most beautiful wedding gown I have ever laid eyes on – you know that, Callie, don't you? It's definitely going to win the competition and you'll see your own design worn by one of the most famous actresses in the world. How exciting is that?'

Despite her natural reluctance to sing her own praises, Callie allowed herself a tiny nod to her ingenuity with a needle, coupled with her God-given talent, which had produced such dazzling results. It was one of her most adventurous creations to date, but every aspect of the gown had merged to form a true work of art. She had slaved through eighteen-hour days over the last three months to get the sample ready for the final judging the next day.

The gown's pale ivory, organic silk flowed like ripples in a summer breeze. The strapless bodice draped exquisitely to enhance Lilac's translucent, swan-like neck and pert breasts. The nipped-in waist would amplify her slender measurements, but it was the A-line skirt that drew the appreciative eye, ruched to the right where a darted panel of inlaid crystals and seed pearls shimmered like a sparkling waterfall whenever the bride moved, especially under the neon lights of Callie's workshop. A fantasy dress for a fairy-tale wedding, putting even Cinderella's to shame.

Of course, if the design won it would have to be custom-altered and remoulded, but she would do anything, work 24/7, if it meant her dress could be displayed to the fashion world on such a famous model. That kind of exposure could jettison the Callie-Louise name into the order books of every style-conscious celebrity in Britain. It was everything she had been working towards. Every single, painful sacrifice she had made would have been worth it.

Except maybe one.

The two girls gently gathered the gown's delicate folds and straightened the underskirt and hem. Callie fought a cauldron of emotions not to shed a tear as she and Scarlet manoeuvred the cardboard wardrobe crate towards the dressmaker's dummy and carefully inserted the textile sculpture.

They draped sheets of acid-free tissue paper around the dress until it was packed as tightly as possible without scrunching the delicate material, and stood back to admire their handiwork before they sealed the door, knowing there would be no further tweaking allowed.

As Callie closed the door and sealed the box with the brown tape, both girls let out a sigh of pleasure and of satisfaction.

'A true masterpiece, Callie. Lilac would be crazy not to pick it.'

Callie couldn't speak. Her throat had tightened around a lump the size of a golf ball. 'Oh, God, I nearly forgot! The paperwork for the courier.'

'Callie? Callie?' Flora's voice floated down from the floor above. 'Call for you in the Tumble Room. Said it was urgent!'

'Okay, Flora, be right there.'

Callie exchanged a smirk with Scarlet as she slipped on her black ballet pumps, stretched her long, colt-like legs and wiggled out the kinks in her shoulder muscles to her full six-foot height. She flicked the sides of her bob behind each ear and slid the pin cushion from around her wrist.

Every call Flora put through was 'urgent'. Despite being the salon's receptionist since its inception three years ago, she invariably fell for the caller's assertive demands.

Rolling her eyes and experiencing a sweep of relief at the conclusion of the most important project of her career, she took the stairs two at a time to their 'ideas' room. It had been nicknamed the 'Tumble Room' because it was where Callie hoped their creative juices and ideas would tumble forth from brain to paper. In reality, it was a small conference room they used to receive their clients and listen to their dreams, decorated with wall art ranging from framed photographs of 1950s brassieres to Callie's prized David Hockney, the celebrated Yorkshire-born artist, which she'd inherited from her father.

'Thanks, Flora. Hi, Callie-Louise Henshaw speaking.'

'Callie, at last! It's Seb,' announced her cousin with none of his usual comedic preamble.

'Oh, hi, Seb. What great timing. We've just put the finishing touches…'

'Callie, it's Mum. Delia's just rung. She collapsed when she was shutting up the shop. She's been rushed to Harrogate hospital by ambulance. You'd better get up here. Delia is with her but she's unconscious. The medics' early diagnosis is a perforated bowel and she'll be going straight into surgery. I'm racing across there now.'

'Oh, my God, Seb, I'm on my way.' An anvil-heavy weight pressed down on Callie's chest, restricting the flow of air to her lungs. She gulped for breath, her body frozen in alarm.

'Callie? Callie? What on earth's happened?' Scarlet rushed to Callie's side, rousing her from her shock and sending her stalled brain into motion.

'It's Aunt Hannah. She's collapsed. On her way to the hospital. Having surgery. Got to go. Now!'

'Oh, Callie, no!'

Callie rushed past Scarlet's blanched face, back down the wooden treads to her workshop and grabbed her handbag and mac. Fear wrenched at her gut. She couldn't lose her aunt, she just couldn't. When her parents had died in a head-on crash when she was only ten years old, Aunt Hannah had surrounded her with a comfort blanket of love and brought her up alongside her two older cousins, Seb and Dominic, in a home filled with chatter and homely warmth. She adored her. She couldn't envisage life without her.

'What about the dress, Callie?' cried Scarlet as she darted in Callie's wake down the stairs to the workroom. 'You need to fill out the forms, and sign the seal and the courier's documentations. It's part of the requirements, as evidence that the entry hasn't been tampered with.'

'Oh, erm, you do it, Scarlet,' Callie called over her shoulder from the top of the stairs, the helix of panic tightening in her chest and throat, her brain ricocheting off into myriad nightmare scenarios.

Scarlet jogged to keep up with Callie's beeline for the exit and the car park at the back of the salon, a visibly upset Flora in her wake.

'Callie…'

'Scarlet. Just make sure it goes. It's packed and sealed. It only needs a signature. I have to get to the hospital.'

Tears sprang into Callie's eyes and trickled down her pale cheeks. Her shallow breathing induced a dizzy spell causing her to pause at the door to draw oxygen into her screaming lungs. An icy drench of panic rose up her arms, leaving goosebumps in its wake.

'Look, Callie, you can't drive all the way up to Yorkshire by yourself – you're in no fit state. I'll drive you.'

'Scarlet…'

'What use will you be to your aunt if you end up in the same hospital after an RTA? Give me your keys!' Scarlet brandished her palm and the expression on her face brooked no further argument.

Callie realised that her objections were only serving to delay her journey. Any further refusals would only extend the time until she arrived at her aunt's bedside.

'Okay. Flora, if you can't find Lizzie, will *you* stay until the courier arrives to collect the gown? All you have to do is fill out the documents and get a receipt.'

'Sure, Callie. I hope your aunt's going to be okay.'

Callie could not recall much of the journey up to Harrogate. Scarlet drove swiftly, the car's headlights tunnelling two piercing beams through the London streets, strangely devoid of their daily bustle on that late March evening, the clientele of the busy bars ignorant of the curling veins of turmoil swirling around Callie's ragged brain. Raindrops splattered sporadically on the windscreen, the blades flicking them away like irritating flies. The amber glow of the street lamps cast their mellow light into the inky black puddles gathered in the gutters and across the rooftops.

She couldn't lose Aunt Hannah, she thought, panicking, especially as she'd already lost her parents. God couldn't be that cruel, surely?

Silence pervaded the vehicle whilst Scarlet concentrated on handling the unfamiliar controls of the Mini Cooper and delivering Callie to the hospital as quickly as possible, her own features pinched and sombre in the half-light. Anyway, what words were there to ease the pain?

At last, Scarlet pulled into the deserted hospital car park. Callie glimpsed the stout figure of Hannah's best friend, Delia, on the stone steps leading to the entrance hall, clearly keeping an anxious lookout for their arrival. Callie leapt from the car, grateful for Delia's foresight – it meant she would not have to wander the neon-bleached corridors, going through the rigmarole of repeated questions to locate her aunt.

'Delia? Where's…'

'Oh, Callie, I'm so, so sorry, my love. So very, very sorry.' Tears streamed down Delia's powdery, wrinkled face, her pale blue eyes gentle as she hooked her arm threw Callie's elbow.

'Delia?' Callie's voice trembled.

'Come on. Seb and Dominic are just in here,' and she steered Callie into a tiny, fluorescent-bright room just off the entrance-hall corridor.

As soon as the door swung back, Seb leapt out of the brown plastic chair and took Callie into his arms. Over his shoulder, Callie swung her horrified stare from Dominic to Delia as icy fingers of dread curled around her heart and squeezed.

'No… no… no…'

'I'm so sorry, Cal. Mum passed away twenty minutes ago during surgery. Heart attack. They did everything they could…'

'No…'

CHAPTER FOUR

A soft breeze laced with the fragrance of spring wove its way through the village of Allthorpe. Shafts of early April sunshine spliced through the leaden clouds clothing the church with a mantle of golden light. It was a picturesque venue and it was no surprise that the parish church, complete with rose-entangled lychgate, was regularly chosen as the venue for much happier occasions. But no ivory ribbons rippled on the gateposts that morning.

How could life dispense such cruelty? Callie wondered as she dabbed away the tears from her cheeks with the scrap of embroidered cotton Delia had given her that morning. First the Director of Fate had snatched her parents, leaving her an orphan, and now he had seen fit to take her beloved Aunt Hannah as well.

Seb and Dominic were her only real family now – her only remaining link to her life in Yorkshire. She laced her arms through theirs as they thanked the vicar for the very moving eulogy he had delivered to a packed congregation. Hannah had been a popular resident of the village of Allthorpe, a committee member of the WI as well as a regular church attendee, and the Reverend Coulson knew her well. There had been genuine sadness in his words of comfort.

The mourners spilled out of the church and meandered their way down the path towards the village green, where the black limousines waited. Those closest to Hannah had been invited to join the family in a toast to her life at her home in Harrogate ten miles away.

Callie had known Theo would be at the funeral to pay his respects to his best friend's mother and the person who had taken his girlfriend under her loving wing when she was only ten years old. Her aunt had possessed an infinite capacity to love and had extended her affection to Theo, the boy who had loved her niece for as long as she could remember. But Callie hadn't anticipated the depth of emotion she would experience when she set eyes on him for the first time in three years as he loitered on the worn-out steps of the church with his parents whilst they chatted to the vicar.

Her first reaction was to turn and run, but how could she?

Seb must have felt her arm tense. He glanced over her shoulder, a smile cracking his face for the first time that day.

'Theo!'

Callie had no choice but to accompany Seb and Dominic to receive the heartfelt condolences of Theo's parents, Geoff and Julie Drake. They shook hands with Seb and Dominic and then turned to hug her to their chests with such compassion that she had to swallow down hard not to open the firmly sealed flood gates. She knew the last thing her aunt would have wanted was for her to be a tear-strewn wreck. She managed a weak smile of appreciation, muttered how grateful she was for their words of genuine comfort, and was keen to move away before Theo took his father's place and enveloped her in his embrace.

'Geoff, Julie, I think Theo and Callie could do with a little space,' announced Seb, his eyes lingering on Theo's as he guided his best friend's parents out of the churchyard.

'Oh, no, Seb, I…'

Callie hadn't intended to meet Theo's gentle, silver-grey eyes. When she did, her heart dropped like a stone down a well before bouncing straight back up again, lodging somewhere between her chest and her throat. Her knees weakened under the strain of her swirling emotions as she drank in his familiar features.

Nothing about him had changed. He was still the teenage boy she had given her heart to. He still spoke with his broad Yorkshire accent, unlike her, who'd worked hard at eradicating it. He still wore his sandy-blond hair on the long side and favoured the designer-stubble look. The smattering of freckles across the bridge of his nose remained, reminding Callie of the time they had spent one summer lying amongst the wheat in a farmer's field when she had counted every single one and had declared there to be one hundred and thirty-two. He'd asked for a recount before grabbing her by the wrists and smiling into her eyes to tell her he was joking. It was the first time he'd told her he loved her.

'Cal, I'm so sorry about your Aunt Hannah. I know how much she meant to you. She was a wonderful lady. When Seb called to tell me about the funeral, I grabbed the first flight back to the UK.' His smile was a peace offering.

'Thanks, Theo.'

He reached out his fingers and gently touched the back of her hand. 'If there is anything I can do to help ease your pain, I want you to know that I'm here for you. I will always be your friend.'

Tears amassed on her lower lashes, but she could think of nothing to say. They weren't the same people they had been three years ago. They led totally different lives. Yet, after all this time, she was still unable to view Theo as just a friend. He had ensnared her heart and refused to return it. Now she realised that it would hurt too much to maintain the civility required to sustain even friendly relations.

A lone tear trickled down her cheek and Theo reached over to brush it away with his thumb. His lips parted as he cupped her chin and lifted her face to his.

'Cal, I want you to know…'

'Don't, Theo. I can't do this. Not today.'

A cloud of regret passed across his handsome features but he respected her request. 'Okay, but we do need to talk. I've got a break in my commitments and I'm home for a few weeks. How long are you home for? That's if you still call Allthorpe home.'

They had reached the village green opposite Gingerberry Yarns, the haberdashery shop on Allthorpe High Street her aunt had owned and run with the help of Delia. 'It's the cosiest little wool shop in Yorkshire,' Delia was forever quoting as her catchphrase. It had certainly been the place Callie had spent her happiest times and its contents had nurtured her passion for all things woolly and had inspired her to follow her dream of a career in fashion.

'The will is being read tomorrow. I've promised Seb and Dominic to go to the solicitors with them, although I don't know why they need me there. Then I'm going back to London. The announcement is being made on Monday.'

'What announcement?'

Callie cursed her lapse in concentration. The last thing she wanted was for Theo to know about her submission to Lilac Verbois's wedding gown competition. She knew he'd tell her that his band had been booked to perform at the evening reception and she didn't think she could take any more trauma that day. The Razorclaws and their music would be for ever linked with Theo's betrayal. She needed to get through tomorrow, then she could leave Allthorpe and eradicate the risk of bumping into Theo again.

'Oh, just something to do with the boutique. Bye, Theo.'

Before Theo could say anything else, she turned her back on him and strode away, jumping into the back seat of one of the limousines waiting to take the mourners to the wake at her aunt's house in Harrogate.

Theo was a spectre from her past and she had to make sure he stayed there.

CHAPTER FIVE

'May I start by expressing my sincere condolences and thanking you all for coming today. I'm Gordon Braithwaite, senior partner here at Braithwaite, Cobbs and Fisher. We're proud to have handled all of John and Hannah Garside's legal affairs over the years.'

Callie cast her eyes around the room. It wasn't what she had been expecting at all. She had envisaged the boardroom of her aunt and uncle's solicitor's office to be lined with mahogany bookcases crammed with weighty, leather-bound, legalistic tomes and the faint smell of dusty parchment fighting for supremacy with the aroma of wax furniture polish like the venue – straight out of a Dickensian novel – that she had been forced to attend for the reading of her parents' wills after the car crash. As she had been an only child, the contents of their last will and testament had held no surprises and she'd wondered at the time why the elderly solicitor had bothered with the charade.

Here she was, a scant fifteen years later, being invited to listen once again to the monotone drone of a probate lawyer as he read through the terms of her aunt's will, but this time she sat, along with Seb and Dominic, in what was essentially a glass cube. The view from the window was spectacular, looking straight out onto The Stray, a large expanse of open parkland in the centre of Harrogate framed by a profusion of pink-flowering cherry trees.

Her aunt and uncle had adored the park so much they'd bought a house which overlooked it. Uncle John had often told her that in Victorian times it had been used as a racecourse, but more recently the area around The Stray had been declared one of the UK's happiest places to live.

She dragged her attention back to the room, surprised to see that Mr Braithwaite was looking over his tortoiseshell spectacles at her with an expectant expression on his face. Seb and Dominic were smiling.

'Erm, sorry, I was just admiring the view.'

'Yes, Miss Henshaw, I have to agree with you, and it's at its most beautiful this time of the year.'

She smiled back, but the silence continued.

'What?' she blurted out.

Seb got up and went to sit next to her. He took both her hands into his. 'Mum has left her house here in Harrogate to me and Dom.'

Callie nodded, smiling into Seb's kind brown eyes, which reminded her so much of his mother that she had to quash the rising panic in her chest. Mr Braithwaite didn't look like the type of lawyer who would appreciate females sobbing onto his smoked-glass conference table.

'And she left Gingerberry Yarns to you, Cal.'

'She… I beg your pardon?'

'Dom and I knew she wanted you to have it. It was half your mum's before she and your dad… well… And you did love the place, didn't you, before you left to chase your fortune in London? You know, one of my earliest memories is of you designing and sewing your own clothes for your Sindy doll from remnants of fabric and ribbon. You even knitted jumpers for our teddy bears, remember? We're not interested in the shop. Mum made the right decision.'

Callie knew her jaw had slackened. She flicked her eyes from Seb to Dominic and back again. The brothers nodded in unison.

'Seb's right, Cal,' added Dominic. 'You adore that place. Whenever I go there it feels weird not to see you sitting at that huge table doing your homework. You spent every spare second there. Well, when you weren't out gallivanting with Theo or watching his band crucify some of my favourite rock anthems.'

'Gingerberry Yarns is mine now?'

Her cousins nodded. The solicitor shuffled his papers back into the buff file in front of him, tied it with a green ribbon and rose from his chair.

'I'll leave you to your discussions. Please take your time and help yourself to coffee. If you need any advice about the disposal of either the property here in Harrogate or the shop on Allthorpe High Street, then my firm's services are at your disposal.'

The door swung closed behind him.

'But I can't run a haberdashery shop in Yorkshire. I live in London. I have a business that devours every second of my time, perhaps even more if my prayers are answered.'

'Mum was so excited about the competition, you know. She told everyone who came into the shop about it.' Seb's eyes sparkled but he managed to hang on to his emotions. 'Dom and I have already decided to sell Mum's house. If you want to sell Gingerberry, you have our blessing. Lives move on, things change. We know that. Just promise to come and visit us up here in Yorkshire once in a while. We miss you.'

Callie couldn't hold on any longer. She'd thought she had no tears left to shed, yet a deluge burst from within.

'I promise,' she managed.

'Oh, and before you go back down to London, why don't you make your peace with Theo? Remember what Mum always used to say? Life's too short to carry grudges. You know, I don't have a single childhood memory that doesn't feature you and Theo together in supporting roles.'

'Seb…'

'And perhaps, before you make any decisions, you should take a good look around the shop. Maybe take a few photos? It'll bring back memories you thought you'd forgotten. It did for me and Dom.'

'I will, yes. Thanks, Seb. Thanks, Dom. But, really, I can't see any other alternative but to sell up.'

'Whatever you decide, Cal, you have our full support.'

She would do as Seb had suggested. She'd go back to Allthorpe and spend an afternoon in the shop. It was the least she could do after such a generous gift from her Aunt Hannah. It would also be an ideal opportunity to check out the stock, to box up anything suitable for Callie-Louise.

Seb was right. She had left her life in Yorkshire behind and carved out a new one in the capital, although it was career-orientated with very little social life. She found herself yearning for the anonymity of London, where the streets were filled with dull, grey office workers unconcerned about their fellow humans' difficulties – in fact, she had become one of them, a member of that overworked, harried tribe. In Allthorpe, on the other hand, everyone knew their neighbours' business, happy or sad, and had a ready word of congratulation or solace to offer.

And she did have a plethora of happy memories wrapped up in Gingerberry Yarns and it would be tough to leave them behind for good. Yet a stab of regret needled her conscience – there was one thing that pained her above all else.

If she did sell Gingerberry, what would happen to Delia?

CHAPTER SIX

Callie paused in Allthorpe High Street to look up at the sign, fashioned from bronze in the shape of a ball of wool stabbed through with a pair of knitting needles. Gingerberry Yarns, it announced. She smiled despite her sadness as she recalled the day it had been delivered; first the shock, then the burst of hilarity her mum and Aunt Hannah had shared.

In a certain light, the signage looked just like a skull and crossbones. Would customers think they were pirates, Hannah had asked. Delia had been summonsed for her valued opinion, but after much deliberation over the big brown teapot, they had all declared they loved it and hung it outside the shop with tongue-in-cheek pride. It would be a talking point if nothing else. They'd christened its erection with a bottle of Prosecco rosé and a Victoria sponge cake filled with oodles of jam and cream from old Tom Wallington's bakery on the corner.

Gingerberry Yarns had been closed for a week as a mark of respect after the passing of her aunt. Shading her eyes, Callie peered through the grime-coated window. The little shop still held a hint of magic for her – once inside the door, the visitor would be enveloped in a warm comfort blanket, safe, just for a few moments, from all the traumas life tossed in their path. She inserted the key Seb had given her and opened the door. The brass bell above her head reverberated with a jaunty chime of welcome but it jarred against Callie's ragged nerves.

'At last, dear, it's perishing out here. What kept you?' Delia bustled in behind her, a rich aroma of warm baked croissants following in her wake and permeating the shop's motionless air. 'I'll just butter these whilst they're still warm. Young Tom Wallington really is proving to be a baking maestro. These croissants of his melt in your mouth. You should taste his cherry scones, Callie, but his cheese and rosemary versions are simply delicious, too. If you ask me, his talents are wasted in Allthorpe after all that training he did in Paris and at Betty's, but, well, his father can't…' Delia's prattling dropped off when she noticed Callie's expression. 'I'll pop the kettle on. See you upstairs when you're ready for a cuppa.'

Callie's eyes followed Delia's plump backside as she disappeared up the stairs to perform the same task she had done every morning for the last fifteen years, only this time for her best friend's niece. She stepped further into the high-ceilinged room, memories crashing through her thoughts whilst she listened to the cheerful tinkling of cutlery and cups as Delia busied herself in the upstairs kitchen, one that was as familiar as her own.

Callie smoothed her palm over the glass-topped counter, its surface reflecting her pixie-like features and the misery swirling in the far corners of her soul. A wave of desolation rippled over her when she realised Gingerberry Yarns would never again be blessed with the smiling presence of its proprietor. The fact that the world could keep on turning despite this devastating knowledge annoyed her.

She cast her professional eye around the room. Her recent absence afforded her the opportunity to scrutinise its outmoded contents with a fresh perspective. What her eyes met instilled no creative enthusiasm. The place was old-fashioned and shabby at the edges. Why hadn't she noticed this careworn façade before?

Puffs of dust and sadness hovered amongst the packed wicker baskets. Garlands of twisted yarn nestled in cubbyholes or behind glass doors with tiny brass knobs more befitting a gentleman's outfitters from the fifties. The shop was well stocked but everything on the shelves depicted a bygone era when communities were tight and pockets tighter. It was a place you would find your granny holding court, not a young mothers' chinwag or a teenagers' coterie of gossip. But then, 'Gran's Woollen Emporium' was exactly what

Gingerberry Yarns was – an old people's social club or a place for the knitting circle from the local WI to persuade their deft fingers to twirl yarn into garments for the needy.

Polished teak shelves ran round the remaining two sides of the room, stuffed with lurid, multicoloured acrylics Callie had last seen on Barbie. Where were the natural lamb's wools, the organic silks, the fair-trade cottons? Even the Aran was synthetic.

Knitting needles had been jammed into spaghetti jars like forests of pasta. Cards of pearl buttons and other assorted fastenings dangled from racks of chipped steel. The sample garments displayed on coat hangers on old mahogany hat stands, clearly knitted by her aunt or Delia, to Callie's trained eye resembled bed jackets for the terminally ill. There were so many trendy designs coming out of Scandinavia at the moment, inspired by the wave of crime fiction that had been serialised for television, and the art of knitting was now a celebrity-endorsed pastime. She thought of the chunky Danish sweaters Scarlet adored; hers was red and cream, a prized possession that had cost her well over four hundred pounds.

Her fertile designer's mind drifted to the Kaffe Fassett designs, works of art every one of them, all sculpted in natural wools, if not organic or locally sourced. She remembered the stitch-and-bitch sessions she had attended when a penniless student in Newcastle, where, for the price of a cup of coffee in the local Costa, she'd spent warm, aroma-filled evenings with a diverse gathering of friends, from eager teenagers to harassed new mums grabbing a couple of hours of sanity away from the baby, and even professional women escaping the testosterone-infused office for a more girly activity that would not be judged against the bottom line.

The shop sported the most magnificent glass-plate frontage with its title embossed in arched gold lettering. But the window was almost opaque with rain-streaked grime and its display of misshapen sweaters did not invite curious perusal by passing window-shoppers.

In the farthest corner of the room, behind the counter where Callie slumped, her elbow supporting her chin, Hannah and Delia had squeezed in an enormous antique mahogany table, complete with green leather inlay as wrinkled as an octogenarian's knees; its tooled edges inlaid with gold leaf and the deep scratches testament to the passage of time. Around this monstrosity huddled a disconsolate selection of equally ancient hard-backed chairs. A couple sported chintzy cushions as a nod to the comfort of their users' buttocks.

Clearly, this was where the serious business of the day was conducted – just not the money-making kind. It seemed as though ghosts still lingered there, at the table, completing unfinished projects before they could rest in peace.

The whole store screamed warmth and comfort; a genteel, English lady's boudoir of the 1950s. Its painted walls blistered and flaky to the touch, its flooring worn and patched. Places like Gingerberry Yarns would not have survived in the metropolises of Leeds and Manchester. They had been replaced by trendy wine bars and the ubiquitous coffee shops, estate agents and nail bars, although even these businesses were struggling now.

Callie glanced out of the front window to the row of shops across the road that mirrored theirs. Marietta's Hairdressing Salon, its windows reflecting the golden glow of the mid-morning sun, displayed three giant black-and-white portraits of cutting-edge hair design. With the bakery producing fresh croissants, Callie wondered whether Gingerberry Yarns was the only shop on Allthorpe High Street that had not moved with the times.

As she straightened up, the realisation came to her with a jolt that slammed straight to her heart. Her aunt and Delia had run this compendium of yarns and ribbons over the years, not as a business, but as a social enterprise. A note of dread rang in the back of her mind for what she would discover in the accounts when she marketed the business. It was blatantly obvious from the noticeable voids on the shelves behind the gargantuan meeting table that very little had been spent on the shop's maintenance. There was no point thinking about that, though, now the building and the business were going to be sold.

Delia appeared at the bottom of the stairs, carrying a tray. 'Here we are, love, one steaming cup of your favourite Earl Grey tea. Warms the cockles of your heart, it does.'

Unlikely, thought Callie. Anxiety and grief had lodged a tight knot in her chest that no amount of alcohol-free beverage could dislodge. Only in the welcoming arms of Jack and Daniel could Callie feel the suffocating weight begin to ease and that was only a temporary reprieve.

'I've made a pot for when Iris and Marcia arrive. They usually pop in after collecting Iris's pension on a Tuesday morning, after a compulsory visit to old Mr Wallington's bakery. Oh, I shouldn't continue calling it that now, I suppose. Did you know he's moved into Heppleton Residential Care Home? Ah, everything is changing in Allthorpe. The passage of time favours no one, I'm afraid.'

As Delia busied herself dusting the shelves with a long feather duster, accompanied by a running commentary of complaints about how quickly the dust settles when not kept on top of, Callie swung her contemplation and analytical eye onto her aunt's best friend of over forty years.

Her hair, the colour of Yorkshire mist, had been cut in a surprisingly modern style – spiky fringe, tufted at the back,

and finished off with the suspicion of gel! In fact, Delia
carried her sixty years well. In spite of her ample hips and
bosom, Callie's expert eye told her that she modelled her
wardrobe on the latest trends; hand-knit apricot cashmere
sweater, embellished with tiny shimmering beads around
the neckline and a pair of flatteringly cut trousers. She
had a suspicion – no, a certainty – that Delia had designed
and hand-sewn them herself to flatter her figure perfectly.
Delia had completed her day's attire with the largest
pearl earrings Callie had seen and a long silver chain
from which her bejewelled glasses swung like an optical
pendulum as she swished away the offending dust.

But there was a tightness at the corners of Delia's
thinning lips and pronounced creases between her
eyes. With a jolt of guilt, Callie realised how anxious
the older woman must be about what would become of
Gingerberry Yarns and, therefore, her own future. Delia
would never have admitted it to Callie, but Callie knew
she had relished the role of the shop's co-chatelaine
over the years. It was what she had lived for.

'Delia, let's sit down.'

Callie strode over to the gigantic table and folded her
six-foot frame into one of the uncomfortable chairs.
Its wooden spindles dug sharply into the small of her
back. Silence extended through the room. It felt weird
because the whole place was usually suffused with
chatter and the aroma of her aunt's favourite coffee
brewing in the corner for customers to help themselves.

Best just launch in, she thought. Natives of Yorkshire were renowned for their straight-talking. 'Delia, Aunt Hannah left me Gingerberry Yarns in her will.'

'Oh, that's marvellous, my dear. Your aunt truly loved this place, you know. She spent more time here than she did over at her house in Harrogate. She adored the yarns, the cottons, the silks, the mohairs. Oh, the way she used to run her fingers through those spools of ribbons and laces. But, most of all, it was the people she loved, Callie, the regulars. Her "posse", she would call them, "Hannah's haberdashery posse".'

Delia stared out of the window, lost in her memories. Her trendy haircut made her look like she was wearing a pewter helmet, but her face reflected the kindness that oozed from her pores. She twisted her rings around her fingers as she reminisced. Her tear-blotched face was pale and drawn, the red spidery veins bleeding across the whites of her eyes evidence of the copious weeping the trauma of the previous eight days had caused.

'I know mere words can't erase your sorrow, Callie. William and I were never fortunate enough to be blessed with children of our own, nor as an only child from a single mother do I have any nephews or nieces or other relatives, but you, Seb and Dominic are as good as family to me.' Delia drew in a deep breath as she prepared to deliver her next sentence. 'We need to open the shop back up. It's been closed for more than a week now and people are asking. I'm happy to stay on, but if you don't want me to... I'll understand.' Her crooked fingers, gnarled by years of gripping knitting needles and the onset of arthritis, continued to twist at her wedding ring, fearful of the response.

'Stay on?'

'Well, just if you wanted to run it yourself, that's all? Or, heaven forbid, sell up. It seems to be what's happening around here in the village.' Delia closed her eyes against the potential heartbreak of not only losing her best friend, but also her reason for getting out of bed every morning.

'What do you mean?'

'Look at the butcher's shop across the road, its frontage clad in a cage of scaffolding. A so-called property developer is renovating the building into "*a desirable country dwelling, boasting wood-burning stoves and a sleek, stainless-steel kitchen; a stylish weekend retreat for a rich city banker*". That's what the sales particulars say – they're not even attempting to market the place as a home to local residents who will become part of the community. I shudder to think what the village of Allthorpe will become if yet another shop loses the fight to stay open. And there's no point in objecting to the planners. We tried that.'

As Callie met Delia's eyes, a barrage of guilt tumbled through her veins. In that instant, her aunt's oldest friend had understood that Callie would indeed be selling up.

'Sorry, Callie, please don't pay any heed to me. I'm a sentimental old woman. You have to be free to make your own decision, unburdened by any feelings of loyalty or, heaven forbid, pity. You have your own life and future to think of.'

'Delia, I'm so sorry. I'm going back to London tonight. I need to get back to work and resume some sort of normality. I want to be at the salon just in case... well... just in case our design wins. Only the winner is going to be informed, to keep things as private as possible for Lilac, so if we don't hear anything tomorrow it means our design hasn't been chosen. Do you think we might have a chance, Delia? It'd be such a fabulous opportunity for everyone at Callie-Louise.'

'I don't know, Callie dear, but I'm sure your design was the most adorable. Your aunt was so proud of all your achievements, you know, not just these star-studded creations. Every day we'd sit at this very table and chat about you and Seb and Dominic; about your fantastic designs, about Seb and Dominic's promotions at work, about Theo's success with his band. It made her happy just to know you were all following your dreams – wherever their paths took you.

'She was just so excited when we closed the shop last Friday. Lots of our customers and friends had called by during the day to wish you luck, before she... before she...' Delia withdrew a lace-trimmed, cotton handkerchief embroidered with a large blue 'D' and dabbed the falling tears away from her papery cheeks.

'I miss her so much. Every day of the last fifteen years since your Uncle John died, we've been running Gingerberry Yarns together. Then, after my William passed away, it was just the two of us. This isn't simply a shop to us, Callie, a means of making a living. Gingerberry Yarns is an integral part of this community. Oh, I know you youngsters think Allthorpe is a dull, parochial village, and it may be, compared to the pull of the bright lights of the metropolis, but your aunt's shop provides an escape, offers solace from the lonely daily routine that we older people find our lives becoming when our children and spouses have moved on.'

'I'm sorry, Delia. I can't run Gingerberry from London, I just can't. Even if my design doesn't win, I have enough commissions to keep me working every hour God sends for the next two years. I don't have a choice. Gingerberry will have to be sold.'

As she spoke those painful words the doorbell tinkled like a wedding ring on a crystal champagne flute, announcing the arrival of a customer despite the sign having been turned to 'Closed'.

With the sun behind him it was a few moments before Callie realised who it was, but Delia knew straight away. She collected her handbag and bustled off, pausing to kiss Theo on her way out of the door.

CHAPTER SEVEN

'Hi, Callie.'

Theo reached out and pulled her into his spice-infused chest. His familiar cologne caused her mind to zoom back to the last time they had been together. He dropped a kiss on her cheek and awaited her reaction.

'Erm, hi,' she croaked as her heart pummelled her chest and a cauldron of emotions whipped through her body, sending sparkles of electricity to her fingertips.

The immediate environs of the shop receded as all Callie could see were those steel-grey eyes that had frequented so many of her dreams. It was as though the last three years of loneliness had melted into oblivion as Theo stood before her, matching her height and meeting her stare. Unlike her heart, her brain refused to process his presence despite the visual evidence of his choppy, tawny-coloured hair and his strong, determined jawline, sporting a suggestion of stubble, not to mention the familiar curve of his lips.

As always, it was Theo's eyes that drew her gaze. Now, face-to-face with the only man she had ever truly loved after three long years, Callie scrutinised his face for a sign that he was a different person to the one she had adored. For confirmation that the passage of time had justified her relinquished love; a love they had sustained throughout their teenage years and the three years of university. But the Theo she saw slouched in front of her was exactly the same, no wrinkles or errant grey hairs, and her heart confirmed with every beat that she did still love him.

She crushed down that unwelcome confirmation, as she was becoming so adept at doing, and cast around for a topic of conversation that wouldn't bring their past screaming back. She plastered on a smile and prayed her voice would not give her away.

'It's great to see you, Theo. I hear The Razorclaws are playing to sold-out arenas now. That's fabulous. Even got a gig at the wedding of the year. Congratulations!'

'Yeah, we're stoked.' Theo stuck his hands in the front pockets of his black Levi's and flapped his elbows, a clear signal to Callie that he was nervous about what his reception might be. He followed Callie to the table, still strewn with culinary debris, and accepted a lukewarm mug of tea from the big brown teapot. 'Couldn't let Finn down. We've been friends since uni.'

Callie struggled to drag her eyes from his soft-pewter stare, annoyed that she still experienced the deep emotional pull of their connection. They had been soulmates, but how could that bond have endured? How could this man's mere proximity still cause her stomach to churn and her nerve endings to tingle after what he had done?

No, she had to pull herself together, act as though he were a treasured friend, as indeed he was. He remained one of Seb's best friends, along with Archie, who played bass guitar in the band. She reminded herself that she had been only twenty-two when their relationship ended; she was now almost twenty-six and a lot had happened to both of them since then. She would deal with this situation with maturity.

She smiled at Theo, intending to continue with enquiries about his band's success or queries about his family's well-being, but what she saw reflected in the depths of his eyes flashed an unexpected jolt of desire around her disloyal body. But she was determined that her head would fight this battle and she pressed on with her attempt to prove to Theo that she had moved on.

'My aunt left me Gingerberry Yarns, you know.'

'Oh, wow, Cal, I'm so pleased. You loved this shop. I have so many happy memories of hanging out here with Seb and Dominic, you and Nessa. I bet you have loads of plans for it. Perhaps it could do with a lick of paint.' Theo ran his eyes over the walls, where the paint blistered like sunburnt skin.

'I'm not keeping it.'

Theo's smile died on his lips. 'You're what?'

'I'm selling up.'

'You're joking, right?'

'No.'

'Hannah adored this shop. I can't believe you would do that.'

'I do have a life of my own, you know. In Pimlico. I run my own bridal boutique now. It's successful.' Callie didn't know why she'd felt the need to add the last sentence.

'Oh, yes, I heard. You make clothes for rich brides to wear.'

'I design clothes. No, not just clothes – haute couture.' She could hear the defensive hint that had crept into her voice, along with the surprise resurrection of her Yorkshire accent. Theo had always known what buttons to press in more ways than one.

'How can you even think of selling Gingerberry Yarns? It's part of the fabric of our lives. And it's more than that. It's an essential part of this whole community.'

'Don't be ridiculous, Theo. When was the last time you were here?' she challenged.

Theo held her eyes for what felt like an eternity. 'Two weeks ago, actually. Three days before Hannah passed away. Unlike you, I still live here. I haven't run out on my friends, or forgotten what home means. I loved Hannah as much as you did, Cal.'

'Well, I've moved on. My life and my career are in London. I'm leaving tonight.'

'Tonight? So you're not even staying on to sort out the shop? What about Delia? And aren't you even going to catch up with Nessa? The Callie I knew would never pass up the opportunity for a chinwag with her best friend!'

'Not that it's any of your business, but I saw Nessa for a weekend of Christmas shopping and partying at the beginning of December and we talk all the time on the phone. But guess what, smartass, I'm not the Callie you knew any more! Something happened to change all that, didn't it? You betrayed me.'

'I didn't betray you, Cal. I loved you.'

'No, you didn't. I was just the first girl you kissed and who was crazy enough to stick around. So if you didn't betray me, what were you doing with that girl? The Tonsil Tango?'

She forced her duplicitous heart to recall the last image she had of Theo; the one that had lingered in her mind over the years like dripping acid, in which he had his arms wrapped around the voluptuous curves of a flaxen-haired fan of The Razorclaws. She could still recall the girl's cat-like eyes gleaming with triumph at her conquest of the lead singer.

Of course, Theo's explanation for that terrible scene had been relayed to her from numerous sources: Seb, Dominic, her best friend, Nessa. Even his bandmate Archie had sent her a text with a plea to speak to a devastated Theo, explaining that what she had blundered in on had meant nothing; that, in fact, it was a regular by-product of being a member of a moderately successful band – that inevitably there would be fans, groupies, young girls who went to extraordinary lengths to gain access to their heroes, and from whom there was often no polite escape. But Archie's protestations and explanations had only served to make her discovery worse and her pain sharpen. The incident and its fallout had solidified her sneaking suspicion that, when she could not be at Theo's side, there was a line of girls willing to walk into her shoes.

'I just knew you wouldn't be able to resist bringing that up. Nothing happened with Lydia. She threw herself at me. What was I supposed to do? Throw her back?'

'Yes, that's exactly what you were supposed to do!'

'But, it didn't mean anything. It just goes with the territory. You promised to be there to watch us play. For God's sake, Callie, it was the night we finally made it into the big time and my girlfriend wasn't even there to share it with me. Oh, no, she had something much more important to do, like sewing sequins on some rich bitch's dress!'

'Well, I suppose now you are famous, that would put you in the same category as a rich bas—Where are you going?'

'I'm leaving. You've done it. You should be able to recognise the signs.'

Theo wrenched open the door so hard the bell jangled on its chain and came loose, dangling down into Callie's face. She slammed the door behind him and reached up to drop the sneck, tossing the bell from her cheek like a recalcitrant fly, only for it to swing straight back and hit her in the nose. She flapped her hand at it again but it returned to give her a sharp and painful blow on the temple.

Her eyes smarted with tears as Theo rolled his eyes at her through the glass and marched off to his battered old Saab.

CHAPTER EIGHT

Callie hesitated, staring at the screen of her iPhone before selecting Scarlet's number. However, she knew her friend and colleague would understand.

'Are you sure you can manage without me, Scarlet?'

'I'm not totally useless, you know, Callie. After all, haven't I had the most fantastic mentor a fledgling fashion designer could wish for these last three years? If you need to stay on in Yorkshire for a couple of weeks to sort out your aunt's shop, then do it. The decision on Lilac's wedding gown is out of our hands; there's nothing more you can do. Anyway, I've got Flora, although she's as much use as a shop-window mannequin, and there's Lizzie.'

'You *will* ring me tomorrow as soon as you hear anything, won't you?'

'It's a promise. Pinky swear. Now do what you have to do. Actually, the break will do you good. You've just had the most devastating shock, and on top of the hours you've been putting in for the last three months, it's enough to drive anyone to the edge of their sanity. And, hey, I'm loving the broad Yorkshire accent, by the way, Callie. How long have you been back up there? You sound like you've just stepped off the set of *Emmerdale*!'

Callie smiled. 'Thanks, Scarlet. You are the best friend ever. I owe you.'

'Well, I might just extract a promise that you'll take me along to every one of Lilac Verbois's fittings as well as the wedding ceremony. That should repay the debt!'

'Scarlet! We haven't won yet.'

'We will.'

***

Tossing back the embroidered cotton sheet and ancient woollen blankets her aunt had favoured, Callie flicked the sides of her ebony bob behind each ear and dragged her sluggish bones to the bathroom to jump-start her senses. She felt as though she had been flayed by a dominatrix's whip.

Her heart leaden, she was aware that today held her fate in its grasp. But misery had enveloped any trace of excitement at the pending announcement, sorrow extinguishing any hopefulness. Every crevice of the tiny flat above Gingerberry Yarns where she was staying resonated with her aunt's presence, her laughter, her jovial personality. The whole day stretched into the distance as she waited for her future path to be sealed.

Nerves tingled their insistence at her empty stomach. The only sustenance she had managed to provide it with the previous evening after her decision to stay on in Allthorpe had been a mug of Earl Grey tea; anything more solid and it would have screamed its objection. As she sagged over the kitchen table, staring out of the steam-covered window, she wondered when the director of her destiny would grant her asylum from grief.

She ran her eyes over that morning's newspaper story speculating on the identity of the designer. It listed the bookmakers' favourite, even though the final choice would not be made public until Lilac Verbois walked down the aisle. The article displayed a selection of photographs from each of the finalists' previous work. It was an impressive spread. The paper was obviously keen to give its readers their daily fix of the celebrity wedding palaver that was sweeping the nation.

Everyone and their granny was talking about it. Astute in their understanding that their special day would inevitably be a media circus whether they liked it or not, Lilac and Finn had decided to embrace this fact by inviting the public's engagement rather than railing against the offensive intrusion of their privacy. They had made themselves available for interviews, photo shoots and had even run a competition for fifty of Finn's lucky fans to win tickets to his concert in Paris a month after the wedding.

On that crisp, clear morning, Callie did spare a thought for the other designers and their supporting teams. Today someone's life would change for ever, if not that of their whole entourage. Of course she hoped it would be her team, but she empathised with the fact that, whoever won, it would mean others who had slogged their hearts out just as she had would be left reeling.

By four o'clock she could bear it no longer. She grabbed her iPhone and, with her hand trembling, called Scarlet.

'Any news?'

'Nothing.'

'Oh, God, that means we haven't won.'

'There's still another couple of hours…'

Callie's stomach felt like it had contracted around a pineapple. Tears, always so ready to breach the surface lately, pressed up from the back of her throat to her eyelids, but she managed to gulp them down.

'We worked so hard, Scarlet – all of us: you, Flora, Lizzie. But you know what? I can honestly say that was the best wedding gown design of my career so far. I couldn't have produced anything better. So if we didn't win, so be it. It's back to the drawing board and I intend to work even harder to reach the pinnacle of bridal couture.' She cursed the audible wobble that had crept into her voice. 'I'm watching the TV as we speak and they've just shown Lilac's PA, Nikki Coates, and her wedding planner, Tish Marshall, climbing into a limousine outside her house in Kensington. Don't you think they would have called the winner before they left?'

'Maybe you're right, Callie. Oh, God, I'm devastated. I really thought we were going to win.'

***

'*Nikki, you're going to have to break it to Lilac that she needs to choose another dress.*'

'*No way – that's your job. You're the wedding planner, Tish.*'

'*But you've been her PA for years. She's going to take the bad news better from you.*'

'*Are you absolutely sure there was no documentation with the gown she selected? Nothing at all?*'

'*Certain.*'

'*What kind of high-end bridal designer goes to the trouble of painstakingly creating such an exquisite sculpture of silk and pearls only to submit their masterpiece without their contact details?*'

'*And what kind of actress just has to pick their dream dress from one of the gowns their wedding planner can't supply?*'

'*What do you mean "one of the gowns"? There was more than one?*'

'*Two of the twenty that were submitted had no paperwork and the documents of one were illegible.*'

Nikki watched from her desk as Tish, kneeling at the coffee table, shoved the scattered papers into a box file and cringed at the girl's lack of orderliness. Whilst her haphazard attention to detail was unlikely to have been the cause of their current predicament, she still despaired of the wedding arrangements being perfect. Tish's chaotic approach to life also extended to her appearance, yet Nikki had to admit she suited the tousled, just-got-out-of-bed blonde curls and not-quite-perfectly-applied blue eyeliner.

'What about asking Lilac to go with her second choice?'

'You were there, Nikki. You saw how she reacted to that dress. And you have to admit, it was stunning – totally made for her. I know she's already a celebrity but she looked like a fairy-tale princess in that gown, didn't she?' Tish's eyes, the colour of liquid sapphires, glazed over as she tumbled into her own fantasy world.

'Tish, quit the Cinderella fantasy. We have to sort this fiasco out ourselves. We can't burden Lilac with the problem. She's got enough to worry about.'

'So what are we going to do? I'm slammed as it is. I've not eaten since yesterday lunchtime. I've got the bridesmaids' bouquets to finalise, the wedding cake topper to chase – you know the confectioner is crazy, don't you? There's the champagne still to source and I have a meeting with the printer tomorrow to finalise the wording on the invitations and orders of service. The invitations need to be sent out by the end of the week

at the latest, although the whole world knows when the wedding is going to be.

'*The only thing that seems to be on schedule at the moment is the music. The organist at York Minster is sorted and he's rehearsed the pieces Lilac and Finn have selected for the ceremony. And the band is booked and the lead singer has even written a song especially for the happy couple that he's agreed to debut at the evening reception. Oh, Nikki, I'm so excited we're getting to meet The Razorclaws. That lead singer, Theo Drake – what a dreamboat. I hear he's unattached. Do you think he has come-to-bed eyes? My sister thinks he has.*'

'*Good grief, Tish, will you calm down with the hearts-and-flowers fixation. You'll have to squeeze some time from somewhere and it'll have to be straight away. We promised to inform the designer they've won the competition as soon as possible. Everyone who submitted will be thinking their design hasn't been selected and they'll start accepting new commissions. There'll have to be a couple of fittings at least and Lilac is a busy girl. She's on location in Croatia for three weeks before the wedding, which, can I remind you, is just three and a half months away.*'

Nikki was used to lurching from one crisis to the next. In fact, she thrived on the daily adrenalin rush. It made her feel worthy of her position as Lilac's right-hand woman – her Girl Friday. She almost hated it when things went smoothly. But this wedding had proved to be the ultimate headache. Tish was so involved in the romance of it all that, on occasion, she had to restrain herself from throttling her.

Okay, yes, wedding planners had to be in love with everything 'planet bridal' to work in the industry, but Tish had taken her obsession to a new level. She was usually to be found floating around the office on the wings of Eros, constantly chattering about diamanté tiaras, personalised confetti (with pictures of the bride and groom printed on it, for God's sake!), and sugared almonds, which she had the perfect excuse to indulge in. Annoyingly, Tish also seemed to have been blessed with a metabolism that ignored the onslaught of sugar. She, on the other hand, despite following a semi-vegetarian diet, still struggled with losing the extra stone that had crept up on her unnoticed – and it had nothing to do with the cupcakes from the Parisian patisserie that had popped up on the corner in the last three months.

Tish had certainly thrown herself into her chosen career, happy to hunt down the most bizarre of requests as she waited patiently to play the lead role in her own fairy-tale Happy Ever After. Of course the girl had her own wedding day planned right down to the toilet paper she wanted in the ladies' cloakroom of the Savoy. Only one tiny detail was missing – there was no groom loitering in the wings, or backstage, or even on the auditions list. So, whilst her own personal hearts-and-flowers scenario was on the back burner, she was content to pour all her energies into conjuring up everyone else's dream wedding.

'But where should I start?'

Nikki rolled her eyes. 'Look, make a list of all the designers who were asked to submit. Then go through the dresses that did arrive with the correct paperwork and tick them off. See what's left. There may be a couple who decided not to submit, but at least we'll have narrowed it down. I'm late for a meeting with Lilac's agent, but I'll be back in an hour and we'll go through the list together.'

'Don't worry, I'll ring them.'

'No! You can't do that.'

'Why not?'

'Well, how do you plan on finding out if it's their dress?'

'Email them a photo – oh, no, right, I see.'

'We've got to be careful not to disclose the final design of the most anticipated wedding dress this year to anyone. Absolute secrecy – we promised Lilac – nothing until it is unveiled to the world on the steps of York Minster. We can't go around emailing everyone a photo. Especially the designers whose gowns failed to make the cut. Think about it!'

'So what are we going to do?'

'I'll think of something. Just get that list sorted and I'll see you in an hour.'

Nikki gathered up the Birkin handbag Lilac had given her for Christmas and a bundle of box files and left Tish

to her task. *This latest development was the last thing
she needed, but her ordered mind was already clicking
through the possibilities as she affixed her new badge of
'Nuptial Detective' to her already crowded breast.*

*Solving problems was her forte, along with a
mild addiction to list-making and fighting off the
media, sometimes physically. Everything she did
was organised with almost surgical precision. There
was no conundrum that outfoxed her. She knew
Lilac's entourage gossiped about her for catering
to the actress's every whim, no matter how bizarre
or outlandish, and her strategies for negotiating the
best price would have embarrassed the head buyer
of Poundland. They would locate the creative idiot
who submitted the gown without the paperwork, but
she'd have something to say to the designer about her
business practices.*

*As she stepped into the glass elevator for her ride
down to the foyer, Nikki allowed herself a faint grimace.
They would probably end up having to tour the whole
country in their search for the elusive designer, which
meant Tish had actually got her wish, after all. This
wedding was turning into a real Cinderella story, just
not the hearts-and-flowers bit – the Poirotesque bit.*

CHAPTER NINE

'Is everything okay, Scarlet? I'll be back at the boutique by the end of the week.'

'Look, why don't you take this opportunity to have some time out, Callie? A sort of short sabbatical?'

'No! After I've sorted out the shop I need to come back and bury myself in the studio. I have to keep designing for my sanity, especially after receiving this blow to my confidence. I need to return to my own life in London. There's nothing left for me up here. I've got lots of new ideas for the Spring/Summer Collection next year. I…' She failed at her attempts to control her emotions and huge racking sobs burst from her chest.

'Callie, you've just lost your aunt, your only remaining parental figure. It's hard to come to terms with the fact there's no safety net to catch you if you fall. You have to take some time to grieve; let it out, don't bottle it up. Of course we'll miss you, but we can manage for a couple of months.'

'A couple of months?'

'Mourn, recharge your creative batteries, organise your family's affairs. Spend some time with those handsome cousins of yours. Market the shop, sell up, or whatever you decide, but don't rush this decision.'

'You can't seriously be suggesting that I run a little haberdashery shop in rural Yorkshire alongside a couture bridal boutique in Pimlico?'

'I'm just saying, take your time. We'll keep in touch, let you know if there are any panics or problems we can't handle. It's only a three-hour train ride away if you need to come down.'

An invisible force pressed down on Callie's shoulders, inducing a dark, heavy lethargy. She had no idea how long she remained at that scarred pine table in her aunt's cosy kitchen, so familiar as the backdrop to many a teenage trauma that had been talked through with the aid of a strong cup of Yorkshire tea from the big brown pot. She, along with Nessa, had lurched from one adolescent crisis to the next; all of which seemed trivial, with the benefit of hindsight, compared to the current turmoil in her life. Sadness lanced her heart and failure sapped her self-esteem, but mingled in with the mix were spirals of indecision about what to do with her aunt's beloved Gingerberry Yarns.

Outside, twilight tickled at the branches of the trees that lined the high street as the traders began to close their shops for the day. If she *did* decide to carry on her aunt's legacy – to honour her memory, to preserve

Gingerberry Yarns for the community – at what cost would that be to her own dreams and ambitions?

She consciously shook herself out of her self-pitying reverie and chastised herself for her despondency. She dragged herself from her seat to dump her mug in the kitchen sink, her mind a scattergun of confused thoughts as she tried to assimilate the consequences of her failure to win the most coveted prize of her life. All those months of unrelenting hard work and unerring focus on one solitary goal that had been disallowed. A goal, she had to admit, she had thought would clinch the match.

Was she arrogant, overly confident in her own creative ability? Obviously, she had been. She had neglected everything and everyone – her aunt, Seb and Dominic, her friends, her love life – in her quest for recognition, notoriety even; for the chance to showcase her design talent to the world, to become a part, however small, of the celebrity circus that was Lilac and Finn's wedding.

If it had been her wedding, this farcical competition would be the very epitome of what she did *not* want. Such an intimate, joyful union demanded only the involvement of those who truly loved and cared for the couple and, as her fragile self-worth plummeted, Callie thought she could count on one hand those stalwart friends who would be in attendance at her own marriage ceremony.

Anyway, what was she doing dreaming about her non-existent wedding? And there was no point in speculating on the identity of any potential groom. There was only one person up there in prime position.

Theo.

But she had no spare emotion to waste on dissecting her relationship with Theo. She shoved that cushion full of pins to the back of her mind for future examination. She had enough emotional pain in her life to be getting on with – neglectful niece to Hannah, uninterested cousin to Seb and Dominic, absent friend to Nessa and Scarlet, and now mediocre fashion designer at Callie-Louise Bridal Couture. Adding failure as a girlfriend to the list would tip her over the edge and she'd be looking at her sanity in the rear-view mirror.

Anyway, she had a shop to get ready for sale.

CHAPTER TEN

'My design didn't win the Lilac Verbois wedding gown competition, Delia.' Callie broke off to inhale a steadying breath and tried to concentrate her attention on the window of the shop, beyond which the day promised warmth. The pavements of the high street were swathed in golden sun as the locals went about their daily business.

She'd found it difficult to elucidate her failure aloud, but was surprised to experience a welcome surge of relief now it was out there. She hoped Delia would grasp the baton of its knowledge and pass it on to the curious, as she knew her aunt had shared her shortlisting in the competition far and wide.

'And also, Scarlet has agreed to look after the boutique for a couple of months to, erm, allow me to sort things out and recover from the duo of shocks.'

A fresh flash of guilt stabbed at her veins that her courage had failed her once again. She couldn't mention the sale of the business to Delia. She experienced a heavy tug of dawning realisation of what kind of person she was – shallow and deceitful.

'Oh, Callie, you don't know how delighted I am to hear that!' exclaimed Delia, releasing Callie from a J'Adore-infused hug. 'I know you have a busy and absorbing life down there in the capital, and colleagues desperate for your return, but you also have a great many friends up here in Allthorpe, you know. I'm so pleased you're staying on for a while. Your aunt would definitely approve.' Delia raised her eyes up to the cracked ceiling. 'Hannah would never have wanted the shop to close down. She was so angry and upset when she heard what had happened to the butcher's shop. She even went as far as objecting to the planning application for change of use to residential – made no difference, of course. But what will happen to this village if *all* the shops close down and are converted into holiday homes and weekend retreats for escapees from the corporate rat race? Allthorpe would become a faded image of its current vibrancy.

'Gingerberry Yarns isn't just a shop selling wool and trimmings; it's a hub of social activity and provides a much-needed service to this community. Don't you remember when you were still at home? All your aunt's friends calling in for a chat, a word of support, of sympathy, of guidance? We're part of the fabric of people's lives. Look how supportive everyone's been these past weeks, rallying round to offer not only a baked pie or a chicken casserole, but a listening ear, a word of comfort, and I have to admit I've succumbed to that offer more than once.'

Tears sprang into Delia's tired eyes as she anxiously tried to get her message across to Callie, who sat, head bent low to the table, studying the dregs of her cold tea. She reached across and took Callie's slender fingers in her own.

'We can't sell the place to a property developer out to make a fast buck. If it has to be sold, then let's try to pass on the legacy to someone who will continue to run it with the same ethos. I'll manage on my own so you can market the business as a going concern, a viable proposition for a potential buyer. It'd probably be worth more that way, or it would be more likely to sell to someone who wanted to keep it on.'

Was Delia right? Was she letting her aunt down by not at least trying to keep Gingerberry Yarns open? Could she handle the guilt of cutting all her ties with her childhood home? She had adored this shop, this village. The people who came were like an extended family to her. Many of her aunt's friends had stopped her on the street to offer their condolences and had been touchingly devastated at her passing.

She recalled bumping into Iris, one of Delia's best friends, and her daughter, Marcia. But what had really surprised her was that they'd been genuinely frightened about what decisions she was going to make about

Gingerberry's future. Marcia had even said it was the only thing she lived for, being able to bring Iris out in her wheelchair to the shop every day, leaving her chatting to Hannah and Delia whilst she ran her errands.

'When was the last time you and Nessa got together for a good old chinwag? Okay' – she held up her palm, her stout fingers glittering with a cluster of rings – 'I know you saw her at the funeral, but I mean really connected? You two were inseparable at school, as close as primer and paint. Pair of devils, you were! You know she'll be at the Fox and Hounds on Friday night. Why don't you go and join her for a drink?'

'Oh, Delia, I'm not…'

'I want you to rekindle some of the love and community spirit Hannah and I were fortunate enough to enjoy, even if it's just for a short time. The community's support has been such an integral part of our lives, especially for your aunt after John passed away. She missed him terribly, as I'm sure you all did. Hannah drew on the comfort and friendship offered by her many friends. It helped to heal her sorrow, if not her heart. And it could do the same for you, Callie, dear. Steer you through this miasma of grief and confusion.

'Fate has a carefully drafted plan for us all, but sadly it must remain confidential.' Delia's eyes peered over the top of her glasses, their silver restraint glinting in the shafts of sunlight forging their way through the dirt-ridden windows.

'I don't believe in fate, Delia. I believe that we should mould our own destiny, not wait until it lands fully formed in our path.'

But she knew Delia had a point. She had to at least try to give the misfortune that had befallen her in the last two weeks a positive spin. Life did go on, and if her aunt could survive after the loss of her beloved husband, then she could stop acting like a puppet clipped of its strings. She needed to quit wallowing in self-pity and put some elbow grease into those filthy windows.

Callie collected a cloth from behind the counter and tentatively rubbed at a small patch of the front window to reveal a sparklingly clear outlook over the road to Marietta's and the scaffolding-bedecked ex-butcher's shop. The blackened stone façades of the depleted row of shops, their painted doors and bay-fronted windows open to trade, spoke volumes. Sadly, the six shops which had thrived for the last thirty years had been slashed to four with the closure of Wainwright's butchers and Greenwood's grocers. The loss of the butcher's in particular had been a grave blow to the community of Allthorpe's Sunday breakfast.

Marietta's Hairdressing Salon was busy, though, churning out hyper-trendy, celebrity-inspired haircuts to the village elders as well as the more discerning teenagers. That just left Hale's estate agents, the bookmaker's and the bank – those peddlers of revolving financial transactions that seemed to be immune from the vicious knives of the current recession.

Delia joined Callie in her toil and they spent the day scrubbing, dusting and reorganising the shop. 'The high street is dying, I'm afraid. It's not only the supermarkets' advance that's draining away our business to their neon-lit cathedrals of consumerism; it's the influx of the weekenders. Those wealthy families chasing the rural idyll for a few snatched hours of calm before they return to their hamster-wheels in the city to churn out more money for their masters or their pension pots. Hannah despaired at every shop closure, every one a shining light extinguished along with the proprietor's dreams. Our lives are wider than one, Callie.'

When the sky dimmed, signalling the end of the working day, Callie smiled her gratitude to Delia as tears brimmed and choked her vocal cords. She waved her off and, as she secured the shop door behind her and pulled down the blind, took a moment to survey the careworn contents of the shop again. The only thing she wanted to do at that moment was abandon herself to the onslaught of nostalgia. The waft of her aunt's favourite perfume still lingered amongst the multicoloured gems of angora and mohair, silk and cotton, jutting from the stands like jewels on a Fabergé egg.

She mounted the stairs to her childhood bedroom, cloaked in a shroud of loneliness. Happiness was a mere apparition that punctuated her life with decreasing regularity. Instead, anguish and heartache stalked her daily path to sleep, the relief in its oblivion always a delayed destination.

Fear gripped her heart as she realised she would now have to live her life without the safety net of her aunt's, or anyone else's, love.

CHAPTER ELEVEN

Callie took a deep breath and pushed open the door of the Fox and Hounds, feeling like a seventeen-year-old about to order alcohol for the first time. The buzz of muted conversation and background music swirled through the air, producing a welcoming atmosphere. She had spent too many nights to recall drinking at the village pub and it was as familiar as an old pair of favourite boots.

'Hey, is that you, Callie? You look like you just walked off the catwalk!'

'Hey, erm...'

'Juliette? We were in the same art class at school?'

'Of course we were. How are you, Juliette?' Callie cast her eyes over the barmaid's fresh face, devoid of any scrap of make-up, her cheeks glowing with the flush of health and her lips a natural rosebud pink.

'I love your top. Where did you get it? M&S?'

'Erm, no, it's one I designed myself...'

'Ah, sorry, yes. I did hear you made clothes now. Callie, I'm so sorry about your aunt. She was a lovely lady and we'll miss her in the village.' Juliette reached over and pulled Callie into a hug. 'Hey, you're all skin and bone. Look at you, like a line prop, bones jutting from all angles. What you need is one of Gavin's Yorkshire hotpots.'

'No! Thanks. No.' Callie hadn't eaten meat since she moved down to London. 'Ah, Nessa!'

Relief at seeing her old friend swarmed through her veins. Callie took in Nessa's familiar features as she pushed her way towards her through the regulars hogging the bar, her long auburn hair flowing free from its usual clasp in honour of her escape from the strict regulations placed on gym mistresses at St Hilda's High School.

'Hi, Callie, great to see you. Come on – Seb and Archie are in the snug playing snooker.'

'Is… is Theo with them?' She prayed that the hint of hopefulness in her voice wasn't too much of a giveaway. Sadly, her friend missed nothing.

'No, but he might join us later. He usually does whenever he's home. You okay with that? He said you'd thrown him out of the shop when he went to see you.'

'A bit of an exaggeration, but that was always one of Theo's charming quirks. I didn't throw him out.'

'Oh, Callie, it's so good to hear your accent's back when you're hyped up over Theo!'

'I'm not hyped up over Theo, Nessa.'

'Okay. What'll you have to drink?'

'I'll have a vodka martini.'

'Sure.'

Callie waited whilst Nessa pushed her way to the bar and returned with their drinks.

'What's this?'

'Pint of Theakston's Best Bitter.'

'But I asked for…'

'We used to drink this stuff by the gallon, remember?'

'Yes, but I… Oh, never mind.' Callie took a sip and ran her tongue over her lips. It was delicious – golden, yeasty, fresh – and she swallowed a long draught, wiping the froth from her upper lip with the back of her hand.

'Now we see her! The old Callie-Louise Henshaw is back with us again!' exclaimed Seb, drawing her into a squeeze and dropping a kiss on her forehead. 'Callie, I'm so pleased you decided to stay on for a few weeks.'

'Hey, Callie! Great to see you.' Archie rested his snooker cue against the table and strode round to envelop her in his arms. 'Missed you, darling. We all do. It's just like old times. Well, it will be when…'

'So, Callie…' Nessa guided her away from a trip down Archie's Memory Lane to a bashed copper table in the corner of the snug next to a museum-standard display of Gavin's best horse brasses and Toby jugs. 'I hear you've decided to sell Gingerberry? Is it really true?'

'Did I hear you right?' asked Archie, who had edged round the table to take his next shot. 'You're selling up? You're leaving again? Aren't we your friends any more, Callie?'

'Of course you are, Archie.' But she couldn't quite meet his accusatory stare.

Another pint arrived and Callie gulped half down in one go. The unfamiliar dose of alcohol was working very nicely at erasing the sharp edges of the local pub. Good grief, she thought, what was Archie doing here, anyway? Why wasn't he living it up in the nightspots of London or Manchester? He was the bass guitarist in one of the most successful bands in Britain at the moment. Hell, The Razorclaws were lucky enough to be booked to perform at the wedding of the decade. If they weren't in demand now, they certainly would be after that. Jealous? Her? Yes!

'I'm so sorry about Hannah, Callie. I loved her, too. We didn't get a chance to talk much at her funeral. How are you holding up?' asked Nessa.

She saw her childhood friend study her over the rim of her pint glass, casting a worried glance over her scrawny frame. They'd been exactly the same build at school, but now Nessa possessed the taut, muscular silhouette of a sports instructor as well as the rosy glow of health and vigour achieved by spending her days on the hockey field with eleven adolescent girls. Securing her position as their old high school's gym teacher was a dream come true for Nessa.

'Oh, well, you know, I'm doing okay, I suppose.'

The scene was a replica of their adolescent dialogues – the welcoming atmosphere of the Fox and Hounds, a ready supply of beer and her friend's soothing words – it was the balm to cure many a teenage heartache. But with the empty space in her heart her aunt had inhabited, Callie doubted any amount of Theakston's Best Bitter would heal the trauma she was experiencing at that moment. The aroma of Chanel Cristal, Nessa's favourite perfume, and the sympathy oozing from her oldest friend conjured up the pain-lashed memories of the last few weeks and caused hot tears to flow down her cheeks.

'I miss her so much, Nessa. I was a useless niece. I've hardly been home in the last three years. Too engrossed in my selfish ambitions, thinking I could run with the pack of celebrity wedding gown designers. Now I'm a true orphan.' Her grief resumed; raw and violent.

'You are not useless, Callie.' Nessa's habitually jolly face, strewn with freckles, reflected the pain she herself was suffering.

Callie saw her friend sweep her eyes over her hair, usually as glossy as liquid tar, but which today hung flat and dull, her fringe skimming her spidery lashes and in need of a salon's attention. She knew she looked a mess. Dark triangular smudges had lodged themselves beneath her eyes that no amount of foundation could disguise, not that she had tried; she sported not a scrap of make-up. What was the point?

'I am, Nessa. Not only as a niece, but as a cousin' – she shot a glance across to where Seb and Archie were studiously avoiding looking in their direction – 'and as a friend. And I might as well add as a fashion designer, too. You heard, didn't you? Delia is this village's one-woman Twitter feed.'

Nessa nodded, her amber lashes sparkling with empathic tears, but she knew Nessa was not going to stand aside whilst she slipped into self-obsessed oblivion.

'Yes, I heard, but it's not the end of the world, Cal. So you didn't make it to the pinnacle of the pile this time, but you *did* make it to the shortlist. That, my girl, is a fantastic achievement and one which two hundred and fifty others would have died to achieve. Your aunt was so proud of your talents.'

'Oh, Ness, all I want to do now is sell the shop and slink back to my old life, hide in the familiar routine of eighteen-hour days and have as little contact with the outside world as I can get away with. Is that so awful?' Callie paused to blow her dripping nose on the tissue offered by Nessa and take a gulp of her beer. She managed to pull herself together and produce a weak smile. 'My plan is to block out my grief in a whirlwind of crazy schedules, deadlines and prenuptial angst.'

The evening passed in a swirl of shared memories, snippets of recent gossip and several more pints of beer.

After a while, Callie began to relax and enjoy herself. She even managed to giggle at one of the stories Nessa told her about dating a guy from the golf club who had helped her to 'improve her swing'.

'Ah, I see Little Miss Dior has decided to grace us with her presence. Thought you couldn't wait to get back down to the bright lights of the big city? What are you still doing here loitering in the dull Yorkshire backwater that you used to call home? Oh, is that beer? I thought designers of bridal couture only drank vodka martini – stirred not shaken, if you please?'

'Theo…' cautioned Nessa.

'It's okay, Ness. Hi, Theo. I've decided to stay up here for a few weeks to sort out some of my aunt's things and then, yes, you're right, I'll be gone.'

'So, you *are* selling the shop. Why are you so keen to permanently erase any memories of your past, Cal? Do I take it from your change of heart that you failed to win the coveted wedding gown competition?'

Callie felt warmth flood her face, but it was accompanied by a flash of white hot anger.

'What business is it of yours, Theo? We're not a couple any more. You don't know what I've got going on in my life!'

'I know you left your friends behind to pursue your dreams without so much as a backward glance. What sort of person would do that?'

'One who was betrayed by her boyfriend!'

Theo held her eyes for a moment, his irises glinting silver with resentment. 'You know, Callie, I'm tired of you throwing that golden nugget in my face every time we meet.'

Callie felt Nessa squeeze her arm.

'I did not betray you, Callie, but you betrayed your friends. These wonderful people' – Theo cast his hand around to include Seb, Archie and finally Nessa – 'who loved you and whom you hurt badly when you left in a fit of fury to focus on your ambitions in London.'

Callie met Nessa's moss-green eyes and a coil of guilt wound through her veins. She opened her mouth to reply but Theo was still speaking.

'I may have made a mistake, but at least I know who my friends are. I would never treat them with the disdain you have by eradicating them from my life, only returning when I *have* to and only staying long enough to extinguish every connection I had with my childhood.'

Theo slammed down his half-finished pint on the green baize of the snooker table and strode from the pub, his long stride assisting in his speedy exit.

Nessa patted Callie's hand as Seb and Archie wound in their necks, closed their mouths and set up another game of snooker.

'He went crazy when you left, Cal,' Nessa whispered.

'I find that hard to believe. He had an army of star-struck young girls buzzing around him like bees to a honey pot. I'm sure he forgot about me straight away.'

'He went looking for you.'

'What do you mean?'

'To London.'

'Theo came to London?'

'Yes. Of course, Hannah respected your wishes and refused to divulge your address. But she loved Theo as much as she loved you and Seb and Dom. She struggled with your decision to cut Theo from your life. He didn't know where you were, but he went anyway.'

'I never saw him.'

'He didn't say much when he got back. We didn't ask, either. He threw every last crumb of his energy into making The Razorclaws a success. As you know, they'd just signed their recording contract so they were caught up in a mad frenzy of songwriting, recording and touring. But, Callie, he always loved you. Theo without Callie by his side took some getting used to for all of us. He still loves you.'

'No, he doesn't.'

Nessa studied her. 'Have you been over to pay your respects to your parents since you've been back?'

'Oh, Ness, you know how hard that is for me.'

'Come on.' Nessa drained her pint and linked her arm through Callie's. She nodded across to Seb and Archie and guided her friend out of the pub.

The night sky was swathed in velvety blackness with scant pinpricks of scattered stars. The cool, fresh air sharpened Callie's senses and she loved the feeling of having Nessa so close to her. For a moment, she felt like she'd never left Allthorpe. They were still the two mischievous teenagers making their way to sit on the wall of Reverend Coulson's churchyard to exchange secrets, divulge confidences, sneak sips from a bottle of cider and giggle at the childish antics of Theo, Seb, Archie and Dominic. Boys, eh?

'I'd forgotten how beautiful it is here. Seems I forgot a lot of things, not just Theo.'

Why hadn't she come back home more often after she'd left? Even if it was just to snatch a weekend with Nessa. Why hadn't she insisted more firmly that Nessa come down to stay with her in the flat above her boutique in Pimlico during the school holidays more often? Suggest they take in a show or a concert or the rugby cup final – Nessa adored rugby; well, all sports really.

'I really am sorry, Ness. I've been a truly awful friend. Will you ever be able to forgive me?'

'Real friends need no apologies, Cal. You were just investing in your dreams. I've followed mine. I'm happy. Only one thing would put the proverbial cherry on top of my cupcake.'

'What?'

It was Nessa's turn to colour up.

'Or should I say, who?'

They had reached the lychgate of the parish church. Nessa lifted the rusty iron handle and they sauntered along the churchyard's pathway, meandering through the moss-strewn graves which protruded from the ground like a set of crooked ogre's teeth.

Then Callie saw it. Her parents' grave. And there, in front of the grey marble headstone, was the white rose bush that Theo had planted for her all those years ago. It had been carefully pruned and well cared for.

'Beautiful, isn't it?'

'Yes,' murmured Callie, allowing the tears to trickle unchecked down her cheeks.

'Theo comes here every time he's home from a tour to tend the rose bush that you planted together for your parents.'

Callie turned in astonishment to her best friend in the world.

'He…'

'It's like a ritual with him.'

Callie was suddenly so overwhelmed by a surge of grief that she dropped down onto her knees and sobbed as though the tears would never stop.

CHAPTER TWELVE

Spring cast its blanket of hopefulness and renewal across the undulating fields but it failed to restore Callie's desolate spirits. Fingers of pale ivory light spread across the horizon promising a sharp new dawn and hinting at a warm sunny Sunday morning. All village activity was confined to the churchyard perched at the end of the village, so Allthorpe High Street was deserted.

Grimacing with annoyance at missing the best part of the day, Callie sat cross-legged on the threadbare Persian rug in front of a scarred red suitcase, its lid yawning wide, stuffed with a plethora of documents, yellowing newspaper clippings, official-looking letters and random receipts, all of which masqueraded as her aunt's business accounts.

She'd been putting it off, but it was time to delve into the murk that was Gingerberry Yarns' finances, such as they were. The task was turning into a feat of financial archaeology that even *Time Team* would have baulked at!

Her mug of Earl Grey tea had grown cold and her neck and shoulders were screaming their objection when her toil was interrupted by a loud hammering on the shop door downstairs.

It's Sunday morning, for heaven's sake, Callie thought grumpily, unfolding her stiffened, jean-clad legs and raising her numb buttocks from the mat. She rolled her neck muscles by twisting her shoulders, before trotting down the stairs to answer someone's urgent call for that last ball of yarn required to complete a project that could not have waited a moment longer.

But it wasn't a desperate customer.

'Nessa!'

'Hi, Callie.'

'Come on in. I'm busy trying to scale a mountain of my aunt's paperwork.'

Callie led Nessa upstairs into the room that served as both kitchen and sitting room. Documents were spread over every available surface, some tumbling like an alpine avalanche from the chintzy sofa down to the rug and the nest-like space in which Callie had been sitting as she thrashed her way through the maze of bureaucracy.

'I had an inkling you've not been eating properly since you arrived home. That is why, my friend, I have arrived on this mercy mission to rescue you from your hunger pangs with these little beauties.' She held aloft a familiar pale peppermint box tied with ivory ribbon.

'Picked them up yesterday from Wallington's bakery. Everyone's talking about it, so I thought I'd make a special detour. Did you know the guy did his training in Paris and then honed his spectacular talent at Betty's, or was it the other way round? You do remember that Betty's Emporium of Confectionary is my most favourite shop in the world, right? These cupcakes are to die for. Erm, I have to confess we started off with three each, but, well, I felt honour-bound to ensure they were up to scratch for my best friend's delectation!'

Nessa had already flicked on the kettle and set about arranging the little sugary gems onto a china plate she'd pulled from the cupboard. 'Earl Grey?' She held the old-fashioned brown teapot aloft, her eyebrows raised as Callie took a seat.

The four chairs around the scrubbed pine table had always invited a good gossip. The unloading of worries into willing ears had been Hannah's cure for the side effects of hanging onto trauma until it gnawed at the gut and allowed bitterness to take its place.

'So, come on then, Callie, reboot your modem and spill the details and I mean every minuscule embellishment, every fold, drape, crease and stitch of this spectacular bridal creation Lilac Verbois did not possess the good taste to select. Do you have a photo?'

Callie smiled at last, her cheeks cracking under the unfamiliar strain and the fact that her skin hadn't enjoyed a smudge of moisturiser in weeks. 'Sure I do.

And I suppose there's no reason not to share the design with you now. The veil of secrecy is redundant!' She fished out her iPhone and scrolled through the images she had stored.

'Oh, my God, Callie, it's stunning. A little on the elaborate side for my taste, but then I'm not a BAFTA-winning actress. This wedding fever has really gripped the nation, hasn't it?' Nessa lifted her mane of copper hair and let it fall in waves down her back, clearly enjoying the lightness and freedom wearing it loose gave her.

'You should eavesdrop on the conversations of some of the girls at school – it's all they talk about. Well, what's not to obsess over? A wedding almost on the doorstep, a whole host of celebrities descending on the county, fashions to scrutinise and criticise. Oh, I've not had chance to tell you. One of our girls, Alicia Walker, has been selected to sing the solo in the York Minister wedding ceremony, no less! With the level of excitement and the raging hormones, needless to say not much academic work is getting done at the moment. Fortunately, Alicia is in Year Ten and doesn't have exams to worry about this summer.'

'It's great for the school, Nessa, but I have to admit I am curious about what made Lilac and Finn choose York Minster for their ceremony. Wouldn't you have thought they'd have chosen a venue in London? Much more central, more convenient for everyone?'

'What do you mean? It's obvious why Lilac chose the Minster. She grew up in Yorkshire – or so her publicity blurb says. She's maybe on some nostalgic jaunt into her childhood, which I assume was "tormented by abusive parents or boyfriends, thus enabling me to bring my real-life experiences into my roles" – you know, the kind of garbage they spout out in these résumés. Anyway, all chaos broke loose when it was announced that Alicia had been selected. Mrs Coombes even had to sedate one of the girls.

'But, I have to admit,' confided Nessa as she tucked tendrils of hair behind her ears, her soft cheeks glowing with pleasure, 'I've also succumbed to following the twists and turns avidly, especially as it turns out I know four of the people involved personally! You, Theo, Archie and Alicia. I wish I could sing, but as you know my multiple talents lie in the sports arena. If only there were a netball, or a hockey, or a golf competition, I'd be right up there with the rest of them.

'However,' she giggled, 'unsurprisingly there's no call for those skills in the circus that is Lilac Verbois and Finn Marchant's wedding. Callie, I'm so sorry your design didn't win but we've still got to go to York to watch the ceremony.'

'I'm not sure about that, Ness.'

Callie had often wondered over the years why Nessa had stuck to training recalcitrant teenage girls on the school sports field. Only last year she had been offered a position as a ladies' golf instructor at one of the newly built courses in Dubai – mega-money compared to her teacher's salary, along with a spectacular apartment overlooking the Burg Al Arab which came with a maid thrown in for free.

But Nessa had not hesitated in turning it down. She excelled in every sport Callie had known her put her mind to, threw herself head first into dating every eligible guy who crossed her path, and generally lived life to the max with an irritatingly cheerful smile, a flick of her hair and a cute wrinkle of her freckled nose. Nessa had always professed to loathe her freckles and Callie recalled with fondness one Saturday night, when they were around twelve, that they'd spent scrubbing her nose and cheeks with her mother's expensive body exfoliator. Nessa's face had smarted with a red hue for a full week but even that had not diluted her zest for life.

Together they had run marathons, swapped secrets and dressed up in the forerunners of Callie's designs made from old cotton sheets and velour curtains donated by Nessa's mum, Audrey. She still squirmed at the memories of the chaffing! Over the years they had each added more items to their wedding scrap boxes – oversized shoe boxes they had covered in sheets of wedding wrap and filled with snippets of fabric and lace, glossy photographs and articles cut from magazines, and sketches of what their individual dresses would look like. On the lid they'd taped a picture of their current crush – first Seb, then Robbie Williams, then a whole string of eligible pop stars and actors for Nessa's, and Theo, always Theo for hers. She still had her box under her bed at home in Pimlico and continued to add to it even now. The latest addition was a photograph of a gorgeous pair of stilettos from the Jimmy Choo bridal collection that had her name embroidered all over their smooth satin toes. She wondered if Nessa still did the same.

A hammering on the door of the shop interrupted their girly conversation.

'Gosh, another visitor. I've never been so popular.'

Callie skipped down the stairs and let Seb in. She pecked him on his bristly cheek and smiled at his pale, pinched face, the smudges of tiredness under his dark brown eyes more prominent when he removed his tortoiseshell glasses to rub the bridge of his nose. He slumped his six-foot-two frame into the chair opposite Nessa and stretched out his legs.

'Hi, Nessa. I'm not interrupting anything, am I?'

'Not at all.'

Callie poured him a mug of tea and pushed one of Tom Wallington's delectable cupcakes towards him. Hers remained on the china plate untouched; its aesthetic perfection felt like an insult to her emotional chaos. She couldn't bear to sully its beauty with her unworthy lips.

'Callie, I'm so pleased you decided to stay up here for few weeks to sort out the shop. What's your plan? I reckon a lick of paint wouldn't go amiss.'

'I agree, I…'

'Then I have the perfect solution. Me, Dom and Archie will pitch in and help.'

'Count me in, too,' added Nessa, her eyes sparkling with possibilities. 'You've got to keep Gingerberry Yarns open whilst it's on the market.'

Nessa reached over to replenish her mug from the pot. She wrapped her palms around its warmth and left her seat at the table to stroll over to the window. She stared at the row of shops across the street, her back to Callie and Seb, deep in thought. After a while she continued verbalising her thoughts.

'After all, Hannah's haberdashery has become the social hub of Allthorpe High Street. Her faithful customers have lost not only a beloved friend, but a stalwart of the local community. Someone who swore she would protect the fabric of this village. I know I don't have to remind you that some people's lives revolve around their visits to this welcoming oasis of calm and acceptance – better than a spa treatment any day.

'There's nowhere else to go. They can't hang out at the bank over there, or the bookmaker's next door, and since the library closed down last year there's nowhere to grab a cappuccino or a latte or a good old pot of tea.

The nearest café is in Heppleton and that's ten miles away. Hey! Yes, that's it!' Nessa swung round to stare at Callie, her eyes sparkling with excitement.

'What?'

'This is your chance to create your dream!'

'What dream?' Callie rolled her eyes at Nessa who, as always, was speeding along on a different tangent.

'The "Gingerberry Emporium" dream – vendor of bespoke yarn creations and aromatic coffee concepts!'

'What are you dribbling on about?' Callie collected their empty mugs and ditched them in the sink before resuming her curled-up position on the ancient rug surrounded by paperwork.

'I'm talking about Gingerberry Yarns, international supplier of custom-made knitted garments to the connoisseur of sculptured yarn and modern creative art, and purveyor of the best cappuccino, latte and espresso for a ten-mile radius!'

'International? Now you're being plain ridiculous, Ness…'

'Set up a website – that'll cover the international bit. Get busy researching a selection of designs worn by the trendy jet set and TV celebrities – like those Danish Fair Isle sweaters from that detective series. You can get the WI knitting circle involved – they love a good challenge. Hey, we could even run knitting sessions here in the shop, start teaching those who are interested to knit and crochet? Maybe market it as an opportunity to contribute to a charity project in the form of a blanket or throw for the Heppleton hospice?'

'Wow, I think Nessa might be onto something here, Cal.' Seb had swivelled round in his seat to join in the discussions. 'The shop downstairs is crammed with miles and miles of ribbon and lace. You could even coach the ladies to sew garments for your bridal boutique in London, such as garters and knickers. Maybe Gingerberry can become the first branch of Callie-Louise Bridal Couture outside London.'

'Fabulous idea, Seb!' exclaimed Nessa. 'We could offer hand-embroidered silk lingerie for a bride's wedding night and honeymoon as part of her trousseau. We could…'

'Hang on, Nessa, hang on, who's going to do all this? Teach people to knit and sew and...'

'You are, of course, you idiot! Have you forgotten you grew up with knitting needles protruding from the ends of your arms? You are your mother's daughter, Callie. And what better way to mark Seb's mum's passing than to design a blanket that everyone can contribute to in honour of Hannah and everything she did for this village, then to present it to the hospice at their annual summer fayre!'

'You are joking, Nessa. I can't…'

'Well, not by yourself, no.' Nessa placed her palm on her chin and drummed her fingernails on her glossy apricot lips. Callie could almost see the cogs whirling behind those emerald eyes. 'You'll need some help.'

'But who would come? No one is interested in…'

'Wrong! In the last year alone, St Hilda's has had more interest in baking and crafts from the students than we can meet demand. All the girls want to get involved in making cupcakes, perfumed candles, fabric design and screen printing, sewing, embroidery and *knitting*!' Nessa's eyes strayed to the untouched perfect swirls of the baby-pink buttercream icing atop the cupcakes on the table.

'It's the Kirstie Allsopp effect. And you should see some of the girls' fashion designs, Callie. They'd give Callie-Louise Bridal Couture a run for its money! I'm sure they'd come up with some awesome designs for bras, knickers, bodies and teddies, if we asked them. Two of our girls were accepted at the Royal College of Art last year, the first students to attend since the person sitting glowering opposite me!' Nessa said, smirking.

'I can't teach a bunch of teenagers to knit and crochet when all they want to do is party in the bright lights of Leeds and Manchester. They don't want to hang out at the village haberdashery shop chatting about threads, buttons and ribbons and whether to use a cross-stich or blanket stick. Anyway, I do have my own social life, you know.'

'What social life is that?' Nessa said accusingly, certain of the reply.

'Well, in London…'

'It pains me to remind you, but you have not exactly been the life and soul of the party since you started work on Operation Lilac's Wedding Gown. And when was the last time you went out on a date?'

'Mmmm...'

'Pardon, I didn't quite catch that excuse?'

'Not since Christmas.'

'I rest my case, Your Honour.' Nessa performed a theatrical bow. 'You can stay here in the flat, run the shop and arrange the classes. Delia will help and so will I. Seb, Dom and Archie, if he's around, will get stuck in with the decorating. We'll give the shop a lick of paint but, more importantly, you can look into restocking the shelves with a decent selection of natural merchandise instead of all that rainbow acrylic that's only fit to dress Barbie's pet unicorn.

'Even if it's not *your* life's ambition, then do this for your aunt! She adored this village and its inhabitants. Every time I came in here it was buzzing with conversation, with laughter, with the aroma of freshly brewed coffee and lavender.' Nessa closed her eyes and drew in a deep breath, apparently hoping to catch a sniff of the nostalgia from her teenage years.

'Last time I was in here was on Christmas Eve. Delia's friend, Iris, and her daughter Marcia were camped out at the table, tucking into a batch of Marcia's home-made chocolate brownies and slurping the most divine-smelling hot chocolate. I stayed for two hours! What an antidote to the stresses of persuading hordes of unruly adolescent females to play hockey on a frozen, mud-caked pitch.

'That's why I think this crafting bug has taken the country by storm. People are sick of the daily grind of anxiety and angst, the clamber to work harder, faster, longer, to earn more in the rush to the top. They're tired of the obsessive addiction to celebrity culture, frazzled with the expelled energy required to strive for the perfection those magazines tout to our youngsters. Did I tell you the head has banned the girls from bringing them into the school?

'People crave a return of real community spirit – the sharing of warmth, mutual support and friendship over a freshly prepared brew and an injection of sugar-sweet confectionary, not a cocktail down at the local wine bar to douse the stress and boast about the last deal. The top rung of the corporate ladder is stuffed with pompous idiots feeding off the talents of those on the step below before shoving them back down with the tip of their boot. It's a world many of us refuse to join now, let alone aspire to.

'Don't close the door on Gingerberry Yarns just yet, Callie. What have you got to lose?'

***

'So you've narrowed it down to three?'

'Yes. Every designer who was asked to submit their sample gown did, so that leaves two who submitted without paperwork and the one who submitted the documents which were illegible.'

'Why were they illegible?'

'Erm, well, they were covered in a sort of yellowy-brown stain.'

'What?' Nikki curled her upper lip.

'I think it may have been a coffee that got spilled, but it could have been whisky. Or maybe something else? And it could have been the delivery guys, not the designer.'

'Okay. So let's look at the photos of the three possibilities.'

Tish produced three pictures she'd printed from her iPhone before Nikki arrived back from her meeting. 'As you are always telling me that I bring chaos to an empty room, I've made a special effort to be organised. I know I'll never get a seat on the top table in orderliness but I can aim for a table mid-room, can't I, instead of one next to the toilets?'

Nikki forced herself not to smirk as she studied the three dresses. They were all gorgeous, but the one Lilac had selected to wear on the most important day of her life was beautiful. Strapless, the bodice shone with tiny crystals that would look stunning under the lights of the Minster. From the back, the A-line skirt was simple with a short train edged in seed pearls that matched *the ivory silk to perfection. At the front, crystals spilled from the bodice to a dart from the waist to the hem, twinkling whenever the wearer took a step.*

'Ah,' Tish sighed, 'the designer may be a dunce in the paperwork arena but she's a wizard when it comes to fabric. Just look at all those sparkles. If I didn't already have my dress sorted, I would definitely go for one like this.'

'You have your wedding gown? I thought you weren't dating anyone at the moment.'

'Oh, I'm not.'

Nikki rolled her eyes.

'Okay. So we have Carla Masconi, Brigitte Gasnier and Callie-Louise Henshaw. So which designer goes with which dress. Have you worked with any of these designers before?'

'No, I haven't. Sorry.'

Nikki placed the headshots of the designers, all printed from their websites by Tish, next to each dress and studied them, then swapped them around. 'It's no good. We can't do it like this. I've had an idea. One of us will impersonate a celebrity who's shopping for her perfect wedding gown. We'll visit each of these designers and ask them to produce a sketch of the gown they would envisage for such a wedding. With any luck, they won't be able to resist producing a similar design to the one they believe didn't win the competition. Why wouldn't they?'

'You're a genius, Nikki. And you'll totally pull that off.'

'Oh, I wasn't thinking of me. You'll have to be the celebrity. I'll play the part of your fabulously efficient, but long-suffering PA. You're the same dress size as Lilac for a start and I'm sure she won't mind if you borrow one of her Stella McCartney dresses. If you tie your hair up in one of her Hermès scarves and wear a pair of dark glasses, I think we can pull this off. Of course, you'll have to be a reality TV celebrity.'

Nikki turned her back on the expression of outrage flooding across Tish's face and couldn't resist a smirk.

'Why can't I be a movie actress like Lilac?'

'Okay, what films have you been in?'

'Erm, well, there's...'

'See, if you were asked that question by one of the designers you'd totally give yourself away. I'll do all the talking. As soon as we're sure we can strike the designer from our list, we leave, okay? No mooning over the gowns. I don't even want you to try any of them on if we can help it.'

'Nikki...'

'Look, Tish. This is a nightmare that should never have happened. We need to rectify the problem as soon as we can and get on with everything else on our lists. Didn't you say you were slammed? You don't have enough hours in the day? Haven't you got the cars to finalise?'

'Yes, I suppose...'

'Okay. It's two o'clock. We'll start with Brigitte Gasnier as she's the nearest, then we'll do Callie-Louise Bridal over in Pimlico. Just pray that it's one of those, as I see Carla Masconi is based in Milan.'

'Oooo, Italy...'

Nikki rolled her eyes. She grabbed her mac, swung it around her shoulders and stalked from the room. By the time she'd reached the pavement outside, her irritation with Tish had evaporated. She chastised herself for her recent propensity towards shortness. It wasn't Tish's fault that since Owen had dumped her she'd disabled her happiness app and downloaded a bitterness one in its place; but still, the girl had to ditch the delusion that she was playing the lead female role in her own romantic comedy.

'Isn't this exciting? We're like a couple of Prince Charmings, touring the country as we search for the foot that fits the crystal stiletto, only this time we're looking for a designer to fit a wedding gown. When we find the right person I think I'll feel like Lilac's fairy godmother.'

Yeah, thought Nikki, as she ran through the kaleidoscope of things on her 'to do this week' list, never mind her 'to do today' list, and glared at Tish's exuberance – and I'm the wicked stepmother.

CHAPTER THIRTEEN

'Delia, would you object if I gave the shop a lick of paint? I'm not sure what colour the walls are *supposed* to be, but nicotine-yellow is definitely not this season's must-have colour.' Callie grimaced as her eyes swept across the dull walls, which seemed to blend in with the coffee-coloured carpet and highly polished teak shelves to portray a sepia-tinted emporium of a bygone age.

'And why do we stock all this candy-pink acrylic? Do we supply Sindy's stitch-and-bitch parties?' Callie unfolded her legs and strode over to grab a ball of the offending yarn, its scratchy fibres clicking the scraped skin around her fingernails. The shelves' contents were a cacophony of the tropical colours more commonly seen in a Caribbean aviary.

'Why not stock a selection of lamb's wool? You know, there's a farmer up in the Dales who has diversified into producing hand-spun organic yarns from his flock of Swaledale sheep. It's expensive; I sourced a batch to weave into one of my designs for the Autumn/Winter Collection, but I'm sure he would guide us to other suppliers, local if possible. And if we can – organic cotton and silk? And where's the cashmere? And what about mohair and angora – but only if it's ethically sourced.' She was vividly aware of the horror stories doing the rounds about the production of angora.

She marched around the drab room, dragging balls of yarn from their resting places, delving into the scattered wicker baskets and cracked leather valises, discarding every specimen as too brash or made from synthetic fibres and imported from China. She felt her inherent sparkle for all things fleece-related begin to return, just not for the type of products currently stocked by Gingerberry Yarns.

Delia's gaze followed her from her position in the throne-like chair at the head of the mahogany table, calm and serene, a faint turn at the corners of her lips, but she said nothing.

'Each one of these brightly dyed balls of yarn is supposed to be the catalyst for the creation of an original garment,' Callie continued, her passion mounting, 'a raw material that can be sculpted into an item to bring joy – from a baby's bootee to a christening shawl, from a grandmother's bed-jacket to a sofa throw – each with a purpose and a story to tell. It's a unique garment made with affection for the recipient instead of the modern attire that's replicated a thousand times and bought for a few pounds then discarded after one wear. If it's worth spending the time creating such a work of art, then surely it's worth sourcing the best materials?

'And why all these mismatched hard-backed chairs? They're like instruments of torture for people who knit. And they make the room look like a junk shop!'

'Well, our customers need somewhere to sit, Callie.' Delia's soft eyes clouded as she continued her explanation. 'Your aunt and I loved to hear the women's stories. They're not just our customers; the majority are our friends, people who have been coming into the shop for the last twenty-five years. Iris and Marcia have been coming in for ten. It's not exactly wheelchair-friendly, but we manage.'

Delia continued, her eyes fixed on the middle distance. 'Then there are our WI friends. They call in once a week – we donate any end-of-batch yarn to their knitting circle and they turn it into fabulous blankets and dementia mitts for the Heppleton hospice.' Unshed tears sparkled at Delia's eyes as she crashed back down to reality and began to gather together the debris of their morning tea break and wipe down the table.

'Ah, here are Marcia and Iris now.'

The brass bell tinkled as Marcia reversed through the doorway, hauling her mother's wheelchair backwards up the stone steps and parking her at the gigantic table. She dragged off her knitted, Inca-inspired hat complete with multicoloured pom-poms on strings. Her curtain of hair fell almost to her waist and her ears protruded through the sides like Noddy's famous best friend.

'Hi, Delia. We called at Wallington's for a box of those cupcakes you recommended. They are gorgeous – today's speciality is peppermint buttercream icing with raspberry stars and edible glitter. We got one for you too, Callie,' Marcia added shyly, having just spotted her crouching in the window display, but unable to meet Callie's eye.

'Oh, thanks, Marcia. Sounds like just what I need,' Callie called over her shoulder. *Especially after the two huge, buttered croissants forced on me by Delia less than an hour ago*, she thought. She jumped down from the window sill to inspect the gems of culinary perfection in the proffered box. They were a masterpiece of sugar-fuelled artistry. Tom was indeed a genius confectioner.

Drawing out a chair to join the gathering at the table, she ran her eyes over the features of the young girl hunched before her. With not a trace of make-up, or a nod to the twenty-first century, Marcia's face displayed the lacklustre pallor of those who did not enjoy enough sunshine or fresh air. Her skin cried out for one of Scarlet's invigorating facial scrubs and her eyes, the same colour as Callie's, were obscured by a pair of overlarge reading glasses that lent her a studious countenance. Any curves she possessed had been well disguised beneath the hand-knitted, black-and-amber-striped sweater with the hint of a thermal vest evident at her neck.

Callie experienced a burst of protectiveness for this caring young girl and realised belatedly that Marcia had been aware of her assumed-covert scrutiny. She watched guiltily as she self-consciously swiped away her glasses and stored them in the appliquéd pocket of her jumper, cut in the shape of a daisy.

'Oh, these are Mum's old reading glasses. I borrow them occasionally.' Marcia swung her sweep of hair forward across her face, anxious to escape from the uncomfortable inspection. 'Is there tea in the pot upstairs, Delia?' She scuttled away, the block heels of her candy-pink shoes clacking on the stairs.

Callie glanced down at her own familiar attire, which could have done with a spin in the washing machine. She chastised herself for failing to pay attention to her sartorial elegance, especially as she was now the figurehead of a high-street shop. She only had to look in a mirror to be reminded that she would win no trophies in a beauty pageant. She, too, wore no cosmetics and she'd lived in her D&G jeans and black polo-necked sweater since she'd arrived in Allthorpe. It was either that or rummage through her aunt's wardrobe, which she hadn't had the courage to do yet.

A few moments later, Marcia reappeared. She set down the cupcakes on a patterned china plate she'd found in a cupboard for them to feast their eyes and then their taste buds on. They were, without a doubt, the most attractive things in the shop. In fact, Callie had to admit the skill and artistry that had gone into their production was nothing short of amazing. The exquisite fairy cakes were definitely not what she'd expected to see produced by the old-fashioned baker's shop on the corner of their row, two doors down from the florist's shop, Buds & Bows.

'These are mini works of art, aren't they? Too good to eat, really.' Iris held her choice aloft for closer inspection, her soft features enclosed by a halo of curls the colour of ash, clearly reluctant to take the first bite and destroy its beauty.

'They are beautiful. Not what I had expected from…' Callie let her voice drift off for fear of causing offence by revealing her true feelings and the extent to which she had outgrown this rural backwater.

Iris smiled. It was clear she knew exactly what Callie had been about to say. 'Me neither, Callie. I thought the same thing when Tom became the third generation of Wallingtons to take over at the bakery. But Delia must have told you that he completed his training at Betty's in Harrogate, after a three-year apprenticeship in one of those glamorous hotels in Paris, whose name, like so many other things nowadays, escapes my memory. These cupcakes are fit to grace any celebrity's wedding reception, don't you think, never mind the tables of the residents of Allthorpe?' Small apples of red appeared on Iris's cheeks. 'If there had been a competition to make Lilac's wedding cake, Tom Wallington would have blown the competition out of the mixer.'

All three faces swung towards Callie and she performed a wriggle of embarrassment under the scrutiny of the gathered ladies. She felt her face become suffused with heat and swore she would never again be caught scrutinising a fellow human being's appearance.

'Well, as you haven't hung out the flags, I assume your own design didn't get selected, dear?' Iris asked.

Callie nodded. She suspected that the time spent confined to her wheelchair had allowed Iris to become sharply attuned to other people's disguised emotions. She saw her sweep a slow, analytical glance around the shop as though, despite having visited it daily for the last ten years, she was seeing it for the first time.

'It's not the same without your aunt, Callie. The shop has lost some of its warmth, a piece of its soul. What will you do with the business?'

Callie squirmed. Iris had clearly been endowed with the same down-to-earth character traits as Delia and many other Yorkshire women. She tensed her jaw muscles at the direct question, but she knew it was not only her own and Delia's futures that depended on her plans, but many of her aunt's old friends' futures too. She just wished she had an answer to hand.

'Well,' said Callie, ruffled by the inquisition about a personal decision. 'First of all, Delia and I thought we'd spruce this room up a bit – maybe a splash of rose-tinted paint on the walls, peppermint green for the shelves, dip those wicker baskets in white paint. We could invest in a couple of leather sofas, a few mohair throws…' She paused.

This was as good an opportunity as any to get the message around the village that her tenure at Gingerberry Yarns over the next few months would be a temporary reprieve only. One thing at least was still thriving in Allthorpe – the village grapevine.

'But I think I will have to start marketing the shop when probate is sorted, hopefully as a going concern.'

'Not likely, though, is it?'

Callie stared at Iris. Her mobility may have ebbed away, but not her enquiring mind; that was still as sharp as a needle.

'I mean, look what's happened to Mr Greenwood's grocery shop; look at old Mr Wainwright's butcher's shop – well on its way to becoming a weekend retreat fulfilling another rich banker's Yorkshire Dales fantasy. These people have no interest in what's going on outside their freshly painted front doors beyond its providing a charming backdrop for their nostalgic village scene – it's like a film set for them. What they don't realise is, they are the ones who are destroying our community, one by one. The lifestyle they find so charming? They are contributing to its decimation.

Mark my words, Callie, if you sell Gingerberry Yarns – it will go the same way.'

Callie was surprised to find that, instead of irritation at being the subject of an economics lecture, she not only agreed with Iris's astute assessment, but experienced a strong urge to protect the little wool shop from the encroachment of disinterested weekenders, and her aunt's legacy from such exploitation. After all, hadn't her aunt felt strongly enough about the subject to petition the local council's planning department when permission was requested for change of use of the butcher's shop?

They sipped the dregs of their tea, licked the sweet crumbs from their fingers and turned the conversation to the more palatable subject of the next WI meeting on Wednesday night. It was to be addressed by Dorri Mathews, a yoga enthusiast, who would speak on the benefits of veganism and a raw foods diet in the fight against every disease known to man. Much giggling ensued when Delia and Marcia described how unhealthy, drawn and washed-out Dorri had looked when they last saw her, concluding that a good dose of home cooking, a balanced diet and chocolate was the source of not only physical, but emotional health – just look at Nigella Lawson, the epitome of a goddess of the kitchen. This observation in turn led the conversation to the subject of the baking craze sweeping the nation on a tsunami of powdered sugar, inspired by the BBC show *The Great British Bake Off*.

'Marcia loves to bake, don't you, darling?' Iris looked proudly at her beloved daughter, who sat hunched forward, shoulders rounded to her chest, the ends of her hair sweeping the table. She had replaced her 'reading glasses' on the end of her nose.

'Yes, I do, but no way am I up to the standard of these.' Marcia wiped away a stray speck of buttercream from her upper lip with her fingertip and licked the end, her eyes crinkling into a smile which transformed her whole face.

'Maybe not, Marcia, but then Tom can't compete with you in the literary stakes, can he? She won't blow her own trumpet, Delia, but Marcia's just had another two of her shorts accepted by *LuxeLife* magazine for their summer holiday issue. That's four stories sold this month. Must be doing something right – but then everyone loves a good romance, don't they?'

Callie watched as Marcia's cheeks reddened, embarrassed at her mother's pride.

'Nevertheless, she won't meet the man of her dreams whilst she's stuck looking after me in Allthorpe, will she?'

'Mum!' Marcia moaned and, as the bell jingled, announcing what Callie hoped would be a paying customer, she took the opportunity to replace her bobble hat and prepare her mother's chair to leave.

'Just saying.' Iris smirked as Marcia fussed with her knee blanket. There was no defeat in those soft blue eyes, only a burning desire to squeeze every last ounce of delight from what remained of her life.

'Don't forget that package we brought for Delia, Marcia, my love,' Iris said, pointing to the Oxfam hessian bag hooked over the handles of her wheelchair, 'and your next two stories for her to proofread before you get them sent off to the editor.'

'Oh, yes.'

Marcia withdrew a large white envelope and placed it on the shop counter before extracting a smaller square package encased in a brown paper bag, passing it surreptitiously to Delia as Callie strode off to serve the new arrival. But not before Callie had caught a glimpse of the meaningful, coy looks being exchanged as Delia stowed the clandestine parcel beneath the counter, her cheeks glowing a deep shade of scarlet.

CHAPTER FOURTEEN

'Hi, Scarlet. How are things at the couture coalface?'

'Everything's fine. No crises to get worked up about. Lizzie is working her socks off on next year's Spring/Summer Collection. Oh, and did I tell you, Jules Gallieri has popped round a couple of times? He said it was to offer us a selection of this season's fascinators, hats and wedding tiaras to display in our window but I know it was just for a gossip. He's a creative genius with bridal headpieces! Would you believe he's talking about being crowned the new Philip Treacy, bless him? I'd die to wear one of his hats at the wedding of the year! And don't you think he's handsome? All that Italian heritage oozing from his pores?'

'Calm down, Scarlet.' Callie giggled. 'How's Flora?'

'Flora is Flora. When she realised we hadn't won the competition she spent the whole day arranging and then rearranging the threads into rainbow order, liberally interspersed with bouts of weeping. She went on and on about her psychic telling her that the Callie-Louise design was going to win and that Madam Clio has never been wrong before. She still forgets you're not here and buys you a vanilla spice latte most mornings – it's costing us a fortune. But we all miss you, of course.'

'Any insider gossip on who won the competition?'

'Well, I heard from Carla Luciano that it might be Brigitte Gasnier, but I don't think that's true. Don't get me wrong; Brigitte's designs are amazing, but they are a little OTT even for my taste. And she's been known to occasionally use animal fur in her trims. Lilac Verbois is not going to want to be associated with any controversy on her wedding day, is she?'

'What about Jacques?'

'He's away in Antibes at the moment, but yes, there's speculation he's gone over there to avoid the possibility of the media digging up any clues. You know he can't keep a secret. But if he has won, he needs to keep his lips firmly sealed. His career depends on it. My money is on him.'

'Yes, I can see Lilac wearing one of his creations on the red carpet. They are very elegant, but I somehow didn't see Lilac walking down the aisle in York Minster in a clingy, sexy sheath dress.'

'No one really knew what she was going to choose.'

'Oh, Scarlet, I'm so sorry it wasn't us. You all worked so hard and it's come to nothing. Perhaps I'm not cut out to be a celebrity fashion designer, after all. I wish I had a thimbleful of Jules's confidence right now.'

'You are an exceptionally talented designer, Callie.'

Scarlet quickly changed the subject before Callie had chance to sail any further down the river of despondency. 'What's happening with Gingerberry?'

'Oh, Scarlet, you'd love it! We're thinking of organising a sort of stitch-and-bitch evening, which should be fun. I've ordered in lots of new stock, too – cashmere, mohair, Aran, angora – all natural fibres. I've also sourced a bolt of that gorgeous cream silk we stumbled on when we were shopping for the wedding dress fabric. Do you think you can email me those designs I did at college for the bridal lingerie range? You know, the baby dolls, the bustiers and thongs, the teddies?'

'No problem, but why?'

'It's an idea Nessa had actually. She suggested we branch out into luxury bridal accessories, lingerie mainly, and I thought we'd make up a few samples at our stitch-and-bitch sessions. Not everyone likes knitting; some might prefer sewing and embroidery.'

'It sounds like a fabulous idea, Callie. We could display the pieces in the shop and any money we make can be sent back up to the ladies. You know, I was actually thinking of talking to you about doing something along those lines after this whole wedding debacle was out of the way. I love that little bolero jacket you designed at Christmas – the one with the high collar and full-length sleeves ending in a point over the hand –

a bit like a virginal Morticia – and maybe we could make up some with gathered, padded shoulders and tiny pearl buttons from cuff to elbow? I was thinking shot silk, but now you've got me wondering. What about ice-white knitted angora interspersed with tiny crystals? Oh, I'm so excited. I'll get Lizzie and Flora together in the Tumble Room and we can work on a new set of designs. What do you think?'

'Sounds great. And Scarlet, that jumper you're always wearing with your jeans? The red-and-white Scandinavian one? Where did you get it and can you remember exactly how much you paid for it?'

'It was a bit of a splurge, I have to admit. I bought it in Harvey Nicks. It was four hundred and fifty. I know it's purse-busting, but I do wear it every day in the winter instead of a coat and everyone who sees it comments on it and asks where I got it from. I wish I could knit. I'd have one in every colour. I think one in emerald green and cream would go with my colouring, don't you think?'

Callie laughed. It was good to talk to Scarlet. 'Well, if you can master the craft of teleportation sufficiently to travel from London to Yorkshire and back again in one night, there's a place reserved at the stitch-and-bitch sessions for you.'

'Count me in, Scotty!'

***

'Oh, don't I look fabulous?' Tish performed a twist and turn in front of Lilac's huge, gilt-framed mirror in the dressing room of her Georgian home in Kensington, smoothing the Stella McCartney fluted crepe mini dress over her hips and experimenting with her best pout.

'Come on, Tish. We can't waste any time. Lilac is due back next week and everything has to be ready for her first fitting. Whoever the designer is, she'll curse us for the delay. Every hour is precious when you have such an important commission to deliver. This gown is going to jettison their career into the stratosphere. It's the pinnacle of anyone's dreams to dress an Oscar-nominated actress on her wedding day.'

Tish pulled a face behind Nikki's back but Nikki saw her in the mirror.

'Okay, we have thirty minutes to get over to Brigitte Gasnier's studio, then, if it's not hers, we'll take a cab round to Callie-Louise Bridal. I've spoken to Callie Henshaw's assistant, Scarlet Webb. Callie has had a family bereavement and is currently away in Yorkshire, but Scarlet assured us that she would be able to show us samples of their previous creations or work with us on a new design. And please, Tish, make sure you leave the talking to me.'

They clambered into a black cab and shot off to Chelsea. Tish spent the whole journey checking her appearance in her compact, patting her halo of blonde *curls and reapplying her lipstick. She was made for a role in reality TV, thought Nikki with a smirk.*

'Hi, I'm Millie Channing.' Nikki introduced herself and shook hands with Brigitte Gasnier, almost suffocating in the cloud of Chanel No. 5 perfume that swirled around the petite fashion designer. 'Thanks for agreeing to see us at such short notice. As I told you on the phone, Miss Gertrude here is keen to decide on her wedding gown as quickly as possible.'

Nikki gave a polite little cough, clearly indicating that 'Miss Gertrude' found herself in a predicament. She struggled to conceal her smile when Tish turned to her, her eyes widened in horror, her cheeks a hot shade of crimson. Was that because she'd called her Miss Gertrude or because she'd spilled the beans about her pregnancy? Nikki didn't care – she deserved a little fun.

'Pleased to meet you, Mizz Gertrude. Won't you come this way, where my assistant 'as a selection of fabulous gownz for you to consider? If nothing suits, I also 'ave a portfolio of designs in my office for you to peruse or we can look at designing something to your precise specifications. Of course, it all depends on your budget,' Brigitte said, her French accent so pronounced that Tish screwed up her nose in confusion.

'My budgie? I don't have a budgie? I have a cat, though – Fluffy?'

Oh, God, thought Nikki. She had to tie up their business here as quickly as possible before their entente cordiale with all things French broke down. 'Do you have anything that's suitable for a celebrity wedding, but that's ready to go? It's just, as I said, we are in a bit of a hurry.'

'Mmm, perhaps I 'ave something. Just wait one moment.' Brigitte disappeared into the back room.

'Why did you have to tell her I was pregnant? Did you see the way her eyes narrowed?' hissed Tish, removing her compact and reapplying a slick of pearly pink lipstick for the tenth time. 'I bet hers is the ball gown one with the lace panelling and the pointed shoulder pads, like Cinderella's but in ivory? Which one do you think it is?'

'Quit talking about Cinderella, Tish. Just concentrate on why we're here.'

Brigitte Gasnier appeared with the most stunning dress balanced over her forearms and an assistant scuttling in her wake supporting its train. It was almost identical to one of the dresses on Nikki's hit list, but not the one they were searching for. Nevertheless, she allowed herself a congratulatory pat on the back and performed an imaginary tick. Now all she needed to do was extricate Tish from her nuptial fantasy with the minimum of fuss and move on to the Callie-Louise Bridal boutique.

She turned to look at Tish. The expression in the wedding planner's eyes reminded Nikki of the hypnotist snake in The Jungle Book. *God, the girl has this wedding fever bad! She decided to turn Tish's silent awe to her advantage.*

'That is a stunning dress, Ms Gasnier. It's certainly a possibility.' Then, with a look of abject horror, Nikki placed her arm around Tish's shoulders and began to guide her to the door. 'Gosh, you don't look very well at all, Miss Gertrude. You've turned the same colour as a frog with a hangover. Let's get you some fresh air. Thank you so much, Miss Gasnier. We'll be in touch.'

The expression on Brigitte Gasnier's face could have been framed and hung in a gallery labelled 'Astonishment', but Nikki didn't have the time or the inclination to think about it. She hailed a taxi and bundled a bemused Tish into the back seat.

'Why did we have to leave so quickly? You're such a spoilsport, Nikki. It was a beautiful boutique. You could have at least let me try the dress on – it wasn't as though Lilac was going to wear it or anything. You know how much I love...'

CHAPTER FIFTEEN

The morning's downpour had awakened the foliage of the trees that lined the high street like a wedding arch of sabres. The fresh green fragrance rose into the warming air, lifting Callie's jagged spirits.

It was Wednesday afternoon and most of the shops in Allthorpe closed for a half-day, another antiquated throwback that didn't fit the consumerism of the twenty-first century, grumbled Callie. She stood just outside the doorway of Gingerberry Yarns, her eyes focused on its stone façade, which had been blackened by the passing years and the Yorkshire weather, but was as familiar to her as a beloved relative, as she tried to imagine how a new customer would encounter the store.

Sunshine now bleached down on the lettering emblazoned across the huge plate-glass window spelling out the shop's title, sending golden shards of light glancing around the shadowy interior. The door, formerly a cheery yellow, had blistered and cracked to a hue of ochre. But it was when she pressed open the entrance door, the tinkle of the bell welcoming her into the cathedral of yarns, and she was presented with its shabby interior, that she sighed. The room was devoid of its lifeblood – its ever-present laughter. In the eerie silence and gloom, Callie battled her rising recollections, battening them down like a game at the fair.

Against the patina of age, the colourful balls of wool crammed the labyrinthine shelving in neat pyramids; from combed mohair to woven bamboo, from baby cotton to brash, chunky Aran – a veritable library of yarn. And yet it was a throwback to past times.

As she took a step into the shop, a gust of outdoor air favoured her nostrils with a waft of lavender and nostalgia. A rose-tinted dreariness suffused the atmosphere – that first glimpse of the glass counter behind which her aunt had always stood – and dealt a thwack of pain to her heart. Gingerberry Yarns without Hannah Garside was like London without Big Ben.

Would a fresh coat of paint be enough to drag the business into the twenty-first century? Was she a fool easily parted from her injection of cash on a few tins of paint, after which she'd sell up and scuttle back to her old life in London?

Pulling back her shoulders, she resumed her critical, professional assessment of the shop's fittings as she decided which would be painted with the peppermint paint she'd ordered and which would not. She ran her fingertips along the varnished surfaces, disturbing the dust, stroking the smoothness of the ribbons, fingering the intricate lace, and allowing the painful memories to assault her senses.

She couldn't wait for the delivery of the pure wools, the tweeds, the fibres that Yorkshire was so famous for. The county's history was steeped in the textile industry. If she could fill these nooks and crannies with natural, instead of man-made, yarns and display sample garments that the trendsetters would give their hard-earned cash for, then maybe, just maybe…

Her stomach hollered its objection to the forfeiture of breakfast so she trudged back up the stairs to flick on the kettle, dragging forward her trusty sketch pad to start planning the renaissance of Gingerberry Yarns. She was determined to keep busy, to focus on menial tasks not the big picture, but disloyal thoughts strained like elastic to return to the melancholy lodged resolutely in her mind. As she sipped on her third cup of Earl Grey and removed a fourth chocolate-coated digestive biscuit from the tube, she pondered on how easily she had succumbed to the oestrogen trio of solace: chocolate, tea and gossip.

She had no idea how long she had been at the kitchen table, mulling over her scribble, when a banging on the door broke through her reverie. She unfurled her legs and slotted the pencil behind her ear, the points of her ebony hair curling beneath her chin. She had made a concerted effort to avoid the bathroom mirror lately, but she knew she needed to arrange her debut visit to Marietta's.

'Oh, hello?' She had expected it to be Marcia or Delia, despite the half-day closing.

'Erm, hi. I'm Tom. Tom Wallington? From the bakery on the corner? Just thought I'd drop by to offer my condolences. I know I'm a little tardy, but well, what with the shop and visiting Dad…' He attempted a conciliatory expression, shuffling his weight from one foot to the other, his gaze focused on a point to the left of Callie's eyes, his diamond stud earring glinting in the afternoon sunlight.

'Hi, Tom, I'm Callie. Come in, come in. I'll make us some coffee.' She eyed the pale peppermint cardboard box he clasped in his reddened hands and could almost feel the drool beginning to form.

'I've brought you these. Just a few leftovers from this morning.' He opened the cake box to reveal the most exquisite, hand-made selection of French patisserie Callie had laid eyes on – and that from someone whose best friend had worshipped the world of Betty's as they grew up.

Tom pointed to a pale pink sugary gem. 'This is a raspberry *Miroir* – raspberry mousse with pink-and-white biscuit, topped with a raspberry-infused glaze, finished with a pink-and-white-striped chocolate square. This one is a *Paradiso* – alternated mango, passion fruit and coconut-infused mousse topped with a rolled white-and-dark-chocolate cigarillo. And these are pistachio and vanilla macaroons.'

In the concentration of the description and the passion it had produced, Tom had emerged from his timid shell to present his culinary creations with the pride of any accomplished maestro.

Callie had kept her mouth clamped shut to prevent the risk of subconscious drooling. 'Wow, they look amazing. Why don't you grab a seat at the table, Tom, and I'll fetch the cafetière?'

She set the glass coffee pot on the huge mahogany table in the empty shop and sank her teeth into one of the tiny sculptures, allowing the symphony of flavours to melt on her tongue and set her taste buds alight.

'Delicious, Tom, you really are a genius. Delia says you trained in Paris and then at Betty's in Harrogate?' She watched Tom nervously lace his elegant fingers around his coffee mug so that he had something to do with his hands.

'Yes, I adore French patisserie. I've been introducing a new product to the bakery every week since I took over from Dad at Christmas. I'm not sure Allthorpe is ready for blueberry-and-lemon *millefeuille* with Madagascan vanilla custard and blueberry jam, though! Dad, of course, tells me I'm crazy and that I should stick with the standard fare of barm cakes and loaves of parkin that customers buy every week, but…' Tom shrugged.

Callie totally got it. If he had to endure banishment to rural North Yorkshire, then he wanted to make an impact on the community's taste buds, just like she did with her natural textiles and crafting sessions. Maybe there was a great deal to be learnt from this ginger-haired giant crouched over the table in front of her.

'I was thinking of doing something new here, too. Like repainting the walls and the shelving, upgrading the stock, suggesting a more modern twist to the customers with the sample garments we display in the window.' She grimaced as her gaze fell on the burnt-orange sweater draped limply over the adjacent chair like a wet flannel. Who could wear orange successfully? 'Maybe even start with a few crafting sessions to bring in a new, younger clientele.'

'But what's the point, Callie? The village is floundering under the onslaught of the hypermarkets. Our high street is in intensive care now. At least you have the option of selling up and moving back to your life in London.' He flashed his moss-green eyes at Callie in apology, clearly not wanting to seem disrespectful. 'With the greatest of respect, once your aunt's probate has been finalised, you *can* sell up. Whereas I'm subjected to daily lectures from my increasingly frail father about what I'm doing wrong in the business and how I have three generations of bakers behind me to measure up to.

'Sorry, Callie, but why bother? Why strive to put all your energy into a dying business when you don't have to. We'll all be slaving for the supermarket masters by the end of the year, working for minimum wage, watching the corporate fat cats drain all the creativity from our veins whilst we comply with their demands for homogenous loaves of bread and cream cakes the texture of polystyrene. The church congregation is flagging, youngsters are escaping to the city, small businesses teeter on the cliff of financial oblivion, like Wainwright's the butcher's did, like Greenwood's the grocer's has. Only the wealthy are beating a return path, buying up renovated weekend homes, bringing their supplies with them. We don't have a hope of competing with that, so why are we flogging ourselves to death trying?'

Tom ran his chapped fingers over his hair and scratched at his auburn stubble. 'Every morning except Sunday, I get up before five o'clock to prepare the dough for that day's bread, to produce the repetitive fare the villagers of Allthorpe have come to expect from Wallington's. If I had any spare time, which I don't, I'd love to indulge my passion for hand-made chocolates, but that's not what our customers want. One of my biggest fears is that I may be losing my culinary edge without the daily stretch of creativity to finely hone my skills.

'And all this is before I limber up for the battle with the paperwork bureaucrats. I ask you, who needs the morning workout of kneading dough when I can flex my brain muscles in the eternal fight with suppliers, delivery guys, bankers, councillors who profess to have the small businessman in their thoughts, not to mention the spectre of the taxman. The government tells us we need daily exercise to avoid an early grave, but it's the red tape that they throw at us that's enough to give anyone a heart attack.'

At last, Tom met Callie's eyes. 'I'm exhausted, Callie. But I'm doing this for Dad. It would kill him if there was even a whiff of a hint that I intended to close the bakery. Oh, I know he thinks my intricate creations are the product of namby-pamby pandering to rich, nouveau-cuisine connoisseurs for whom he has no time. He used to cringe when I was a teenager and he saw me carry out my confectionary autopsies to ascertain the precise mix of ingredients and then attempt to reconstruct them with more panache than the original inventor.'

Callie dropped her gaze from his eyes to his pianist fingers, picturing Tom mixing together a symphony of flavours all his own, a true genius with a wooden spoon but minus the smooth social skills and engaging personality of the celebrity TV chefs. His lack of self-confidence ensured he would not be taking part in the Great British Pageant of Patisserie any time soon.

Tom leaned towards her. 'Callie, listen to me. You don't need to plough all your money and energy into refurbishing or wasting your design talents on a parochial shop catering to the needs of the old dears who use it as a community centre. No one would think badly of you. They all loved your aunt, but this is about *your* life, *your* ambitions. It's not worth it. Don't throw your dreams away, Callie, like I have!'

'But, Tom, running your Dad's bakery clearly isn't preventing you from experimenting with new recipes. We adore your cupcakes – they are divine creations of sugary art,' she enthused as she wiped away a crumb from her lips.

'But do the discerning customers of Allthorpe want a steady diet of pistachio macaroons and tiramisu pyramids?' he asked.

'Never underestimate the hungry customer, Tom. They may be elderly, but they, like everyone else, can be lured to partake of a delicious *petite madeleine* or glazed fruit tart. Many still bake from scratch at home, you know, unlike the teenagers, although I am reliably informed by Nessa, my friend who teaches up at St Hilda's, that the girls are *loving* the cookery classes they have reintroduced into the curriculum and they're struggling to meet demand. Hey, and *GBBO* fever is sweeping the nation, too. Why not tailor your forensic culinary experiments each week to produce your own twist on one of the recipes featured on TV?'

'Don't be ridiculous. Who would be interested in that?'

Callie rolled her eyes at the scepticism and the lacklustre response from this quiet, self-effacing man with the elegant fingers. 'Well, *I* would, for a start, and so would Delia, and Marcia – oh, and Nessa and her students in the cooking class. Maybe you could offer to give a cooking demonstration to the class at the school, mixed in with a soupçon of gossip from your exploits in the kitchens of Paris and Betty's?'

Callie paused in her organisation of Tom's future business exploits as a look of pure horror invaded Tom's face, making her laugh for the first time that week.

***

'*Don't forget, Tish, let me do the talking at the next boutique,*' warned Nikki as she clambered from the back seat of the black cab onto the pavement outside Callie-Louise Bridal.

'*Oh, isn't this an adorable little shop?*' Tish cooed. '*I love the peppermint-and-gold theme. I bet this is where the fairy-tale gown was designed. It has to be.*'

'*Tish, stop with the romance claptrap, will you? Someone needs to break it to you that there's no such thing as "true love that lasts forever",*' Nikki said, signing the universally accepted two-fingered speech marks of sarcasm.

Tish's lower lip trembled with annoyance, but she rallied. She tossed her curls behind her ears and fixed her eyes on Nikki. 'Finding a soulmate is a tough task, I get that. It can take years. Hell, you're right; some people may never find "the one". But you know what? I'm never going to stop looking and when I do find him, I'm going to use every weapon in my armoury to hang on to him. If the choice is happiness versus loneliness, I know which I'd rather invest in.'

'But what's the point? There's nothing you can do if your soulmate decides to run off with a shop assistant from the local department store, is there?' asked Nikki.

Tish ignored her; she was on a roll. 'My theory is that the more love you give, the more you receive. The more you expect it to fall into your lap when you're not looking, the less likely it is that you'll find it. You need to let people into your heart, Nikki. Sure, I adore weddings, but don't misunderstand me – I love romance more. I love happiness more. I love being in love more. After all the glitz and hype, even actresses and rock stars have at some stage to go home and cook dinner and wash the dishes. And those mundane tasks in life are made much more interesting if your soulmate is at your side slicing the sushi.'

Nikki stared at Tish as though she had gone stark raving bonkers. 'Tish, will you pull yourself together? Don't you understand how serious this is? Your first celebrity client, Lilac Verbois, is getting married in three months' time. She has no gown. Don't you think she'll have a problem with walking down the aisle in her lingerie? I've about had enough of this "make-believe" fairy tale you insist on living in. Get over it. Life isn't a picture-book story with a Prince Charming just waiting in the wings to whisk—What?'

'Lingerie!' Tish covered her mouth with her hand. 'I'd completely forgotten.'

'But surely, Lilac...'

'She asked me to do it,' she squeaked.

'Oh, for heaven's sake...'

She'd just about had enough of Tish. Didn't she realise there was no such thing as true love? Even when you thought you'd found it – it could still vanish in an instant, borne away on the wings of a blonde Scandinavian girl who worked in the china department of Liberty's. Yet, sadly, you just couldn't control who you gave your heart to, no matter how much you tried to stack the odds in your favour.

However, what she could control was her job. As she stood on the pavement in Pimlico, looking up at the pretty peppermint signage announcing in curly golden lettering that they'd arrived at Callie-Louise Bridal Couture, she drew in a deep, steadying breath. She pushed open the door, a petulant Tish stomping in behind her.

'Ah, you must be Millie Channing. I'm Scarlet Webb – we spoke on the phone.'

Nikki shook hands with Scarlet and introduced her to Tish who simply nodded. Nikki watched Scarlet run an expert eye over Tish's dimensions.

'And I think I might have the perfect dress for your client.' Scarlet smiled at Tish but got no response. 'Please, come through. Would you like a glass of champagne? It's English sparkling wine, actually – Callie insists on it. I can assure you it's just as delicious.'

Tish's frosty mood evaporated. 'I'd love a glass of champagne! Thank you!'

Flora appeared with a silver tray and offered a flute of the effervescent elixir to Tish, who took it and drained it in one. Nikki shook her head to refuse, but, before Flora could whisk the glass away, Tish had grabbed that one, too. She smiled like the Cheshire Cat at Nikki as she relaxed on the huge cream chesterfield sofa, crossed her slender, stockinged legs and waited for the gowns to be paraded.

Nikki's stomach growled. She hadn't eaten since supper the previous evening and then only an attempt at cheese on toast. There was never anything in her fridge anyway. She usually tried to stock up on fresh salads, fruit and fish on a Saturday, but by the following Friday, she'd not had the chance to eat any of it and had to throw it away in the bin and start the circle all over again. She knew it was a waste but, as far as food was concerned at least, she was an eternal optimist – one night she would get home at a reasonable hour and cook a decent meal for herself. It just hadn't happened since Lilac had announced she was marrying the handsome hunk that was Finn Marchant and was holding a competition to select the designer of her wedding gown. If it had been she who'd been lucky enough to be getting hitched to a rock star, Nikki would have opted for a quiet, intimate wedding, perhaps in a tiny church on the beach in some exotic location, like Bali or Hawaii. Even the dress was superfluous if you had the man of your dreams standing next to you, barefoot in the sand.

Her uncharacteristic sojourn into nuptial oblivion was brought to an abrupt halt when an exclamation erupted from Tish's lips. 'Yes! Yes! Yes!'

Nikki focused her attention on the dress Scarlet was displaying and leapt from the sofa. 'Oh, Scarlet, I could kiss you! That's it! That's the one! It's a Callie-Louise!'

Unlike Nikki, Tish had no reservations on the kissing front. She clutched a shocked Scarlet to her chest and slapped a loud kiss on both cheeks. 'Thank God, thank God. You are an absolute saviour. I love you.'

'Erm, I'm glad you like it. Do you want to try it on?'

'No!' screamed Nikki. 'No! Sorry, let me explain. I think you should sit down.'

Nikki guided Scarlet to the couch and perched next to her. She scrabbled around in her Birkin for her business card and her ID. 'You're not going to believe this. I'm Nikki Coates. I'm...'

'You're Lilac Verbois's PA. Oh, and you're Tish Marshall, her wedding planner. I thought I recognised you. I wasn't sure, but... Why are you here?'

'The Callie-Louise design has been chosen by Lilac as the one she wants to wear on her wedding day.'

'Oh, my God! Oh, my God! Flora, get back in here!' screamed Scarlet.

Flora appeared at the door, her eyebrows raised in mute enquiry.

'We've won!'

'Won what?'

'The Lilac Verbois competition.' And Scarlet promptly burst into tears. 'I'm sorry. It's just such a shock. We thought, we thought when we didn't hear anything that...'

'Well, it's taken us some time to find you.'

'What do you mean?' Scarlet asked, dabbing at the corners of her eyes with the tissues they usually reserved for tearful brides-to-be.

'There was no documentation with your dress when it was delivered to The Dorchester. Is this the dress Callie-Louise submitted?'

'Yes, it is, but I don't understand. Why... Oh.' She turned to look at Flora's pale, almost translucent face, her eyes wide, her fingertips resting on her lips. 'You forgot to fill in the paperwork? Flora!'

'Oh, God, I'm so, so sorry, Scarlet. I know you mentioned it, but remember, we were in a panic about Callie's aunt and I was upset and I suppose I just...'

'No harm done,' interrupted Nikki, 'except the time that's been lost. Lilac has a tight schedule. These are the dates she's available for fittings. As you know, the gown has to be ready for the thirty-first of July.'

'Callie usually asks for a minimum of three fittings. This first date is not until two months' time. We need to do the first fitting straight away.'

'I'm sorry. That's not possible. Lilac is flying out to Croatia as soon as she and Finn have finalised everything with the Bishop at York Minster next Tuesday.'

Scarlet's brain whirled. They couldn't start work on the gown until they had an idea of Lilac's exact measurements. 'Callie is currently taking a short sabbatical to finalise her late aunt's affairs. Her aunt passed away recently and left a haberdashery shop in Yorkshire to Callie. I'll call her to tell her the fantastic news. I'm sure she can come back down to London this week to see Lilac before she leaves the country.'

'*But Lilac isn't in London. She's filming in the Outer Hebrides. When that's in the can, she's being flown by helicopter to Leeds/Bradford airport for the meeting at the Minster, and then she's flying straight out again from Manchester. Did you say the shop was in Yorkshire?*'

'*Yes, Allthorpe.*'

'*Right. I'll arrange to collect Lilac in York when she's through with the arrangements and drive her over to the Yorkshire branch of Callie-Louise. Shouldn't be too difficult.*'

'*Oh, it's not a branch...*' *Scarlet caught the meaning in Nikki's stare.* '*Yes, I'm sure the Yorkshire branch of Callie-Louise Bridal Couture will be ready to receive Miss Verbois whenever she is available.*'

'*Right. Can I ask you to do one last thing? Miss Verbois has said she would like to congratulate the winner in person. Could you keep this a secret for a couple of days? So that Lilac can inform Callie-Louise herself? I'll be in touch and many congratulations.*'

'*I think we should stay and celebrate!*' *announced Tish, grabbing another flute from Flora's tray.*

Flora smiled and joined her, tears of joy – but mostly of relief – trickling down her cheeks. She'd just got away with almost losing the most prestigious order Callie-Louise Bridal Couture was ever likely to get, by the skin of her teeth. To say she looked relieved was an understatement.

Nikki glanced at the two girls knocking back the champagne and then at Scarlet. She shrugged her shoulders. Perhaps she did deserve a glass. Hadn't she just pulled the proverbial rabbit out of the hat?

CHAPTER SIXTEEN

The doorbell jangled its introduction and both Callie and Tom turned their heads to see Marcia, without Iris in tow, blushing at the door.

'Oh, Callie, sorry – I didn't realise you had company.' Marcia hid behind her hair as she hesitated in the doorway, clearly wanting to flee but not sure if she dared, dragging her mother's oversized tweed coat across her rounded shoulders like a shield.

'It's okay, Marcia. This is Tom Wallington, from the bakery on the corner?' Callie shot up to prevent Marcia from leaving and guided her to a seat at the table, realising that if she spent any more time listening to Tom's take on life then she would be joining him on the pulpit of the village's bridge. 'And I was in the process of persuading him to present a few cookery demonstrations to the students at St Hilda's. Don't you think that's an excellent idea?'

'Callie, believe me, I'm no good at that sort of thing. I don't have the time or the confidence to…'

'Why don't you draw up a detailed lesson plan for an after-school club? Include a choice of recipes, sweet and savoury, a list of the ingredients each one requires and a set of clear, concise, easy-to-follow instructions. Maybe you could add in some photographs of the finished article and a few words about the history behind every cake, a sort of story of its birth? You know, like where does parkin originate from, how do Florentines get their name, that sort of thing. Nessa can then show it to the head teacher. She's always complaining that all the after-school activities are sports-based. It's perfect!'

Tom's face had alarm written across it. 'A story – for a cake – what a ridiculous idea! No, that settles it, Callie. Thanks for the vote of confidence, but no way.'

'I can help you, if you like?' Marcia offered, her soft voice muffled as she stared down at her fingers twisting the strings of her woollen hat.

'What do you mean?' Callie pressed, keen to involve Marcia.

'I can help Tom write the lesson plans and the stories. I am something of an expert, after all the official documents I've had to complete over the years to get a community care assessment for Mum and my carer's assessment and allowance. We've had to appeal the council's decision on her personal budget plan on several occasions and that really does sharpen your pen, so to speak.'

Marcia chanced a flick of her jam-jar-covered eyes across to Callie, studiously avoiding any direct contact with Tom. 'And I can write the cake histories, too. I've had loads of romance short stories published, so…' Her voice trailed off as she dropped her eyes back to the table and re-hunched her shoulders.

Callie was forced to address the top of her head.

'Marcia, that's wonderful…'

The bell tinkled again and Callie heaved a sigh. What was the point of closing the shop on a Wednesday afternoon when she had more visitors than she had customers in the intervening days?

'Saw you were enjoying a gathering so I thought I'd grace you with my presence.'

'Erm, right, and you are?'

Callie slid her eyes over the handsome young guy who had already grabbed a chair and turned it backwards to sit astride it. With his immaculately barbered, jet-black hair, skin lightly tanned and clean-shaven jaw, he could have been a catwalk model but for his height. He smelled delicious, too. His pristine, candy-pink shirt had been laundered to perfection and he wore a dove-grey cashmere sweater draped artfully around his shoulders, his black Armani trousers moulded perfectly to display a taut behind. But it was his heavy gold-link bracelet that caught Callie's eye and caused the corners of her lips to twitch.

'I'm Marc Bairstow, darling. I own the florist's next door to the bakery – Buds & Bows? Oh, hi there, Tom, didn't see you there. Oh, and is this your girlfriend?' he asked with an unmistakable glint in his coal-coloured eyes, his lilting tone curved into a tease.

'Hi, Marc. No, Marcia is not my girlfriend.'

All three swung their eyes to survey Marcia, whose deep flush had suffused her blanched complexion as she dipped her eyes back behind a curtain of hair. Callie could have murdered Marc.

'Well, anyway...' Marc's eyes danced in the knowledge he'd hit his mark. 'I'll take a skinny cinnamon latte, Callie-Louise, my dear, and one of these divine little amuse-bouches! Even though it will *not* enhance my waistline, I'm anxious to see what it'll do to my discerning taste buds. I'll just have to endure an extra half-hour of Pilates tonight; no punishment, really – the tutor has buttocks of steel!'

Callie plonked a fresh cafetière of coffee on the table in front of Marc with a challenge in her hazelnut stare. She was not making him a skinny cinnamon latte. What did he think she was running here, a Costa franchise?

'So' – he flung his flexed wrist around the shop – 'what are your plans for this cathedral of commercial gloom? I do hope you *have* renovation plans, Callie dear? We are the three musketeers of Allthorpe High Street, charged with its salvation. Yes, you may laugh, but I ask you this: What if we also took the easy road instead of the right road? What would be left of the Great British High Street then?

'Here I'm thinking Marie Antoinette French boudoir, marshmallow pinks and creams, a splash of that delightful peppermint green. Perhaps an espresso machine over there in the corner?' He raised his neatly plucked eyebrows and rushed on when he saw the expression on Callie's face, refusing to be diverted from his interior design project. 'And Tom, darling, you could supply a baker's dozen of these delectable French fancies for the discerning customers, couldn't you? What say you, Callie? Drag this little antiquated emporium into the twenty-first century?'

'You just said eighteenth-century boudoir!' she reminded him.

'Eighteenth century-*inspired*! And you know I'd love to assist in this transformation, but...' – Marc shot a glance around the table to ensure he held everyone's undivided attention – 'I've just been commissioned to supply Hugo Marston and Avril Carter's wedding flowers!'

Marc rolled his eyes at the blank expressions around the table. 'Philistines. Hugo Marston is one of our county's most talented operatic tenors. And I've wheedled two invitations to the evening reception for me and Jacob! It'll be such a blast. Anyway, must dash. Bye, my sweeties!'

Marc drained his coffee with a grimace befitting a drama queen and flounced out. Callie met Marcia's eye and they crumpled into giggles. Tom, however, remained stony-faced, swinging his glare from one girl to the other as he waited for them to get a grip on their laughter.

'If I agree to let Marcia draft a lesson plan for the school, then you, Callie, have to organise those stitch-and-bitch sessions this week.' That stopped their hilarity in its tracks. 'I've got a pal over in Heppleton who owns the printer's shop. I'm sure Jon will be able to run off a few flyers for you. Who were you thinking of targeting?'

'Well,' Callie said, wiping her eyes with the cuff of her sleeve, 'Nessa mentioned the girls at school and there are Hannah's WI friends in the knitting circle.'

'And there's my reading group and writers' circle friends,' Marcia offered, sitting up straight in her chair, excitement written boldly across her features.

'Okay…'

'And Delia's Friday night girls and my mum's friends from the MS support group at the hospital?'

'Great,' said Callie, with diminishing enthusiasm.

'And maybe Tom can supply the cupcakes, you know, just for the launch? "A Sweet Temptation"?'

Callie never would have believed Marcia could become so animated about a project and it sent a surge of delight through her chest. It was true – she did have the organisational skills to match those of an army general.

'So, next Tuesday, then?' Marcia continued. 'Shall we say seven o'clock? I'll design the flyer and email it across to Tom's friend. Will you call Jon tonight, Tom?'

'Erm, sure, okay, Marcia.'

Was that a steamroller retreating from her crushed bones? wondered Callie.

From their seats at the table, Callie and Tom watched like frozen goldfish as Marcia tripped from the shop, neither of them quite realising what had happened and how Marc and Marcia had got away with it. She might look like a shy bookworm, but Marcia was no slouch in the bulldozing stakes.

'Thanks for the coffee, Callie. I've got to visit Dad. Bye.'

Tom disappeared, leaving Callie with her swirling thoughts. Ripples of ivory and indigo stretched across the retiring sky as she dropped the sneck on the door and pulled down the blind. She heaved a heavy sigh, wishing she could turn the clock back twelve months when her life had been dull and boring, with no celebrity wedding gown to design and no haberdashery shop to run – even if it had been nicknamed 'the cosiest little wool shop in Yorkshire'!

As Callie reached to flick the light switch, dreaming of a hot bath and a glass of Merlot, her eye caught on the brown paper package Iris had given Delia the previous week, which she'd shoved under the counter and clearly forgotten about.

She picked up the large white envelope, drawing out the neatly typed sheets of paper and glancing at the heading, her lips curling into a smile. *The Lustful Lancelot by Clementine Johnson* – fabulous; a good romance was exactly what she needed to accompany her bubble bath and wine. She hoped Marcia wouldn't mind; as she'd had many short stories published, she didn't think so.

She tucked the envelope under her arm and was about to leave when she remembered the brown-paper-encased bundle. She lifted it from its shadowy confines, a stab of guilt causing her to pause and wonder if she was trampling on Delia's privacy. But as she peeled back the wrapping to take a peek, she saw it contained nothing more personal than a trio of paperback books.

Curious as to the sort of novels Iris and Marcia were sharing with Delia – and why they were encased in brown paper – Callie turned the books out onto the glass counter. Her eyes bulged from their sockets. An instant tickle of amusement breached her throat and burst forth into peals of laughter, culminating in tears of mirth.

Oh, what a relief it was to laugh out loud, she thought as she picked up one of the books to study the jacket blurb, wiping her eyes on one of the pink serviettes left by Tom.

She mounted the stairs, the books tucked securely under her arm, to enjoy her first foray into the trilogy that was *Fifty Shades of Grey*.

CHAPTER SEVENTEEN

Tuesday. Delia flicked the sign on the door to *Closed* at precisely five o'clock. The pearly sheen of condensation on the front window masked the hive of activity within like a bride's veil. There were so many things to organise before everyone arrived at seven o'clock. They worked in tandem to clear the area around the huge mahogany table, dispersing chintz cushions for those with delicate bottoms.

Seb and Dominic had performed miracles. They had blown in on Saturday teatime as the shop closed, armed with litres of paint, which they assured Callie had been wallowing for years in their mother's garage. As it was the exact same shade of pale rose Callie had agonised over for the walls, and the identical pale peppermint she'd selected from the Dulux paint chart for the shelving and wicker baskets, she doubted it. She suspected either Nessa or Delia's hand in its production and was immensely grateful.

With the sustenance but not the precision offered by a dozen bottles of hand-crafted Hambleton ale, coupled with a late-night Indian takeaway and an eclectic selection of music, Callie, Delia, Nessa, Seb and Dominic had decorated and gossiped until the early hours of Sunday morning. The gang, minus Delia, then broke for a couple of hours' kip on the floor of the flat upstairs, before returning to the task the next morning. It was trite, but true; many hands did make light work.

By six o'clock on Sunday evening, with aching limbs and weakened muscles (apart from Nessa), they stood back to admire Gingerberry Yarns' transformation from serene old lady to energised princess. Callie had to brush away a tear when Marcia produced a string of hand-embroidered bunting, each pastel-green polka-dot flag stitched with a letter spelling out 'Gingerberry', as she performed the rebirthing ceremony by draping the garland over the front of the glass counter.

Now all Delia and Callie had to do was display the new stock that had arrived that morning in the hope they could make some sales at the crafting session that evening. They'd had seven confirmations – three ladies from the knitting circle of the local WI, two of Delia's Friday night posse, and Nessa was bringing two teacher friends from St Hilda's. So, with herself, Delia, Marcia and Iris, it would make a very respectable twelve. But, as the clock edged towards seven, Callie's confidence began to wobble and she regretted the misdirected impulse to do this. No one would come, she was certain of it, and she struggled to quell her rising panic.

This time the tinkle of the door chime, far from being an irritant, was a welcome relief. Callie wiped her hands on a tea towel, shot a nervous glance across to Delia, and rushed down the stairs to welcome in the first student.

But it was Tom, weighed down with a large silver salver of assorted confectionary. His offerings would not have disgraced a chic Parisian soirée.

'Wow, Tom, these look awesome. I expected a batch of cupcakes!' In keeping with the theme, Tom had produced rose-and-pistachio macaroons nestled next to vanilla-cream-and-peppermint-jam *millefeuille* and a selection of kiwi and raspberry glazed tartlets finished with curls of dark chocolate.

'I'm grateful for the chance to practise, Callie. I can't afford the time to bake these every day and the risk of them not selling makes them financially unviable. So I thought, well... I'm sure the ladies coming tonight all possess discerning taste and I really need your venture to be a success.'

Tom thrust the tray of culinary gems into Callie's hands, his reddening face clashing unattractively with his ginger hair.

'Stay and have a coffee, Tom,' Callie offered, desperate to detain him in the empty shop. It was ten past seven and still no one had arrived. What if no one turned up? A helix of nerves began to wind through her abdomen, but she gave herself a shake – that path of thought was an idiot's journey and one which she had no intention of travelling down that evening.

'Oh, no, I'm not staying here!' Horror replaced the embarrassment on Tom's face, now a vivid puce. He rotated on his heels to make a swift exit, only to end up bumping chests with Marc, who had arrived weighed down by a profusion of pink Stargazer lilies.

Marc smirked at Tom's mortified apology before turning to Callie.

'Darling! I brought you these. They will be Gingerberry's crowning glory and their fragrance is divine.' He landed a kiss on each of Callie's cheeks before turning to greet Tom, who had beat a hasty path to the door.

Sensing Tom's discomfort, Callie stepped into the breach when she noticed Marc's black eyes glinting with mischief. 'Why don't you help me pop these in water, Marc? They are gorgeous, thank you.'

'Oh, and what are these scrumptious little delights? Mmm… flowers, sweet treats and gossip! Now that the holy grail of female delights has been established, the evening is bound to be a dazzling success!' He reached over to select a pale pink macaroon but Callie slapped his hand away.

'Not yet, Marc! This tray is just as much a work of art as your magnificent bouquet.'

'Of course, but us artisans can't be too precious about our creations, can we, Tom? They are but temporary offerings for our patrons' delectation. Well, where is everyone?' He swung his gaze around the refurbished shop, his arms flounced in theatrical style. 'Oh, I love what you've done with the place, Callie; pink sorbet and peppermint are two of my favourite shades. I'm so pleased I chose those lilies – they're just perfection. Icing on the cupcake!'

Delia appeared in the shop. She greeted Tom and Marc and fussed around the flowers.

'You know, Tom,' said Marc, 'you should really have submitted a proposal to be appointed as Lilac Verbois's wedding cake supplier. You would have definitely been shortlisted. Ms Verbois is known to have the most exquisite taste.'

Marc's dark eyes met Callie's and his hand shot to his mouth. 'Oh, I didn't mean…'

'It's okay, Marc, but thanks for the motivational direction. And yes, Lilac does have an eye for exquisite design.' She squeezed a smile into her eyes for Marc and then Tom, who lurked like a frightened lamb caught in a wolf's lair over by the door. 'Are you sure I can't persuade you to stay?'

'Erm, no, thanks,' and Tom disappeared through the door in a flash.

'Oh, don't worry, I'm staying right here. I wouldn't miss this party for all the tulips in Amsterdam. Jacob is out celebrating with his tennis gang tonight, but I demurred and promised to meet up with him for cocktails when we're done here.'

Marc strode over to inspect the new merchandise that had been crammed into the freshly painted cubes of shelving and piled into the dipped bamboo baskets. He selected a soft-spun natural lamb's wool yarn and held it to his cheek, appreciating its texture.

'Oh, I'm thinking a cream-and-peach Fair Isle sweater, Callie. Have you been watching those Danish detective shows? Perhaps I could knit one for Jacob for Christmas? Or maybe I should go for one with a picture of Rudolph on the front? I simply adore the annual craze for festive knits!'

'Marc, I think we should begin our sessions with something a little more basic, don't you? But as it looks like it will just be me, you and Delia tonight, perhaps we can…'

CHAPTER EIGHTEEN

When the tinkle of the brass doorbell reverberated through the shop, Callie was so relieved she resolved there and then never to be irritated by its cacophony of chimes again.

'Hi, Callie. Hi, Delia. Sorry we're a little tardy, love, but Grace had to wait for her daughter to arrive to sit with Arthur.'

The WI sisterhood of yarn bustled into the shop. Delia had reported how anxious they had been to lend their support so their sanctuary would survive even if its proprietor sadly had not. They fussed over the sweet-smelling floral display, swooned over the cakes and dragged out the seats with the cushions. They were just settling in for the session when Delia's friends arrived, pink-cheeked and breathless, followed swiftly by the giggling trio from the school, which included Nessa, who had clearly been at the wine.

'Hi, Callie,' they chorused. 'Wow, did *you* make these?'

'No, of course not. Tom Wallington brought the cakes and Marc Bairstow from Buds & Bows donated the floral display.' She indicated Marc who waved a fingertip greeting whilst dissecting the girls' choice of attire as though possessed of laser-vision.

Marc stepped forward to receive their enthusiastic praise, in his element with so many women surrounding him, before claiming the seat at the head of the table, poised to learn his first stitch on the way to the promised Christmas sweater.

'I think we should begin, Callie,' Delia said.

Callie pressed the tightened coil of nerves to the back of her mind. She suspected she might be about to explain to her aunt's WI friends how to suck eggs, but hey, in for a penny...

'Can I first of all thank each and every one of you for coming here tonight. As this is our first session and we have a diverse range of talents here, I think we should begin with the basics and those who are more experienced can help the beginners before we break for coffee and some of these delicious cakes and a gossip?

'What I'd really like us all to do is work on two different projects. For the first part of the session, I'd like everyone to concentrate on a six-inch knitted square that can be practised on at home and brought to the next meeting. We can make use of the acrylic and man-made yarns Gingerberry used to stock. I hoped we could create a blanket from the samples we make, which could then be donated to the hospice in Heppleton in memory of Aunt Hannah?' She glanced across to Delia for her approval and saw a sparkle at the corners of her pale eyes.

'I am grateful to the ladies from the WI, who together knitted this gorgeous navy-and-cream Aran-style sweater for us to display in Gingerberry's window. Our new stock arrived this morning and I have to admit, it's gorgeous.'

Callie passed around the sweater for the group to inspect, followed by balls of soft-spun angora and cashmere to appreciative oohs and ahhs. 'I truly believe that if we are to spend our time in any artisan pursuit, then we should produce a garment worthy of our labour, in natural and not man-made yarns. Not only do we now stock cashmere, but also mohair, pure organic cotton in four-ply, a selection of bamboo yarns, which produces a lovely drape when knitted up, and organic lamb's wool sourced from a farm high up in the Yorkshire Dales.'

Callie held up a photograph she had printed from the internet of a Nordic-patterned sweater. 'These hand-knit sweaters are flying off the shelves at Selfridges and Liberty's. And they sell for over four hundred and fifty pounds apiece.'

'Four hundred and fifty pounds? Ridiculous! Who would pay that sort of money when you can knit one yourself?' exclaimed Iris.

'That's just the point, Iris. People are either too busy to make their own garments or have never acquired the skills to knit, and believe me, these sweaters have been carefully designed by the fashion houses that produce them. Then, there are the one-off pieces of couture. In fact, this one I'm showing you here' – Callie held up a photograph from *LuxeLife* magazine of a blonde Scandinavian woman sporting navy-blue, calf-length flares and a hand-knit cropped sweater fashioned in white angora with crystal detailing around the yoke and the cuffs – 'retails at seven hundred and fifty pounds.'

'That's gorgeous!' gasped Julia, one of Nessa's friends from school.

'Well, there's no reason why you couldn't have a go at that, Julia.'

'Where do I start!' she exclaimed, grabbing a pair of needles from the centre of the table, slotting them under her arms and making a clicking noise.

'With the basics,' Callie laughed.

'What is the second project you have in mind, Callie?' asked Nessa.

'Well, as you all know, I own a small bridal boutique in London.' Murmurs of acknowledgement looped around the room. Callie saw the expressions of sympathy on a couple of the WI women's faces and pressed on. 'Aunt Hannah has amassed a cornucopia of pretty embellishments over the years – seed pearls, tiny crystals, sequins, beads, ribbon, lace – in every colour imaginable. I thought we could use some of it to make bridal lingerie.'

Callie bent down and extracted the bolt of ivory silk that Scarlet had FedExed up from Callie-Louise that just happened to be the leftover fabric from the ill-fated Lilac Verbois wedding gown. Scarlet had also emailed her the lingerie sketches she had worked on at college and not had time to develop. Callie handed round the designs she had photocopied.

'Wow, these are gorgeous. Look at this garter, I love it. Shame they are only worn for weddings nowadays,' declared one of the WI women. 'I adore this nightwear. What's it called?'

'That's called a baby doll and that one's called a teddy, Kath. I thought we could have a go at stitching a few samples and see if they'll sell at Callie-Louise. The salon only stocks silk in cream, ivory and white, but I could maybe source some fabric in peach, pink, even scarlet?'

'Sounds wonderful,' declared Kath and a ripple of excitement spread around the table.

They spent the next thirty minutes learning how to cast stitches onto a needle using the thumb method, as Delia insisted this technique produced a neater edge. Kath and her friends helped Nessa's friends to keep the stitches on the needles to much hilarity and giggling. At the end of their first hour, the WI women had finished two squares each and Nessa's friends had managed five lines filled with holes, but new friendships had been forged.

For the second part of the class they moved on to sewing and embroidery. They rolled out the silk and helped Callie pin out the paper patterns for the lingerie onto the fabric before taking it in turns to carefully cut out the pieces. They selected spools of ribbon and lace from the shelves and draped each over the silk, admiring the effect and offering suggestions.

'Okay, I think we should break for coffee now,' Callie called above the hum of contented chatter. Yarn and needles were stowed away and the silk pieces placed gently in a leather trunk lined with Liberty print. The remaining paraphernalia was cleared from the table and replaced by the huge brown teapot and a cafetière, along with the silver platter that everyone had been drooling over since they arrived.

'Hey, don't you think our meetings should have a name?' proposed Nessa as she poked her tongue around her crumb-laden lips. 'I vote for "The Knitting Ninjas"! What do you think?'

'Great idea!' laughed Delia. 'But we are sewing bees, too!'

'What about "Cupcakes & Couture"?' suggested Marcia to a chorus of approval.

The doorbell jingled, causing everyone to swing their scrutiny to the unexpected intrusion.

'Hi, I hope we're not too late to join in the fun? Oooh, what fabulous little cakes!'

'Girls!' Nessa shot up to greet the trio of teenagers from St Hilda's, her auburn hair swinging in a ponytail, her school mistress's hat firmly on. 'You've totally missed the lesson. We've moved on to the coffee, treats and gossip part of the evening!'

'Eh? Thought it was an eight o'clock start, Miss?'

'No, seven, and anyway it's eight forty-five!' Nessa assumed her best 'patient teacher's' voice as she rolled her eyes at Alicia, Polly and Megan, the gang who adored their crafting sessions at school.

'Oh, Megan's dad's dropped us off and adjourned to the pub so we'll just have to stay for the coffee, cakes and gossip bit then.' Alicia looked anything but regretful.

The girls swooned over the melt-in-the-mouth delicacies, then fingered the ivory silk and drooled over the lingerie photos. They placed orders of their own for the teddies, suggesting leopard-print and tiger-print satin, and joined in with the gossip as though old friends.

As darkness crept up unnoticed and the amber glow of the street lamps suffused the gathering with a golden sheen, Callie sank down into a chair next to Delia and surveyed the scene. The room had come alive that evening with the swirl of chatter and laughter that wrapped a cloak of comfort and serenity around the group. The shop shone with the promise of a bright future; several friendships had been forged that would never otherwise have been contemplated. For the first time in months, Callie experienced a boost to her flagging spirits and the anvil-heavy weight that had clutched at her chest began to crumble.

This night had been for her aunt and, as she head-counted the participants, she knew it had been a great success. She had made no money as she had donated the acrylic yarn for the hospice project and the ivory silk from Callie-Louise. However, the silk would hopefully be turned into items she could sell under the Callie-Louise brand and the money would be shared between the ladies who decided after this evening to take part in the new enterprise. Delia had in any event signed up every attendee for the next session of Cupcakes & Couture.

'Okay, okay. Can I thank every one of you for showing your support this evening? Delia and I truly appreciate it.' Callie was shocked to find her throat had choked up and she struggled to swallow down her rising emotions.

Delia pressed her palm on Callie's forearm and continued on her behalf. 'Many of you here tonight knew Hannah as more than the proprietor of Gingerberry Yarns. She was a loyal and supportive friend endowed with a warm, welcoming smile and a listening ear for all our highs and lows as we pass along life's treacherous journey. I, and I'm sure you all, miss her dreadfully, but I hope that our little haberdashery shop can continue to move forward into the future. I know you've all enjoyed the evening and learnt something new. Cupcakes & Couture will return in a week's time and I hope everyone will come back with renewed vigour for the world of Gingerberry. Thanks, everyone.'

Callie swiped away a tear on the cuff of her black polo sweater and began to gather the discarded crockery as the class scraped back their chairs and prepared to leave with shouts of thanks and promises to finish their homework squares.

At last, the bell became silent.

'Delia, I…'

'It's okay, dear. I know Hannah was with us this evening and was bursting with pride at what you've achieved. I know I am. Oh, here's Seb. I thought he'd promised to drop in.'

'Wow, look at this place. What a wonderful transformation. Gingerberry is definitely going to remain a thrumming hub of creativity and chatter. What, no cakes left?' Seb hugged Callie to him. Before drawing away to greet Delia, he whispered in Callie's ear, 'Hope you don't mind – I brought a friend with me.'

Still retaining her welcoming smile, Callie brushed her now almost shoulder-length hair from her cheeks to behind her ears and focused her tear-reddened eyes on

Seb's companion. Without warning her heart shot like a stone down a well into her stomach and bounced back up again, causing her knees to weaken under the sudden onslaught of emotion.

Theo!

CHAPTER NINETEEN

'Can we talk?' Theo asked.

Callie nodded, snatched her jacket from the hook by the door and followed Theo out of the shop, leaving Seb and Delia watching them like a pair of gobsmacked goldfish.

It was a mild night for early May. They sauntered down the high street, a soft breeze licking at the eaves and lifting Callie's overlong fringe from her eyelashes. The moonlight glanced against the shop fronts and lit up their path.

Neither spoke. Callie was relieved as her throat was so tightly constricted that any reply would have come out as a squeak worthy of Tweetie Pie. Theo's proximity had sent her heart into a frenzy of unfathomable emotions. They reached the churchyard and paused at the lychgate where the clematis wound its sinewy stems up the wooden posts to the slated roof.

'Remember when we used to frighten ourselves stupid playing hide-and-seek in the graveyard?' said Theo.

'I do.'

'Remember when Seb dressed up as a ghost and you threw a rock at him? He's still got that scar in the middle of his forehead.'

'Served him right,' Callie smirked, chancing a glance from beneath her fringe at Theo. 'Have you been pruning the rose bush we planted for Mum and Dad?'

Theo nodded, staring through the darkness towards the plot where Callie's parents were laid to rest.

'Thanks.'

'We loved them, too, Callie. Seb, Dominic, me. It was the least I could do whilst you were… away.'

'I should have come back more often. I should have spent more time with Aunt Hannah before she…'

Theo lifted Callie up onto the moss-covered stone wall and jumped up next to her, studying his fingernails.

'I told her it was my fault. If she had to blame anyone then it had to be me.'

'It wasn't your fault, Theo. If anything it was me who jumped to hasty conclusions. Always reacting before thinking, that's what Aunt Hannah used to say. She was right. Why do things have to be so difficult?' Tears slid down her cheeks.

'They don't have to be, Cal. You could come back home, run Gingerberry…'

'I can't. I love my life in London. I adore the buzz, the nightlife, the people, even the traffic! And I love my boutique. It's the culmination of all my dreams from as far back as I can remember, you know that, Theo. You were there. But now I'm back here, it feels like this is where my heart truly is.'

Callie couldn't look at Theo but she knew he was staring at her. It felt like the last three years had slipped into oblivion; that they had simply been apart for the weekend and were now back together. They had so much shared history, so many mutual friends and experiences. 'A girl can't have everything, though.'

'Even when I'm on stage playing to thousands of fans, all screaming my name, asking for one more song, you know what I'm thinking? When can I jump on that plane and fly back home to Allthorpe? Mum and Dad despair of ever getting rid of me. They've even taken to leaving estate agents' sales particulars lying around the house where I can find them. But do you know what? Every one of those glossy brochures is for houses within a ten-mile radius of home.

'This is where my heart is, Cal, where it will always be. No matter how far I travel, or how successful the band becomes, I will always come back home. And I think you feel the same way. You've just been in denial these last three years.'

Callie met Theo's eyes at last and almost fell from her perch on the wall. Her breath quickened and longing flashed through her veins and sparkled out to her fingertips. This was her Theo, the man she had given her heart to when she was a teenager and who had refused to let her have it back. He was the first boy she'd kissed and, she realised with a smile, his picture was still sellotaped on that ridiculous wedding scrap box she and Nessa had made all those years ago. She still had it, hidden under her bed. She wondered if Nessa had kept hers and whether Robbie Williams' picture was still pasted on the lid, or whether a new photo had taken its place.

'Look…' Theo jumped down from the wall and turned to look Callie in the eyes. He reached into the inside pocket of his black denim jacket and produced a pair of tickets. 'I've brought you these. They're tickets for a gig The Razorclaws are doing in London. It's the last one before Finn's wedding so it's more of a rehearsal, really. Just a few members of the official fan club, and friends and family members of the band and our management team. Come, please. Bring a friend?'

Theo's silver eyes held a question but she looked away.

'We're expecting about two hundred people. Tickets are like gold dust. I want you there this time, Callie. I want to see your face in the audience. I need to hear your feedback on one of the songs I've written. It's the forerunner of the song I've composed for Finn and Lilac's wedding celebrations and it'll be the first time it's been performed in public, even though I wrote it years ago. I think you'll like it.'

Theo pressed the tickets into her hands and curled his fingers around hers. She looked down at their entwined hands. It felt so easy and natural to be this close to Theo. She knew every contour of his handsome face, every curve of his muscular, slender body. She had to fight the urge to run her fingers through his spiky sandy hair. Her nostrils prickled as a whiff of his citrusy cologne rose up and sent her emotions zooming back to her past.

'Did you ever wonder what would have happened if you hadn't run out that night?'

'I had to get away, Theo,' she whispered. 'The image of you with that girl on your lap, her arms wound round your neck like a lioness protecting her cub, has remained branded on my soul ever since.'

Theo looked like he was going to say something straight back but he refrained.

'You've done so well. Callie-Louise is a fabulous success. I'm proud of you, Cal. I'm sorry that this happened to us. If I could turn back the clock...'

'I know.'

Theo's mouth was inches away now, his eyes locked on hers.

'Can't we...'

He lowered his head, his breath warm on her cheek. Ripples of desire flooded her veins and heat surged through her body as his lips brushed hers and then touched at her ear lobe. She closed her eyes, allowing every one of her senses to sparkle with pleasure. His mouth moved back towards hers and their lips almost joined.

'No, sorry, Theo, I can't do this!'

Callie leapt down from the wall, grazing her knuckles on the stone. What the hell was she doing? Nothing had changed. Theo was still the lead singer in one of the most famous bands of the moment and she had a boutique to run in London. Why was she even considering opening up old wounds that had taken so long to heal, if indeed they ever had? Hadn't she been hurt enough? Did she *want* to put herself through that agony again?

She stepped away but held his eyes, pausing long enough to see the confusion and hurt reflected deep within. Then she ran, ran as if her life depended on it, tears flowing down her cheeks, her heart breaking in two.

CHAPTER TWENTY

Callie sat at the mahogany table, practising the new stitch that she would be demonstrating to the Cupcakes & Couture ladies at their next session in an hour's time. She had also laid out three sample garments of the baby doll and teddy lingerie that she'd put the finishing touches to last night for them to inspect. Under normal circumstances she would have been honoured that so many people were prepared to hear her ideas, but since her wedding gown design hadn't won the competition she was upset to find that she struggled with creating new designs. It was the reason she'd asked Scarlet to email her old lingerie designs for the Cupcakes & Couture ladies to work on instead of sketching new ones.

For Callie, who had been dressing her Barbie dolls in her own wacky designs since the age of four, the withering of her passion for fashion had surprised her. A persistent lethargy had invaded her creative dexterity so that even putting pencil to sketch pad had been a tremendous effort which produced nothing of merit.

What was the point? Lilac Verbois's wedding dress had been one of the most inspirational creations of her career and yet it had been rejected; she had been banished from the salon, even if it *was* only temporarily; and now she found herself skulking in Yorkshire, compelled to manage a high-street business until it could be sold – an act of extreme hostility towards the community that had taken her to their hearts.

Her head reminded her that grief was a personal journey, an unnavigable maze impossible to share with even the closest confidante. Until the barrage of sorrow abated, she knew she could not recover her equilibrium or her flair for design.

But there was a glimmer of light on the horizon. The lingerie was exquisite and she was certain there would be a market for it in her boutique in Pimlico as well as hand-sewn garters, basques and silk bra and knicker sets. If she could inspire the Cupcakes & Couture ladies to turn their skills to embroidery and lace-making, it could be the start of an exciting cottage industry. There was already an established outlet with a readily available clientele and whilst the cost of a hand-made piece of lingerie would have been baulked at by a Yorkshire woman, residents of the capital had deeper pockets. She could perhaps even run the businesses side-by-side, each feeding from and into the other.

But was it too little too late? Despite having restocked the shelves with modern yarn and updating the window display, the shop's income did not cover expenses. The fee for that evening's Cupcakes & Couture class barely covered the cost of a coffee and a selection from the tray of Parisian marvels Tom had dropped by earlier.

Tom's words of warning floated back to her. Should she have bolted whilst she'd had the chance to leave without a backward glance or a slice of guilt? Should she really be spinning a fantasy of false hope to these lovely people? Wouldn't it have been less painful for everyone if she'd just kept Gingerberry closed after her aunt's death and told everyone she was sorry, but her life was in London now and the continued operation of a tiny shop two hundred miles away was not a viable proposition?

Why was she doing this? Her aunt, bless her, would never know what her niece had done with her beloved shop. She'd never had the opportunity to note down her wishes. But who was she trying to kid? Her aunt would have wanted her to keep Gingerberry, probably just as it was.

Her ricocheting thoughts alighted on Delia whom it seemed was enjoying a new lease of life. With a jolt, Callie realised that she, like her aunt before her, had grown to love Delia and her trendy haircut, her leopard-print-clad bosom, her bejewelled spectacles swinging in rhythm to the sway of her ample hips as she teased the newbies' stitches into something presentable. This was why she was still here in Allthorpe; the community and their unerring support of her and of Gingerberry Yarns.

The bell jangled and Callie raised her eyes to the door.

Nessa.

It seemed she had arrived early to commence a one-woman crusade to reboot Callie's love life, conveniently brushing aside Callie's arguments that she wasn't interested as she was only back in Allthorpe temporarily.

'Look, Nessa, stop nagging, will you?'

'Callie, I've spoken to Seb, and Archie confirms it, too. Theo is not involved in a relationship at the moment. You really need to get over that one mistake when he…'

'How do you know it was once, Nessa? Don't you think it's stretching coincidence that his one-time lapse in loyalty just so happened to be when I walked in that night and caught him?'

'Things are different in the music scene…'

'You don't have to lecture me on the quirks of the music industry. I dated Theo for years until… Well, I'm not in the slightest bit interested in what Theo chooses to do with his life. Stop matchmaking! And anyway' – Callie decided attack was the best form of defence where Nessa was concerned – 'people who inhabit glass houses! Who are you dating at the moment?'

Nessa flicked the sides of her hair behind her ears, a gleeful smile lingering on her apricot lips. 'Well, there's this professional at the golf club; firm abs, taut butt, great swing, sends ripples around my…'

'Okay, okay, sorry I asked.'

'Callie, life is short and there's a goody bag of guys out there with whom to share the journey. Come on, why not let Dominic set you up with his friend Fraser? He's single, he lives in Paris. What better place for a fashion designer to call her base?'

'Nessa…' Callie paused in her task of laying out the bamboo needles and colourful yarn on the gargantuan table to fix Nessa with what she hoped was her most fearsome expression. 'I'm… not… interested! I've got enough to think about at the moment with sorting out Gingerberry and then getting it on the market.'

'So, you are still selling up, then?' asked Nessa softly.

Callie sank her lanky frame into the scruffy second-hand leather sofa she had purchased after last week's success of Cupcakes & Couture and draped with a neon-pink throw. Her anguish over her prevarication about Gingerberry's future had risen slowly like a creeping, ceaseless tide, but a decision had to be made.

'I don't think I have any choice, Nessa. I can't split my time between two businesses so far apart. But I have to accept that I've been putting it off, arguing that it'll be more attractive to potential buyers if I just spruce up the décor, maybe improve and replenish the stock, revamp the window display, increase the income, run crafting sessions. But none of this will make any difference if the person who buys Gingerberry intends to turn it into a holiday let, will it? So I'm wasting my time and my money.'

Nessa opened her mouth to add her own soliloquy of criticism of the property developers who had taken over Allthorpe High Street, but Callie was saved from hearing it by the jingle of the front door bell and the next session of Cupcakes & Couture getting under way.

Ten minutes later the room was crammed with enthusiastic participants. The ranks were swelled by a married couple from the next village and two girls from Marcia's reading group. Every one of the dedicated crafters from the previous session had arrived armed with their completed square of knitting, revealing varying degrees of competence. As a comfortable swirl of cheerful banter wove around the shop, two of the more experienced WI women proudly displayed an intricately knitted Fair Isle sweater that they had collaborated on to a great deal of murmured appreciation.

'As good, if not better, than anything you can get in any of your fancy London stores, eh, Callie?'

'Absolutely gorgeous, Kath. I love the peaches-and-cream colour palette. Could you hold it up whilst I take a picture of it to email to my friend Scarlet? Be prepared to get your first order!'

After she had sent the photo to Scarlet, Callie took a moment to surreptitiously survey the diverse but happy gathering.

First Nessa, arched over the glass counter with her friend Julia as they spread out and pinned the woolly squares, ready to sew together for the hospice blanket project. Then there were the students from St Hilda's, Alicia, Polly and Megan, giggling as their ducked under the table to retrieve their burnt-orange yarn like the naughty schoolgirls they were.

But it was in contemplation of Marcia that Callie stalled. Whilst her tawny hair remained long and unstyled, she had ditched her mother's reading glasses and her face glowed as she patiently guided Marc's hand through each stitch until, with a whoop of delight, he completed a row of moss stitch. A smile turned the corners of her lips as she exchanged a silent glance with Iris. When the class broke for their coffee and patisserie treats, Callie continued her study of the shy young girl and realised the change was not merely physical. Callie had never seen Marcia so content.

'Those girls from St Hilda's are a hoot, aren't they?' Delia said as she curled her fingers around a mug of coffee. 'I'm delighted to see that youngsters are rediscovering the crafting bug. Polly said three more of their friends will be along next time. At this rate, as long as Callie stops giving away these delicious pastries and coffee and starts charging proper prices for them, we might just manage to turn this place around.'

'Oh, I hope so!' Marcia interjected. 'It's shocking what's happening to the high street, just shocking. Mum didn't want me to say anything before the meeting, Callie, but this morning we received notification from the council about another application for planning permission, this one for the petrol station on the corner of our street. You know, Hargreaves & Sons that closed down eighteen months ago? Well, no prizes for what's being proposed – a block of eight executive apartments.

'All the houses round there are Victorian, stone-built terraces and semis, and they want to throw up a four-storey, brick-built monstrosity! Well, if it has anything to do with me, it will *not* happen.' Marcia emphasised the last four words. Her cheeks burned as she lowered her lashes. She twiddled with the hand-knit scarf around her neck. 'I've drafted a written objection to the council, setting out the reasons for our objection, but with all the businesses closing it creates a circle of collapse. The properties are renovated into housing only city dwellers can afford as weekend retreats which perpetuates the problem of dwindling resident numbers and lack of daily trade.'

'You are absolutely right, Marcia,' Callie said, nodding. Then, wrestling with her conscience, she decided to add her own submission of persuasion to the conversation. 'Marcia, I hope you don't mind but I read one of your short stories the other night. It was excellent, absorbing. I adored Lance, fell in love with him actually, and I loved the twist at the end. Could I just make a suggestion?'

Marcia raised her chin and met Callie's eyes. She nodded, awaiting her pronouncement without a smidgeon of nerves. And why should she be nervous? After all, she was a published author with a national magazine.

'Have you ever thought of extending the story into a full-length novel? I can see you are an accomplished writer of short stories for the women's magazine market, but I firmly believe that if you submitted your work to a book publisher they would snap you up in a millisecond. Why don't you give it a try? What have you got to lose? You already have an army of fans, me included!'

'Thanks, Callie. I'll think about it.'

Before anyone else could comment, the doorbell rang and all eyes swung to check out the new arrival.

'Oh, hi, Tom, come on in.' Callie swooped across to the coffee machine, anxious to thank him for the tray of baked goodies and offer payment. 'Cappuccino?'

'Thanks, Callie. I just popped by for the tray. It's from my window display and I need it for tomorrow morning. You can keep the cupcake pyramid until later in the week, though.' His green eyes spotted Marcia and swiftly averted their gaze to fix on Callie as a crimson blush seeped across his unshaven cheeks. 'Erm, how was your evening? What's your team of knitters and sewers called again?'

'Cupcakes & Couture!' Callie laughed. 'So I actually have you to thank for half of it. We've had five new students join the ranks tonight, although I suspect it was your culinary delights that brought them here rather than my knitting and dressmaking skills.'

Callie smiled at Tom but he was studying his feet so she glanced across to Marcia. She realised immediately what was happening and why Marcia had seemed to exude an uncharacteristic glow that evening.

As it seemed no one but she intended to aid the path of conversation, Callie ploughed on. 'Any news from St Hilda's about the after-school-club cookery lessons, Tom?'

'Not yet, but Marcia did an awesome job writing down the recipes and the methods as well as designing the lesson plans. I'm just not convinced my skills are what the school is looking for and, anyway, every bit of my time is already taken up with running the shop, visiting Dad, doing the books…'

'Tom, you're exactly what the school needs,' said Nessa. 'I'll have a word with the head tomorrow and get back to you. She's been deluged with paperwork for the forthcoming OFSTED inspection.'

'Thanks, Nessa,' said Marcia, flashing a triumphant smile in the direction of Tom.

'Come on now, everyone, we need to get back to work,' urged Callie. She unfolded a sheet of acid-free tissue paper to display her lingerie samples. 'I've finished the teddies and the baby dolls I showed you photos of last week. What do you think?'

'Ooohs' and 'aaahs' rippled through the room as the class stroked the silk and marvelled at the workmanship.

'These are just beautiful, Callie. Is this the sort of thing you have in mind for your shop in London?' asked one of the WI women.

'Yes, as well as a selection of hand-sewn silk garters, bustiers and basques, and embroidered bra-and-knicker sets. Every penny that is made will be filtered back to those members of Cupcakes & Couture that wish to contribute.'

'I'm in.'

'Me, too.'

'You can count on me, too.'

'And I'm going to be your first customer, Callie. I have to have that teddy, it's just gorgeous,' said Julia. 'And can I order one in bronze for my sister?'

'Sure,' Callie smiled.

A wave of appreciation washed over her. Perhaps her love of all things fashion hadn't deserted her after all. She flopped down onto the couch and tilted her head against its back, twisting to her left as a sudden movement at the shop window caught her eye.

What the…

***

'Is this it?' asked Lilac. 'The Yorkshire branch of Callie-Louise Bridal Couture?'

Nikki and Tish stood on each side of Lilac as they peered into Gingerberry Yarns. The plate-glass window had steamed up and trickles of condensation ran in parallel lines from top to bottom, collecting in tiny pools on the window sill.

'I'm not sure what I'm seeing exactly, but it looks like a bunch of old ladies sitting around a table, knitting. What do you see, Nikki?'

Nikki groaned inwardly. For the first time she found herself cursing her ever-present need for efficiency. She'd anticipated the meeting with the bishop would take a lot longer than it actually had – it seemed he had an even more punishing schedule than a BAFTA-winning actress. When they'd emerged from the Minster, she'd called their limousine service and they'd dashed across to Allthorpe. She'd thought that Callie could probably utilise the extra time with Lilac after she'd made the announcement. She checked her watch. Eight-thirty. Clearly, Callie was busy doing something else.

'Do you think those ladies are her assistants?' asked Tish, her mouth gaping as she watched a lady in a

wheelchair roll over to the table by the door and help herself to a selection of cupcakes from a giant pyramid to take back to the gathering.

'Maybe,' replied Nikki, her hand over her eyes as she strained to understand what was going on inside. 'I think some of them are sewing.'

'It looks like lingerie,' murmured Lilac.

'Oh, God!' spluttered Tish.

'What?'

'No, nothing.'

'What?' Lilac tucked her wavy bob, the colour of liquid caramel, behind her ears and placed her hands on her hips. 'You've forgotten to order my lingerie, haven't you, Tish?'

'Yes.' Tish scrunched up her shoulders and creases appeared across her brow as she waited for the blow to fall. 'Sorry.'

'Doesn't matter; I'll sort it. Now, are we going to risk being labelled a trio of sad voyeurs or are we going inside?'

'I think we should go back to the car and wait until this, erm, this meeting has finished,' suggested Nikki, striding back towards the sleek limo with blacked-out windows and the most handsome driver she'd set eyes on. It was probably the uniform that did it, though... it was one of her weaknesses that she was working hard on eradicating. Or maybe it was the spicy cologne, or his broad muscular shoulders, or his...

'Oh, God, let me through.' Lilac pushed past Tish and Nikki and opened the door. The bell tinkled above her head. 'Quaint!'

The chatter ceased and all heads swung in unison to look at the elegant, six-foot-tall movie star who had stumbled into their world from another planet.

'Oh, this is adorable. You must be Callie-Louise?' Lilac stepped into Gingerberry Yarns and was immediately enveloped by a sense of calm and comfort. 'I'm Lilac Verbois. I love your shop! Are you having a party? Oh, wow, these cakes! Do you import your pastries from Paris?'

Callie rose from her place at the head of the gigantic mahogany table and took a couple of steps forward. 'Yes, I'm Callie-Louise. What can I...? What are you...? Why?'

Lilac drew herself to her full height, straightened her shoulders and cleared her throat. In her best presenter's voice, she said, 'I'm here to announce that Callie-Louise Bridal Couture has won the Lilac Verbois Wedding Gown Competition! Congratulations!'

There was a moment's silence. Callie's hand flew to her mouth but Nessa was quicker off the mark. 'Oh, my God! Awesome!' she shrieked, and the room burst into noisy chatter, only now it was a full octave higher than before the announcement.

Nessa and Delia gathered a stunned, silent Callie into their arms and kissed her. 'Well done, Callie!'

It took half an hour for the ladies to calm down and have a variety of items autographed, by which time their Cupcakes & Couture session had ended and they had to start packing away.

'So, Cupcakes & Couture,' mused Lilac, who had been given the Throne of Honour at the head of the table where she was being shown the various finished products of the group's toil. 'I love this bridal lingerie. I think you might have just saved someone's skin, ladies.' Lilac smirked as she shot a look across at Tish, who was loitering next to the cake table, her hand held under her chin to catch the crumbs from the fifth pistachio macaroon she'd indulged in. 'Are they silk?'

'Yes, it's organic silk. I source it for the salon in London from a small women's collective in India. Everything has been hand-sewn and embellished by the Cupcakes & Couture ladies.'

'I particularly like this teddy. I'd like to order seven, please, in different shades, one for each night of our honeymoon. And could you design me a bridal basque in this fabric please, and matching knickers?'

'Erm, yes, of course.'

'Don't tell me you make these delectable little cakes yourself as well, Callie?' Lilac bit into a cupcake topped with the palest pink icing and sprinkled with edible glitter. 'Absolutely heavenly. How are the macaroons, Tish?' Lilac giggled at the look on her

wedding planner's face when she realised she'd been caught in the act.

'Delicious,' Tish mumbled through a mouthful of buttercream, 'and these peppermint millefueille are to die for, if a little difficult to eat.'

'Oh, no, Miss Verbois. These are supplied exclusively for our Cupcakes & Couture evenings by internationally trained pastry chef, Tom Wallington,' announced Marcia. It was the first time she'd spoken since Lilac and her entourage had arrived, but the pride in her eyes on Tom's behalf caused Callie's heart to flutter.

'Wow, you do have some fabulously talented people in this village, don't you? I have my five-tier wedding cake ordered already.' Lilac raised her eyebrows at Tish, just to check, but she was teasing her. 'Do you think it would be possible for your supplier to prepare, say, twenty-five of these cupcake pyramids? The children that we've invited to the wedding will adore them – it's a much better option than stodgy fruit cake. Oh, I'm so excited!'

Lilac kicked off her shoes and sat back in her chair, casting her eyes around the women. 'You know, I really do miss all this female camaraderie. Getting together with a group of friends to spend the evening gossiping, swapping secrets, asking for advice. You're lucky, Callie. Now I understand why you have a branch of Callie-Louise in Yorkshire. It's your home; these are your friends who are willing to support you through life's ups and downs. I was born in Yorkshire, too, but sadly I don't have a bunch of friends to come home to.'

Callie smiled at Lilac, but tears prickled at her eyes. Why had it taken such a devastating loss for her to realise how fortunate she was that she still had roots in her home town? That there were friends here who loved her no matter how long she'd been away? Nessa, Seb, Dominic, Archie – even Theo, if she let him. It was time she started to appreciate her good fortune and gave something of herself back.

She shoved her guilt at her recent behaviour into the far crevices of her mind for later dissection. Tonight was an evening of celebration. It was the best night she'd had for years.

She made a decision.

As she would now have to return to London to start working on Lilac's wedding gown, she would accept Theo's invitation to attend The Razorclaws' rehearsal concert and take Nessa as a thank you for being her best friend.

CHAPTER TWENTY-ONE

'Wow, look at this place. It's magnificent! I really can't decide whether to faint at the architectural splendour of it all or drool with envy. Like everything else about this wedding, Harewood House is such a perfect venue for an actress and rock star to hold their fairy-tale wedding, don't you think?' Scarlet clutched her chest and performed a theatrical swoon.

Callie giggled. 'Stop it. You're reminding me of Tish.'

'Of course, our very own twenty-first-century Cinderella would have ordered the Georgian façade to be bedecked with a cornucopia of pink ribbon and lily-of-the-valley wreaths, and the coats of the prancing ponies welcoming us out front would have to be dyed to match the bridesmaids' dresses.'

'Oooh, that sounds so romantic, Scarlet,' sighed Flora before she executed a wide yawn in Callie's face.

Flora had complained the whole journey from King's Cross to Leeds about missing out on her requisite nine hours of sleep and how early mornings played havoc with her delicate body clock. Sadly, her psychic had not seen fit, or indeed been seen at all, to warn Flora of the unexpected last-minute jaunt up to Yorkshire.

Callie had received a call the previous day from Nikki to inform her that Lilac and Finn were visiting with the chef at Harewood House the following afternoon for a tasting session of the menu they'd chosen for their wedding breakfast. If Callie could get up there in the morning, Lilac could squeeze her in for an extra dress fitting. It was an opportunity Callie couldn't afford to refuse and it also meant she could call in and see how Delia was getting on at Gingerberry.

Since being informed of winning the wedding gown competition, Callie had been bouncing between Allthorpe and London, trying to keep all the plates in her life spinning in unison. But mostly she'd been spending her time holed up in her workshop with Scarlet as they made numerous tweaks to the dress in accordance with Lilac's wishes. It was shaping up to be the most complicated design brief Callie had ever had, but she was definitely up to the challenge.

There was a real buzz about the salon, which they'd struggled to keep under wraps for fear of giving the secret away and finding the paparazzi camped out on their doorstep. Unsurprisingly, Flora was the weakest link. She really was the worst secret keeper ever. Apart from that morning when she'd been deprived of her beauty sleep, she tended to spend her days smiling and humming to herself. One of their newest bridal clients had even asked if she had mental health issues and added how lovely it was that Callie was acting as her mentor.

They climbed the worn stone steps of Harewood House to the columned entrance, pushed open the surprisingly unimpressive front door and found themselves in the entrance hall. Callie stared up at the ceiling and smiled. It would be a wonderful place to hold a wedding reception.

'Hi, you must be Callie-Louise Henshaw? If you follow me, I'll show you up to Lilac's suite. Tish and Nikki are already there. There's been a bit of a hitch, I'm afraid, but I'm going to let them tell you about it. Oh, I'm Craig Carver, by the way – Lilac and Finn's wedding photographer and videographer. Come this way.' Craig smiled at them, displaying perfectly even teeth, and his gentle chestnut eyes crinkled attractively at the corners. With his stocky build and broad shoulders Callie suspected that in his spare time he played prop forward for the local rugby team.

They followed Craig up the sweeping staircase. His rear view was even more impressive than the front and confirmed Callie's theory that he was probably more comfortable on a sports pitch than in a stately home, herding recalcitrant wedding guests into group photos. The fact that his muscular legs took the stairs two at a time only served to enhance the tautness of his buttocks.

'Do you think the lady of the house would let us slide down the banister after we've seen Lilac?' asked Flora, running her hand along the smooth mahogany wood.

'Maybe not, Flora,' giggled Callie, who'd had the exact same thought.

'Here we are. Before you go in there I feel I should warn you – Nikki Coates is not a happy PA bunny. If you see her with anything in her hand, you might want to duck. Maybe I'll see you in the bar before you leave?' Craig suggested, his eyes lingering on Flora. 'Good luck!'

He cracked open the door to Lilac's suite and fled.

'Hi,' said Callie, the word dying on her lips. 'Where's Lilac?'

'Upstairs puking in the en suite bathroom,' snarled Nikki.

'Oh, erm, poor Lilac. That's awful.'

'Well, it is for the chef. We made it absolutely clear to the catering company we engaged that Lilac had an intolerance to shellfish. It was even included as a term in their contract. And what did the moron offer on the tasting menu? Mini Thai fishcakes. She'd popped one in her mouth before we realised. She's throwing up for England. But that's not the worst of it – you should see her lips; "bee-stung" doesn't even cover it! Looks like she's indulged in a course of extreme Botox, and you know what Lilac's position is on chemical enhancements.

'Finn's with her and he's fuming. And she's had to cancel her flight across to Croatia tonight, which has set the filming schedule back. The producer's having a hissy fit, screaming about budget, timescales, the changing light, you name it. And of course the chef's stormed off screaming and swearing that no one told him about any dietary issues, so Tish has another item on her already infinite to-do list – finding a replacement chef who can coordinate the catering for one hundred and fifty discerning guests from the movie and music business in just two weeks. Talk about Mission Impossible!'

Callie cast a glance over to the full-height windows overlooking the gardens where Tish stood with her iPhone clutched to her ear, her voice wobbling as she pleaded with the person on the other end to help her. The poor girl looked exhausted and had certainly lost weight since the last time Callie had seen her. She wondered if this wedding would be the one to finally cure Tish of her hearts-and-flowers obsession.

'You should have been here when the chef left. It's been a long time since I heard such a tirade of vibrant language during the working day. The air almost thrummed with verbal electricity, I tell you. Gordon Ramsay, eat your heart out! But Tish stood her ground marvellously. It was a masterclass on how to keep your temper when everything around you is crumbling. She was amazing. To be honest, I didn't think she had it in her.'

'Are you Callie-Louise?'

Callie turned to the door where the most handsome man she had ever laid eyes on had appeared, scratching at his short, trendy beard. His eyes were so startlingly blue they seemed to draw her towards him and she couldn't help staring, her jaw gaping unattractively.

'Yes, that's me,' she stuttered.

'Lilac's asked me to come down and fetch you. She's still tinged with an attractive hue of green, I'm afraid, but she says she's feeling well enough to stand up in her wedding gown. She wants everything to be just perfect. If you ask me, though, I still say we should've grabbed that jet out to Hawaii. I know her mother would have killed her, but now it seems the chef has got there first.'

Callie dispatched Scarlet to fetch the dress and followed Finn up to the bedroom suite with Flora scampering in her wake. It was the swiftest and quietest fitting Callie had ever performed, but she was grateful to Lilac for making the effort. She did not look very well at all as she took occasional sips from a glass of tepid water and forced a weak smile onto her swollen lips. They left her to rest as soon as the fitting was done.

'Thanks, Callie,' Lilac muttered, climbing back onto the bed and pulling the sheet over her head.

'Let's hit the bar,' suggested Scarlet.

'God, yes, please,' said Flora, skipping ahead of them down the corridor, clearly keen to reacquaint herself with the hunky photographer. She wrenched open a pair of double doors with a flourish. 'Oooops, not in here. Looks like a ballroom.'

The girls peered inside the room. Two men clad in black jeans and Black Sabbath T-shirts were busy unravelling coils of cable as they worked on setting up what looked like a stage for a disco that evening. A third man was fiddling with the dry-ice machine, sending bulbous clouds of vapour floating out onto the polished dance floor.

Eventually, they found the bar. Tish gave them a wave of acknowledgement as she hunched over a corner table, her phone glued to her ear. A huge glass of white wine – more a goldfish bowl, really – rested on a pile of box files in front of her.

Nikki was laughing at something the wedding photographer was saying. He looked so incongruous sitting amongst the antiques and the Chippendale chairs in his khaki flak jacket, the pockets hopefully filled with a variety of camera lenses rather than grenades.

'Can I get you ladies a drink?' Craig offered, standing up to greet them.

'Oh, yes, please,' breathed Flora, concentrating her attention on the optics behind the bar before turning to the barman. 'I'd like a Mai Tai. Do you have any of those cute little umbrellas?'

The sides of Craig's lips twitched, but he said nothing. He raised his eyebrows at Callie and Scarlet.

'White wine would be great. We'll share a bottle of Pinot Grigio.'

'Coming right up.'

'Be back in a minute,' said Callie, giving Scarlet's arm a squeeze. She made her way to where Tish had just finished her telephone conversation and was running her fingers distractedly through her curls as she scribbled notes on a jotter in front of her.

'Oh, hi, Callie. I don't suppose you have a best friend who is a Michelin-starred chef who has nothing else to do with his time but drop everything to cater for a hundred and fifty celebrity guests, do you? No, I thought not.'

'Actually, Tish, that's what I wanted to tell you. Whilst I don't think he has a Michelin star, I do have a friend who has trained in the kitchens of a five-star Parisian hotel. Would you like me to introduce you?'

'Oh, my God! Yes! Give me his number and save a girl's life – or her sanity at least!'

'Here. His name is Tom Wallington and he's already supplying the wedding with the most magnificent cupcake tiers for the younger guests. Just tell him you got his number from me.'

'Thank you, Callie, thank you.' Tish was already keying in his number and Callie left her to it.

She settled down at a bashed copper table with Scarlet, Flora, Nikki and Craig and, as the wine flowed, she began to relax.

'Oh, God, what was that awful noise?' squeaked Scarlet.

'They're testing the sound system in the ballroom. The crew have been up there all day,' Craig explained, before turning his full attention to Flora. 'So, has this whole food-poisoning fiasco put you off weddings?'

'Only weddings like this one. If it was me getting married, it would be a tiny church in the country with a handful of special friends – or, no, elopement to somewhere exotic!'

'At last, a girl after my own heart.'

'What do you mean? You're a wedding photographer, for Christ's sake,' laughed Callie. 'You must adore all this romance stuff. Capturing that perfect, dreamy "look of love" between the bride and groom with your camera lens for all eternity.'

'You'd think so, but no. Actually, I'd much rather be out on an assignment in Iraq or Afghanistan, recording the facts as they happen and informing the world about the desperate scenes of terror that are unfolding out there. I was a war photographer before... well, before I got injured in the line of duty, so to speak.'

'Wow, like a soldier?' Flora's eyes widened.

Craig laughed. 'No, those guys are the real heroes. I'm nowhere near as brave as they are. But I have seen my fair share of action. Anyway, enough about me.' Craig turned his attention to Flora. 'You must have a fantastic life being a bridal fashion designer in the bright lights of London?'

As Callie sipped at her wine she had the strangest feeling she was intruding. Something about the way Craig's eyes held Flora's, the way his body language screamed sexual desire. She wasn't sure whether Flora herself had realised it yet, but he was certainly besotted. She decided to grant them some alone time.

'Scarlet, Nikki, come on. Let's check everything we brought with us has found its way safely back into the hire car.'

'Callie, I haven't finished my… oh, yes, right, okay.'

They trotted from the bar but Flora and Craig barely noticed. As Callie closed the door she heard Craig say, 'As Lilac is incapacitated, would you mind helping me out by posing as a stand-in for a few shots in the gardens out front? I need to check the variety of backdrops that are available. I could give you a tour of the house and grounds afterwards. The gardens are beautiful, designed by Capability Brown…'

'I'm starving. Do you think they do afternoon tea here?' asked Scarlet.

'Well, if you think we should risk it,' smirked Nikki, 'I'll join you.'

'I'm not hungry. You two go ahead. I'll go check the car and be with you shortly.' Callie jogged outside.

A gentle summer breeze wafted through the canopy of trees that hugged the rear of the house. It really was a stunningly romantic setting for a country wedding. Down to her right, the surface of the lake glimmered like a piece of tin foil reflecting the clear blue sky above. Her eyes picked out a tiny boathouse on the lake's shore from which a short wooden jetty led, with a rowing boat bobbing serenely on the water next to it.

For the first time in years, her surroundings made her wish she had someone to share this day with. Someone she could link arms with and saunter around the estate, exclaiming at the blossoming flowers, marvelling at the works of art dotted around the estate, taking in the bird garden and chasing around the maze. Preferably Mr Darcy, if he was available – well, there was the lake, and maybe he could...

She returned to the house and sought out the bathroom. All that wine had gone to her head. She could do with splashing her face with cold water and retouching her make-up. She'd not had any spare time lately for personal grooming. Her hair had grown longer than she'd worn it since she was fifteen years old and she'd simply taken to wearing it pinned up. And Scarlet, the undisputed queen of waxing, would have palpitations if she could have seen the state of her legs.

She mounted the stairs, smiling to herself as she envisioned Flora whizzing down the sweeping banister, her hair flying behind her as she whooped for joy. When she reached the top, she paused at the vast window overlooking the pristine gardens to drink in the view out over the rolling hills of Yorkshire and her heart ballooned. How could she have stayed away from her spiritual home for so long? How could she have been content to live amongst the urban sprawl and swirling smog of pollution in London?

Her eyes fell on Flora and Craig in the gardens below the window. Flora stood on a stone bench giggling as she twirled left then right in a variety of increasingly comedic poses as Craig scampered around in front of her clicking his camera. He reached up to help her down and together they wandered to the edge of the balustrade. As Callie watched, Flora spun round to say something to Craig, but instead, her hand flew to her mouth and she burst into laughter, pointing at the bronze statue of Orpheus that stood as the magnificent centrepiece of the garden, a leopard draped over his shoulders. From where she stood, Callie only had a rear view of the naked Greek god, but that was certainly impressive. She made a point of adding a swift detour to her itinerary to appreciate the full splendour of the sculpture from the front.

It was the first time for months she'd seen Flora relaxed and having fun. The smile on the young girl's face as she posed wide-eyed in front of the statue was a joy to witness. A rush of pleasure surged through Callie's veins. She hoped that when this circus of a wedding was over she could resume her easy-going friendship with her ditzy trainee who professed to be vegetarian but whom she'd seen devouring a chicken tikka salad on more than one occasion, not to mention the illicit bacon sandwiches dripping with brown sauce.

As she turned away from the window, she tried to think back to the last time she'd had fun. A wave of melancholy swept over her but she shoved it from her mind with a grimace of irritation. She had no time to indulge in such self-focused introspection today. She pushed open the door to what she thought was the bathroom and immediately found herself enveloped in a cloud of swirling fog.

What was going on? The door swung shut behind her and clicked. She peered to her left and then her right, trying to see through the murkiness.

'Hello?'

'Sorry,' called out a voice. 'The ice machine has gone haywire. Just give us a couple of minutes, love. We've opened the windows and it should clear shortly.'

She recognised the room now. It was the ballroom where the tech guys had been setting up a sound stage. She was reaching for the brass door knob when her eye caught on a figure emerging from the smoke like a ghostly apparition alighting from a steam train: six-foot-two, slender, his hair tufted into familiar spikes, a grin stretching his cheeks, those dimples evidencing the delight he experienced at seeing her.

'Callie! I thought it was you I saw on the steps earlier. What are you doing here?'

'I could ask you the same question.' Her heart hammered a concerto of pleasure against her ribcage and her mouth had suddenly become dry.

'We've been given permission to set up the stage and do a sound-check. Finn's here with Lilac so I thought I'd drop in and we could have a beer and a catch up before I hotfoot it over to my gig in Leeds tonight. He's not had time to sort out a stag night so it'll be the last opportunity we have before the wedding.'

Theo was standing so close to her she could feel his breath on her cheek. He hadn't touched her – no welcoming peck on the cheek, no grabbing her hand to guide her from the room. He simply stood in front of her, his steel-grey eyes concentrated on hers, his lips parted slightly, waiting.

Callie's thoughts ricocheted around her brain. She had no idea what to do, but she knew Theo was waiting for her to make the first move. She could smile and make small talk about Lilac's predicament. She could ask about his family, his band, the concert in London next week; tell him she'd invited Nessa and they were both excited. But if she was honest, in that precise moment, she had no interest in his answers. Throughout her life, her head had always ruled her heart. Was now the time to experiment with allowing her heart a chance to star in the decision-making show instead? Would that lead to a happier existence? How would she know until she tried it?

She inhaled a deep breath, clenched her fists and took a tiny step forward. She sought his lips with hers and when they met she experienced a crash of such pure happiness her knees weakened. She grabbed Theo's forearms and leaned into his chest, desperate to prolong their kiss as sparks of desire shot out to her extremities and sent tingles to her fingertips. Their bodies still melded together perfectly, their embrace as familiar as ever. Callie felt like the last three years had evaporated with the dry ice and they were still together, still in love, still a couple.

Callie and Theo. Theo and Callie.

She broke away for a second to scour his face, picking out the blemishes, the freckles, the tiny scar on his left temple, to reassure herself that this was still her Theo. She was surprised but relieved to see that nothing had changed. A feeling of total security enveloped her, as if all her troubles had been snuffed out simply by Theo's presence; that the safety net which had been whipped from under her by her aunt's death had been rolled back out by Theo.

'Theo, we're late. We need to get... Oh, sorry, I thought...'

'Callie, we have to talk before we...'

'I know.'

'I have to go. I've got my gig in Leeds. Can I call you? Or were you thinking of coming to the concert in London next week?'

Callie nodded. She didn't trust herself to speak. It took all her willpower, such as it was, to keep the lid on her emotions and not crumble into an embarrassing heap of tears in front of Theo and his crew, who stood in a line only six feet away, staring expectantly at him.

'Then perhaps I can take you out to dinner afterwards?'

'Great.'

Callie watched Theo turn, slap one of the tech guys on his back and stride from the ballroom. Was her heart, which had been an enemy for so long as far as Theo was concerned, now her friend? If the warm feelings swirling around her chest were any kind of barometer, then it was.

But one thing she knew now with absolute certainty. She still loved Theo. Always had. He was the first person she'd kissed all those years ago and she wanted him to be the last.

CHAPTER TWENTY-TWO

'Do you need me to model one of these for you again, Callie?' asked Tish as she ran her fingertips over the delicate embroidery of a pale lilac bustier that hung on a rail in Callie's workshop alongside a selection of bridal lingerie that had just been delivered to the Callie-Louise in Pimlico from its Yorkshire branch.

Every piece was perfect. The women of the Cupcakes & Couture sewing group had proved to be true maestros with a needle and thread and they had followed her intricate designs to the letter. The resulting garments were beautiful and Callie was not surprised Tish couldn't resist the urge to touch them. She hoped others would feel the same way, too, as she had surrendered to Scarlet and Flora's nagging and agreed to deliver a selection of the teddies and chemises and cami sets to one of the luxury lingerie boutiques in Knightsbridge. If they liked them, then the future of Gingerberry would be secure. Did this mean she intended to keep it?

Despite the dark smudges under her cobalt eyes, Tish still possessed an inexhaustible vigour for the wedding arrangements which had now moved on to the 'final frenzy' stage. Panic had set in and she had taken to zooming around the streets of London on a second-hand moped, checking that every order was on schedule, every detail had been adhered to, right down to the individual sugar-craft flowers on the wedding cake, which had caused a near catastrophe when the lilac blossoms had not been the right shade of purple.

Callie experienced a surge of sympathy for the young girl. Tish had told her that, out of necessity, she had to eat, sleep and breathe Lilac's wedding. She'd even had to turn down a date with a potential Prince Charming, despite being so keen to find 'the one' and star in her own dream ceremony. There wasn't a bridal supplier in the capital she hadn't scoured for inspiration. She had even taken to emulating Nikki's penchant for extreme list-making and made copious notes that grew longer by the day. But despite her frantic schedule she had still found the time to call in to see Callie and shop for her future wedding lingerie.

'No, thanks, Tish. It's kind of you to offer but Lilac's trousseau has been finalised. It's just the dress that needs a last fitting. But if you pop next door to my office you might find something to put a smile back on your face,' teased Callie.

Tish screwed up her nose questioningly but obediently trotted off into the office.

Scarlet smiled at Callie as she adjusted one of the most expensive diamanté tiaras Callie-Louise had to offer and inspected her appearance in the mirror. The headpiece looked amazing nestled in her halo of auburn curls. 'Don't you think Jules is a millinery genius? This is his most fabulous artistic creation to date.'

'Scarlet, do I detect...'

Before Callie could finish her question, a squeal of delight erupted from the room next door and Tish came running back into the workshop holding aloft a gorgeous satin teddy fashioned from the same pattern as Lilac's but in a delicate blush pink – Tish's favourite colour.

'Oh, my God, thank you, thank you so much. That's another item I can strike off my "must-have" list. I love it! I'm trying it on now!' And she disappeared into the changing room.

Callie exchanged a smirk with Scarlet and Flora as they waited for her to reappear. When she did, tears were trickling down her pale cheeks.

'It's gorgeous, Callie. You are so talented. Thank you a thousand times.'

'Oh, don't thank me – thank the ladies from Gingerberry who made it up for you.'

Tish rushed forward and flung her arms around each of the girls in turn as the door to the boutique swung open with a gust of warm summer air and a dense waft of Chanel Pour Monsieur cologne.

'What? Another hugfest? What is it with you girls? Can't you get through a day without succumbing to a bout of excessive physical contact?' Jules Gallieri rolled his eyes but then fixed them on Tish's svelte figure and gave an appreciative whistle. 'And I don't just mean the millinery masterpiece!'

The girls giggled and Tish shot from the room to get dressed.

'Are you planning to wear that tiara anywhere special?' Jules enquired, experimenting with a nonchalant look but failing to pull it off.

'No,' said Scarlet, gently removing the headpiece from her hair.

'Why do you ask, Jules?' said Callie, a mischievous glint in her eye.

'Erm…'

Callie laughed. It had been a long time since she'd seen the handsome Jules blush.

Tish appeared fully clothed and ready to leave. She reached for her handbag and waited whilst Callie slotted the lingerie into one of the Callie-Louise peppermint-and-gold bags and tied the ribbons into a bow.

'Thanks again, Callie.'

'You are welcome, Tish. I'll see you in just over a week's time at the hotel in York on the morning of the wedding.'

'Sure. Bye.'

'Hey, Scarlet, seeing as you like that tiara so much, why don't you permit me to escort you round the corner to my humble establishment and talk you through some of my other designs for the more budget-conscious consumer of all things sparkling? It would be my pleasure.'

'Oh, yes, please!'

'Your wish is my command.'

The expression on Scarlet's face as Jules raised her fingers to his lips told Callie that Scarlet might just have found her prince.

CHAPTER TWENTY-THREE

July was Callie's favourite month, not least because it included her birthday. The day of the concert, from its first breath of crystal light bursting through the blinds of her flat above her studio in Pimlico, promised warmth and exhilaration. As if directed by the concert's organisers, a cerulean sky, dotted with wisps of spun cotton, had appeared arched over the London rooftops, casting angular shadows over the streets and pavements and lifting its residents' mood.

'Hey, girls!' A bearded stranger leapt out from a shop doorway into their path.

Nessa let out a cry of alarm and reached out to grasp hold of Callie's arm.

'Bet you've got tickets for The Razorclaws' gig tonight, haven't you? Want to sell them? I can go up to three hundred quid.'

'No, thanks,' Callie said, not daring to meet the man's eye. She tucked Nessa's arm through hers and guided her down the narrow alleyway to the stage door of the

West End theatre where Theo had assured her their names would be on the backstage guest list.

They were late. Scarlet, Flora and Lizzie had insisted on a belated celebration of the Callie-Louise competition win with copious champagne cocktails in Covent Garden. Her friends were tinged green with envy that she and Nessa were specially invited guests of The Razorclaws. Flora had asked if Callie would sneak her in under her coat.

The doorman squinted at them like a hunched vulture eyeing his lunch having forgone breakfast. He took an inordinate amount of time scrutinising their passes before reluctantly waving them through. A surge of excitement coiled through Callie's veins as an explosion of memories of all the concerts she'd attended with Theo and the band came screaming back. But those gigs in the backrooms and basements of pubs and social clubs around Yorkshire had been nothing like this.

The support band had just leapt onto the stage and the level of excitement in the theatre had reached fever pitch. The place was so crammed with screaming girls that the security guys were already stalking the aisles muttering about fire regulations and ticket fraud. Backstage buzzed with technicians, backing musicians, even a TV crew, and a sprinkling of dignitaries and hangers-on anxious to be seen where the action was.

Callie glanced down the corridors hoping for a glimpse of Theo. She knew he would be waiting in the wings and, despite the awkwardness when she'd spoken to him on the phone the previous night to arrange dinner, she wanted to wish him luck. After their meeting at Harewood House she had spent a lot of time wondering if forgiveness of Theo's actions three years ago would be the route to salvaging some kind of relationship. Hope had been an elusive friend these last few months, but she still retained her belief in its restorative power. However, as she peered round the corner towards the band's dressing room, she saw they were protected from the braying public by several burly security guards.

'I'm sorry, ladies, this is a sterile area. No one goes in, not even the band's mothers. You'd better go find your seats. Late arrivals will be locked out,' the guy threatened with a soupçon of glee.

'Come on, Cal. Let's grab a drink in the bar whilst the support band's playing.'

They made their way up the majestic staircase swathed in plush claret-and-gold carpet, to the Grand Circle bar, where they ordered two glasses of Prosecco rosé, which produced no change from a twenty-pound note.

'Hey, Nessa? Is that you?'

A gloriously handsome man in his late twenties with bouffant blond hair and startlingly blue eyes strode over to where the girls were perched on bar stools sipping their drinks. He held his palm outstretched to greet Nessa, who smirked at Callie's raised eyebrows.

'Harvey! What are you doing here?'

'Oh, God, I'm in desperate need of an alcoholic injection of strength to endure the privations of the next hour. I'm here with my niece and two of her friends. My brother took out a mortgage to pay for the tickets for them to see The Razorclaws and it turns out he's away on business in Germany tonight so he couldn't come. I suspect foul play.' Harvey smiled and tiny dimples appeared in his cheeks like commas around his plump pink lips. 'I have to admit, I'm surprised to see *you* here, though. A sporting event at Wembley or Twickenham or Lord's, yes, but not at a rock gig filled with screaming adolescents! Don't you see enough of them at school?'

'Oh, Callie and I grew up with a couple of the band members. Sorry, Harvey, this is my best friend, Callie. Callie, this is Harvey Adams. He was a drama teacher at St Hilda's before fame came calling and he scooted off to the bright lights of Manchester.'

'I'm delighted to meet you, Callie.' Harvey lifted her fingers to his lips.

'Yes, I'm an ac*tor*.' He flicked his floppy blond fringe from those bright blue eyes and graced them with his bleached smile. Callie felt Nessa stiffen at her elbow, knowing she was stifling a chuckle.

'You may have seen me in *Death in the Aire* – the gritty detective series set in West Yorkshire?'

'Oh, yes, I have,' Nessa said, much to Harvey's blatant delight. 'On BBC Four? What part did you play?' She scrunched up her nose as she tried to recall the series.

'I played the murder victim. A difficult and challenging role to get right, but of course I managed to nail it. I'm nothing if not professional. The director told me I have a bright future playing the dead and dying,' Harvey boasted without a hint of irony, 'and those scenes are often pivotal to the plot, I find. If you're interested, Nessa, perhaps you'll allow me to talk you through my last role as a firefighter who fell to his death whilst tackling a blazing clock tower. The demands on the actor can be strenuous, but fame and celebrity must be secondary to the sense of pride at having contributed to the whole ensemble.'

Callie sucked her lips between her teeth to prevent her mouth from twitching as she felt Nessa shaking with an onslaught of barely repressed giggling.

'Can I offer you ladies a drink? You know, I have some promotional photographs I could autograph for you. One never knows when one might be recognised and it's prudent to be prepared. Wouldn't wish to let a fan down. Fame is an onerous burden, but us actors must bear our responsibilities with stoic fortitude.'

Harvey flashed his pearly whites again at a nonplussed Nessa, who'd been rendered temporarily speechless.

'Erm, thanks, Harvey, but I think we need to go and find our seats.'

'Toodle-loo, then. Have fun. Maybe we can catch up later?'

Inside the airless auditorium, the noise was incredible. Every perch was occupied; every gilt-framed box had been pressed into service. The crowd was made up of ninety per cent teenage girls and ten per cent concerned parents who'd been unwilling to allow their offspring to attend the concert unchaperoned and who wore expressions of reluctant stoicism.

'I think you've made a friend.'

'You mean Harvey?'

'Yes. He's very attractive, if a little overconfident. I think he might wear coloured contact lenses, but I saw the way his eyes lingered on yours. And you already know each other.'

Nessa gifted her best friend with a roll of her eyes as she pushed her way along the third row to take her seat.

'I'm so excited,' she squeaked in Callie's ear. 'This is the first time I've been in a West End theatre. Do you remember that pantomime we staged in Year Ten? What was it? Oh, yes, *Peter Pan*, remember? You were a full-blown pirate and I was a lowly deckhand. We had a blast!'

'You had a blast, Nessa,' Callie corrected her. She'd hated every minute of being on the stage. 'I'm not blessed with the same bare-faced confidence you are. Never again! But I tell you who *was* excellent and a huge surprise. That girl who played Captain Hook from Year Nine? What was her name again?'

'Lillian Greenwood?'

'Yes, I'd never noticed her before. Always thought she was one of those geeks who kept herself to herself and preferred the more cerebral pursuits. Nose always stuck in a classic? She certainly never ventured onto the sports field, unlike you, Nessa – the girl who's won every trophy going'.

Nessa giggled. 'Remember when we made Mr Barringer walk the plank for a laugh at the end of the show?'

'I do, and I'd be prepared to bet my last pound that the experience will live on in his nightmares until the day he leaves the earth. That was a nasty ankle sprain.' And the girls doubled over in fits of laughter.

'I couldn't do what Theo and Archie do, though. Stand up there in front of all these people and sing their hearts out. I'm not sure which is the most terrifying – performing to an arena full of avid, all-forgiving fans or to a more discerning audience at a celebrity wedding where the groom is a world-famous musician. Both are gut-wrenchingly scary!'

'Totally agree. All *I* had to do was deliver my wedding gown creation along with a little piece of my soul, wrapped in tissue paper in a cardboard trunk, and then sit back and await the devastating rejection of my talents, not parade it live in front of a room full of music industry professionals.' Callie indulged in an involuntary squirm of sympathy.

'But your design wasn't rejected, was it?'

'No, but for a time I thought it had been. It's a painful experience that I have no wish to repeat any time soon.'

As the noise reached maximum decibel level, a beanpole-thin guy clutching a clipboard like a shield, decked out in the black uniform of all stage and screen crew, his microphone strapped to his cheek with a Band-Aid, stepped onto the stage and proceeded to ask for quiet.

Immediate silence ensued.

'Okay, ladies and gents, as you know this is The Razorclaws' rehearsal gig for the wedding of the decade between Finn Marchant and Lilac Verbois, which will take place up in Yorkshire in two weeks' time.' A huge roar of approval rolled out of the stalls and reverberated around the room. 'You are about to hear a selection of the band's bestselling songs and, I'm excited to announce, a ballad that is being debuted this evening, written by their lead singer, Theo Drake!

'Ladies and gentlemen, I give you... The Razorclaws!'

CHAPTER TWENTY-FOUR

A tsunami of screams roared into the auditorium coupled with whistling and foot-stomping. Callie exchanged a glance with Nessa and they joined the throng in leaping from their seats and applauding. A surprise swirl of nausea assaulted Callie's throat and chest. Her heart pounded and her stomach muscles clenched with a mixture of excitement and nerves, and something else she was reluctant to name. She attempted to stretch her lips into a smile but failed. The hairs on the back of her neck prickled as the crystal-clear notes of a bass guitar seared through the air.

But it was when Theo, her Theo, strode onto the stage, grabbed the microphone from the stand and stared out into the crowd that her knees crumbled from under her. As he launched into a rendition of their most recent number one, she sank down onto the burgundy velvet seat, drawing in huge gulps of oxygen to steady her emotions, annoyed with her reaction to seeing him up on the stage after three long years apart.

For God's sake, she had seen him perform with The Razorclaws hundreds of times when they were at school and university. Okay, she knew nothing of his new material and had had no idea what to expect that evening. But the years rolled back and he looked exactly the same as when she'd fallen in love with him, with his eyes that sparkled like silver buttons and his quirky personality, not to mention his spiky, honey-blond hair and honed, muscular body.

As she peered between the breaks in the crowd, she drank in his onstage presence. He exuded an almost ferocious magnetism. He'd chosen black Armani jeans and a matching shirt, open at the neck to reveal not only a glimpse of golden chest hair, but also a glint of silver that caught Callie's eye and whipped her breath away. There, poking from the folds of his shirt, was that stupid St Christopher chain she had bought him for his eighteenth birthday and which he had sworn to her he would never remove.

Callie leant towards her knees, her forearms clenched into her stomach.

'What's up, Callie?'

'Oh, erm…'

Nessa sat down next to her. 'I know, darling, I know. You still love him, don't you?'

'No, no, I…'

'Come on, stand up or you won't be able to see anything.' Nessa linked her arm through Callie's reluctant one and dragged her back to standing.

The next forty minutes flashed by like a dream. Callie was swept away on a tidal wave of memories stretching back fifteen years to the first time Theo had held her hand in the playground at their primary school. The music playing tonight was the accompanying score to every important event of her life; something she had found solace in when she'd cried herself to sleep on the days when the loss of her parents was the most acute, like on their wedding anniversary or at Christmas or on her birthday.

She'd made a half-hearted attempt not to follow Theo's most recent success, as reading about him in magazine or newspaper articles only brought the pain of losing him flooding back. But she was a masochistic fool and had downloaded a selection of his music to her iPod, listening to the lyrics endlessly to dissect their meaning until her brain was fried and the pain once again became ragged and raw.

She was jolted back to reality as she realised the auditorium had quietened.

'Thank you, everyone. Have you all had fun tonight?' Theo's familiar voice boomed over the sound system.

A roar of approval rippled over the crowd.

'Okay, this is our final song. It's a ballad I wrote several years ago, but every word is still valid today. I hope you like it.'

Theo nodded across to Archie who struck the first chord. He smiled at his childhood friend and then flicked his eyes along the length of the third row until he'd picked out Callie's face.

She tried to avert her eyes but the music demanded her attention with a mesmeric force. She stood motionless, captivated by the powerful rock ballad Theo was belting out right at her. Goosebumps spread the length of her body and the roots of her hair prickled against her scalp. As she listened to the poetic lyrics she wondered whether each word was really directed at her. She was tempted to discard the thought as egotistical nonsense. Since they'd split, Theo had no doubt had his pick of attractive and available girls, she knew that. Even though he frequented her dreams, it did not mean she still inhabited his.

As the final notes of the song died away, there was a brief pause before a burst of thunderous applause erupted into the auditorium and the crowd surged forward with whoops and whistles. The Razorclaws stalked from the stage and the audience continued to scream, clap and stamp their feet as they demanded an encore. It took a full five minutes for Clipboard Man to restore calm and ask everyone to leave the theatre in an orderly fashion.

Callie's emotions boiled over. She could no longer hold back the tears of joy for the magic Theo had created on stage. The lyrics he'd sung spoke of the intensity of love, the cauldron of emotions its many guises stirred and the agony of its loss. In that moment, she knew he had suffered just as much as she had during their separation and she could hold back her true feelings no longer.

If nothing else, she needed Theo's friendship in her life. Her heart escaped from its prison of misery and loneliness and her spirits lifted. She felt jubilant at The Razorclaws' success that evening and about the forthcoming honour of playing at Lilac and Finn's wedding reception. And she would be there to see them perform, she promised herself. It was time to make amends with Theo. This night would go down as one of the best of her life.

'I'm so happy for them, Nessa. They deserve all their success, especially Theo. I think it's time I made my peace with him, don't you?' Tears smarted at Callie's eyes as she sought her friend's reassurance.

'At last! Come on. Let's use those backstage passes!' Nessa screamed, dragging Callie against the flow of the departing throng to the corridor that led to the rear of the stage. The girls flashed their privilege passes at the surly security guard and rushed to the door of the band's dressing room. Someone had pinned a huge golden star to its glossy exterior on which the band members' names had been scrawled with green glitter pen – Theo, Archie, Rick, Danny and Serge.

'Ready?'

'Ready.' Callie nodded as her heart hammered out a rock anthem of its own.

The first thing she planned on doing was congratulating the whole band on a fantastic performance, but a close second would be delivering a heartfelt apology to Theo for her inexcusable absence from his life over the last three years. She also wanted to slide into the conversation a question about his inspiration for the ballad he'd performed for the first time that night.

She wiped her palms down her thighs, inhaled a steadying breath and plastered a smile on her lips. She was so nervous her thoughts began to spiral away from her so she mustered every last ounce of her courage and pushed open the door.

The dressing room was packed wall-to-wall with a congratulatory swarm. Men in designer suits and dark glasses, a bunch of wardrobe and make-up girls, and the guy they'd seen on stage holding the clipboard had all crammed into the room to offer their individual congratulations. There was also a coterie of giggling fans, who'd been lucky enough to win tickets to meet their idols after the show, pressing their lithe bodies around the band members.

She could see Rick and Serge lounging on a pair of leather swivel chairs, holding bottles of champagne to their lips as a crowd hustled them for an autograph. Archie had been backed into a corner by a group of girls handing over cellophane-wrapped roses and teddy bears clutching red hearts.

'Any sign of Theo?' whispered Nessa, twisting from left to right on her tiptoes as she tried to see over the heads of the crowd in front of her, unable to make any headway into the room.

'If it's Theo Drake you're after, girls, you'll have to take your place in the queue,' smirked one of the entourage, shoving his thumb over his shoulder. 'It's like this all the time, especially for Theo. Crazy, but, well, he *is* the lead singer. I suppose he has to get special treatment. And anyway, he loves it!'

Callie's joyful smile melted from her lips to be replaced by a grimace of horror. Through the tightly packed throng, she could just glimpse Theo lounging in his own swivel chair, his snakeskin boots propped up on the dressing table with a bottle of Moët in one hand and a red rose clasped between his teeth as he signed a fan's autograph book with a flourish. She watched as he drew in a mouthful of the bubbles, swallowed and ran the tip of his tongue over his lips in a familiar, yet for Callie shockingly intimate, gesture.

She endured a wave of nausea so strong she felt it breach the back of her throat. A concrete block took up residence in her chest and her heart rate quickened. She felt threatened. The mass of warm, undulating bodies packed so tightly together made her feel light-headed. Could she do this? Could she stand by and watch Theo become the object of such adulation night after night? Loitering in the background like a spare part, an object of pity, the discarded girlfriend hanging on to her boyfriend for dear life? Or worse, battling against the assumption that she was simply following in his wake in the hope that a little of his stardust would fall onto her shoulders?

Had she made the right choice in coming to the concert tonight? Clearly, she had been naive at the very least in her anticipation that Theo would be waiting for her – and her alone – in his dressing room. Heat filled her cheeks when she acknowledged that she had hoped, after their kiss in the ballroom at Harewood House, that tonight would be the first step on the journey to rekindling their relationship. How could she have been so foolish? Nothing had changed – nothing at all – so why did she think this time around things would be different? Theo was even more successful now than he had been three years ago, with thousands more fans demanding a slice of his attention. She still craved success for Callie-Louise and was even running an additional branch of the shop! They both had more demands on their time than they had ever had before. It was almost inevitable that if they pursued a long-distance relationship, just like before, it would end in betrayal as they sought solace in other avenues. She couldn't put herself through that pain again.

She turned to Nessa, parted her lips to say something, but no words arrived. She slipped back into the dimly lit corridor, annoyed by the intensity of the spasm of jealousy the tableau in the dressing room had aroused in her. Her head told her that leaving was the right decision, despite the vehement objections raised by her heart. In fact, if she thought about it, she had so little time for socialising right now that it wouldn't be fair to expect Theo to be happy with whatever crumbs she could spare him. She wasn't in a position to prioritise a relationship at the moment. What on earth had she been thinking? The past was simply repeating itself – and their inevitable separation would be her fault once again.

As tears gathered along her lashes she determined to make as swift an exit as possible. But it was not to be. She chanced a final backward glance over her shoulder and caught Theo's steel-grey eyes boring into hers. She saw him leap from his chair and plough his way through the crowd, almost knocking Archie to the ground in his determination to stall her escape and prevent a repeat of what had happened before.

'Callie, wait!'

Theo caught up with her at the exit door of the theatre. He hooked his arm through hers and spun her round to face him. He nodded to the burly security guy, who cracked open the door, checked their route was clear and guided them into the empty tour bus that was parked at the back of the venue. They fell into the front seats together, their presence obscured by blacked-out windows, as the security man stood guard at the door, nonchalantly smoking a cigarette.

'Callie, I'm so sorry, that was a bit manic. It's not always as bad as that. It's this wedding fever that's got everyone overexcited. Just let me finish signing autographs and posing for selfies and we can share one of those bottles of champagne.'

'Theo, I'm not sure…'

She decided not to add that she had thought he'd promised to take her to dinner so they could talk. She stood and took a step towards the exit but Theo grabbed her by the waist and dragged her back into his arms. He held her tight to prevent her from walking away. His eyes delved into hers and she was surprised to see his lower lashes sparkling with tears.

'Callie, you know that I've loved you since we were kids. I still love you. And there's never been anyone else – you are all I care about. This distance between us is agony. Please, please, give me another chance to prove how much you mean to me.'

'Theo…'

'I wrote that song for you, you know that, don't you? Every word, every syllable was crafted with the image of you firmly centre stage. I've reworked a few of the lyrics for Finn's wedding, but it's a homily of love from a man who prays every day that he can be reconciled with his one true love. Can we, Callie? Can we start again? I know you feel the same way I do.' Theo's eyes held a heartbreaking plea.

'Theo…'

She felt her tears slide down her cheeks. Theo reached up, cupped her face with his palms and brushed them away with his thumbs. 'I met my soulmate when I was thirteen years old and I've never stopped loving her since.' His eyes bore deep into the crevices of her soul and she could feel his breath on her lashes.

'How can we start again, Theo? Nothing has changed. We're both still concentrating all our efforts on our careers. The demands on our time are heavy. It's for the best, Theo – for both of us. I know how hard it is to walk away, but believe me it's the right thing to do.'

'It's not the right thing to do! I know you; this is not what you want – what you really want. I can see it in your heart, feel it in your veins. Why are you always running away from your true feelings and forcing your head to rule over all of your decisions? Let your heart have a chance for once!'

Callie let that scorchingly delivered home truth pass. 'We're just not in the right place for a relationship to work right now, Theo. Callie-Louise will be busier than ever after the wedding and The Razorclaws will be booked for gigs all over Europe. I can't bear to think of another girl winding her arms round the neck of my boyfriend whenever he's away touring. It breaks my heart, but...'

'Then come with me, Callie. Tour with the band. You know them almost as well as you know me and they love you. The fans will always be around. Whether I like it or not, they're part of the tapestry of life as a musician. But they don't mean anything. I've not had a date since we split, not a proper one, not one where all I wanted to do was kiss her until we were chucked out of the Fox and Hounds. You were the first person I ever kissed Callie, and no one else has ever come near to inducing the feelings I have for you.'

Theo's mouth was inches from hers. Their eyes locked as he lowered his head and brushed her lips with his for the briefest of moments.

'Theo, I can't...'

'Theo! There you are. Put her down and get your butt out here for an interview with the Channel 4 reporter. He's been waiting for half an hour already. Where have you been? Theo?'

'Okay, Martin, I'm on my way. Callie, I have to go. I'm sorry, I can't do dinner. I forgot that the band's flying back to Germany tonight. Can we meet up for a drink before the wedding?'

'Theo, I'm not sure it's a good idea...'

'Theo, darling, you're needed.' A blonde PR girl appeared at the door and hooked her arm proprietorially through his. 'Come on. Everyone's waiting.'

'I'll ring you.' Theo made the sign of a phone with his fist as he was led away and Callie was finally able to make good her escape.

As she searched for Nessa in the theatre foyer she realised Theo was right – it had always been, and would always be, thus in the music industry. But that knowledge didn't insulate her from the feelings of insecurity and mistrust it instilled in her. She knew she would never be able to get used to sharing Theo with a throng of screaming girls who would stop at nothing to get to their hero, nor did she want to. It hurt too much.

Anyway, that wasn't the life she had worked so hard to achieve for herself. She had carved out her own successful career that she adored. How could Theo be so incredibly selfish as to ask her to go on tour with him?

No, sadly their lives were on diverging trajectories that it was too late to alter. She would just have to redouble her resolve and harden her traitorous heart to the potent effect Theo Drake had on her. She had no intention of meeting him for a drink and a 'talk' before the wedding. She acknowledged her decision was the coward's route, but all her spare time and energy now had to be lavished on Callie-Louise and finalising the most spectacular gown possible for the wedding of the year. It was time to concentrate on her career dreams and spend some time at her boutique in Pimlico. Scarlet and Flora were doing an admirable job, but the shop was her responsibility.

She also had to work on forgetting Theo and moving on – and the only way she knew she could do that was by dating other people. She would start by asking Scarlet to set her up with the cousin she'd mentioned numerous times as an ideal date.

She spotted Nessa chatting animatedly to Harvey on the burgundy-carpeted steps. She smiled in response to her friend's raised eyebrows and resolved there and then that she would put her head down and focus on her enduring passion for all things couture, not Theo.

CHAPTER TWENTY-FIVE

Allthorpe village still possessed the power to lift Callie's spirits and for that she was grateful. Warmth flooded her cheeks when she recalled the look of scepticism on Scarlet's face when she'd made a feeble attempt at an excuse about checking stock levels at Gingerberry, jumped into her Mini Cooper and driven home to Yorkshire. She was desperate to put as much distance between herself and Theo as she could to garner the headspace – or more truthfully, the heart-space – she needed to process the aftermath of the Theo debacle.

Flora and Scarlet had rallied round, suggesting trips to the theatre, visits to the wine bar, even a day out at the Harry Potter Studios in an effort to divert her attention away from dwelling on Theo. She couldn't even begin to come to terms with her resolution to move on until the wedding was out of the way and Lilac was safely on her honeymoon. Then she would think about dating. She'd seen a photo of Scarlet's cousin on his Facebook page and, although he wasn't really her type, she had to start somewhere. Anyway, she knew no one was going to be a perfect match because they weren't Theo.

But he was in her past and she had to make sure he stayed there. However, it was proving a lot more difficult than she had expected. After the success of the concert, photographs of the band seemed to be appearing everywhere – even in the broadsheets. She struggled to focus on anything that did not relate to the battlefield her private life had become. So, the only alternative was to seek out a change of scenery and what better way than to go back to Allthorpe. This trip up to Yorkshire was exactly what she needed to put her life into perspective. Delia would regale her with her own brand of down-to-earth advice on the unpredictable ways of the world and Iris would no doubt add her two pennies' worth.

She parked her car next to the village green and leaned her chin on the steering wheel. There was Gingerberry Yarns, the pretty bunting Marcia had hand-stitched draped across the window and the display festooned with samples of knitwear in rich, bold colours. A knot tightened in her stomach. She loved this village, but she loved Gingerberry Yarns more. Not just the shop – although that was sporting its Sunday best now – but the people who made it what it was. The place was a mixture of the foundations her mother and Hannah had built and what she, Delia and Marcia and all the Cupcakes & Couture ladies had subsequently added to bring it roaring into the twenty-first century. She knew in that moment with absolute certainty that there was no way she could contemplate letting it go. It was a part of her, of her life, of her roots. Selling it to someone else or, heaven forbid, closing it down was unthinkable. She would just have to promote Delia to manager and shuttle between the two shops, working 24/7 to make it work. Maybe Flora could help out, too? Perhaps she would even jump at the chance if it meant she could spend some quality time with Craig who had already driven down to London twice to take Flora to the ballet, and enjoyed a flight on the London Eye and a trip to the Harry Potter Studios in return. The pair were clearly smitten with each other and relocating Flora to Allthorpe was the perfect solution.

As Callie lifted her head from the steering wheel, she caught a burst of light out of the corner of her eye. She squinted through the fly-splattered windscreen, searching for its source. She ran her eyes along the row of shops that included Wallington's bakery, Marc's little flower shop, Buds & Bows, and Gingerberry Yarns. She was about to put it down to a car wing mirror flashing in the evening sunshine until she saw a second flash from the doorway of Marietta's Hairdressing Salon, which had closed for the day. It was a camera bulb.

It took a few further seconds of concentration before she distinguished that the long lens of the camera was directed at the shop window of Gingerberry. Her first assumption was that a holidaymaker was entranced by the beauty of the rural village of Allthorpe and wanted to preserve his memory of a happy holiday away from the daily grind. However, it wasn't long before a second sceptical, but more accurate, thought arrived. The owner of the camera was dressed head-to-toe in black and wasn't just sheltering in the shop doorway – he was *lurking*.

What the…

Then it hit her. Oh, my God! No!

She restarted the engine, shoved the car in gear and cannoned to the high street. She leapt out of the car, her hair swinging around her cheeks, and strode towards the cameraman. Or should she say paparazzo? A flash of blinding light erupted in her face and she screwed her eyes tightly.

'Hey, what do think you're doing?!'

The man smirked, gathered his holdall and sprinted off down the street.

Mmm, perhaps approaching him all guns blazing hadn't been one of her smartest ideas. If she had taken the time to think it through, she realised, she would have played it differently. Now he had a photograph of her reacting angrily, which was tantamount to admitting she was the designer of Lilac's wedding gown. Why else would she have been so suspicious of a man with a camera in an idyllic country village in rural North Yorkshire?

Chastising herself for her stupidity, she returned to her car, dragged her overnight bag from the back seat and hoisted the handles over her shoulder. She really should have been more prepared. If, as she hoped, business at Callie-Louise and Gingerberry took off after the publicity of the wedding, then she would have to be thinking of a strategy to deal with such scenarios. She did hope to attract more celebrity interest and she couldn't have inquisitive photographers camping out on the doorstep of Gingerberry every day!

As she reached for the door handle a burble of conversation trickled from within and, with a jolt of guilt, she remembered that it was Tuesday night. She had left London in such a hurry that she'd overlooked telephoning Delia to tell her she was on her way. She had even forgotten that the Cupcakes & Couture session would be well underway by the time she arrived.

The familiar tinkle of the brass bell welcomed her and for the first time in days she felt the leaden weight on her chest shift and the corners of her lips curl upwards. She took a step forward and Gingerberry wrapped its comfort blanket around her shoulders and all her troubles seemed to melt away. She briefly closed her eyes and drew in a strengthening breath. She loved it here.

'Hi, everyone!'

'Callie! Hi!' came a chorus of welcome.

'Callie! What are you doing here? Why didn't you call?' Delia dashed towards her followed by Marcia and Callie had to fight an urge to crumble into tears, she was so relieved to be home.

'Oh, it was just a spur of the moment decision. I really wanted to attend the last Cupcakes & Couture session before the wedding. I've brought a few samples of organic silk from Callie-Louise that arrived last week and wanted to know what you all thought.' Delia's grey eyes narrowed and Callie knew she didn't believe her. 'I'll just drop my bag upstairs. I could really murder one of your cappuccinos, Marcia? Oh, and I see Tom has been here, too! I want you to dish all the gossip about his catering for the wedding of the decade at Harewood House. Be down in a minute.'

Callie trotted up the stairs, feeling Delia and Marcia's eyes scorching holes in her back, but the ripple of chatter resumed as the ladies got back to their chosen projects. She was delighted to see that the ranks of the Cupcakes & Couture sessions had swollen even further. She'd performed a swift headcount, which had told her there were seventeen women and five men, including Marc and his partner, who were in the throes of knitting their longed-for Fair Isle jumper on the scruffy chesterfield. She released a sigh of relief. Now she had made the decision she was definitely keeping Gingerberry, these sessions would not only pay for themselves but would add a decent profit.

She dropped her holdall onto the sofa and, as she turned to go back downstairs, her eyes landed on a pile of mail on the kitchen table awaiting her attention. She grabbed it and skipped back to the shop, anxious to catch up with everyone. She resolved not to mention the appearance of a lone photographer with a long lens trained on Gingerberry's window. She knew he would be gone by now. She only hoped that Lilac would not be too upset – after all, it wasn't as though she was carrying her wedding dress!

'So, how was The Razorclaws concert?' asked Marcia, her eyes scrutinising Callie's reaction as she handed her a mug of coffee and one of Tom's chocolate eclairs on a decorated china plate.

'Fabulous! Awesome! Nessa had a great time, too. She even met an old teacher friend, Harvey, at the gig. He was there with his niece and her friends and...' She knew she was gabbling. It was one of her well-known tactics for avoiding difficult conversations, but she wasn't fooling Marcia who nevertheless had the grace not to press her on it.

She shuffled the letters addressed to Gingerberry Yarns in her palms, deciding which of the invoices to open first. There was only one envelope that wasn't an ominous buff colour.

'Come and see the hospice blanket, Callie,' called one of Nessa's high-school students. 'It's almost finished. We're planning on presenting it to the residents at the Heppleton summer fayre next week. Will you be there with Nessa?'

'Of course, I will, Alicia! I wouldn't miss… Oh, my God!'

A flash of shock reverberated through her veins sending painful sparks out to her fingertips. Her knees gave way from under her and she slumped onto the chesterfield next to Marc, the letter she was holding fluttering to the floor.

'What is it, sweetie? What's happened? Are you okay? You're not going to faint on us, are you? Stick your head between your knees! Would someone bring Callie a glass of water?'

'I'm fine, I'm fine. Oh, thanks, Marcia, thanks.'

She took a gulp of the cool water, letting it trickle down her throat as she waited to regain her equilibrium. When her heart rate had finished its ferocious symphony she bent down to retrieve the letter and reread it slowly, carefully, savouring every word. It was only when she had read 'With Warmest Wishes' that she realised a cloak of silence had descended as the Cupcakes & Couture attendees waited for an explanation of her strange behaviour.

A wide smile split her face as she surveyed the gathering. Whilst she was overjoyed at the news she held in her hand, she knew it was not hers to keep. It was for everyone.

'In fact, Marc, I'm more than fine! I'm ecstatic, euphoric, over the moon!'

'So come on – spill the beans, my dear! Don't keep us all in suspense!'

Callie stood up from the sofa and turned to face the people who had come to be like her family.

'Delia, Marcia, could you join me?' Callie gestured to the huge mahogany table where Delia presided over the finalising of a beautiful pair of leopard-print silk cami knickers. She stuck her needle and thread into the pin cushion she wore around her wrist and, along with Marcia, came to stand next to Callie.

'Before I read out the contents of this letter' – Callie shook the thick sheet of luxury cream writing paper – 'I want to announce that Gingerberry Yarns will remain an integral part of the Allthorpe community for the foreseeable future. I know some of you were concerned about what would happen, especially after a number of shops have closed, but this will not happen at Gingerberry whilst I have any say in it.'

'Yay!' chorused Alicia and her friends.

Callie smiled. 'And from today, if she agrees, Delia will become Gingerberry's manager, ably assisted on a part-time basis by Marcia and potentially one of my colleagues from Callie-Louise, Flora, whom I suspect will be delighted to spend more time here due to her blossoming interest in a certain young photographer she met at Harewood House last time we were here.'

'That's fabulous news, Callie, but I can hardly bear the suspense. What's in that letter?' Marc clapped his hands and scooted to the edge of the sofa.

'Before I read it out, I also want to say a heartfelt thank you to each and every one of you for the support you have given to my aunt over the years and also to me when I needed it most. These Cupcakes & Couture sessions have not only revitalised Gingerberry, but have also given me a new perspective on life. But not only that! You already know that orders for Callie-Louise Bridal lingerie have been increasing over the last few weeks and I'm getting fantastic feedback. I hope you are all spending your share of the profits wisely!' There was a tinkle of laughter. 'And here is the icing on the cupcake, so to speak!'

Callie waggled the letter in the air and ostentatiously cleared her throat.

'Callie!'

'Okay, okay.

'*Dear Ms Henshaw,*

I am grateful for the opportunity you gave us to consider your new product line for inclusion in our Autumn/Winter Collection. Our buyer loved the hand-knitted sample sweater you provided and even more so the story behind its production. We pride ourselves on having a discerning clientele whom we believe would appreciate not only the beauty of the design but the local origins of the natural fibres and dyes used in the final product and the fact that each item is hand-crafted and therefore unique.

I wonder if initially we could discuss the supply of the Fair Isle sweater in a palette of colours to be agreed upon in consultation with yourselves and our designers. If our collaboration is successful we would be looking to move on to working with you on the design of other hand-crafted items, such as Aran sweaters, matching hats and scarves, and even Christmas-themed jumpers.

Congratulations, Ms Henshaw. Perhaps you could contact our Mr Gallagher to arrange for him to visit one your Cupcakes & Couture classes and maybe even take part.

With Warmest Wishes,

George Gallagher

Head of Collaborations'

Callie raised her eyes from the precious piece of parchment in her hands that secured the future of Gingerberry, maybe even of Callie-Louise, for years to come. But the reaction from her audience was muted, with none of the celebratory whoops she had expected. The sea of faces in front of her wore a blank, confused expression and her elation at making the announcement seeped from her veins.

'What?'

'Well, that's lovely, dear,' offered Iris, scooting her wheelchair forward to give Callie a hug.

'But…'

Marc swung his head from left to right, squeezed Jacob's hand and then stood up from the sofa. He drew Callie into his cologne-infused embrace before twisting the letter from her fingers and scanning its contents.

'Oh, my God! Oh, my God! Oh, my God! What Callie has neglected to tell you, peeps, is that this letter is from Liberty's – only *the* most wonderful department store in the whole of the UK! Wow! Congratulations, everyone! Jacob – get those knitting needles clicking. We are about to become internationally renowned crafters for Liberty's!'

And, at last, the room erupted into cries of delight, interspersed with a few tears of joy. After hugging everyone, twice, Callie managed to slip out of the shop and call Scarlet, the instigator of the whole project.

'Wow, Callie, that's fabulous news! I'm thrilled for Gingerberry. Maybe I should put my order in now for my emerald and cream one before your prices skyrocket!'

'It'll be my treat, Scarlet. If it hadn't been for you and your jumper…'

'This is your project, Callie. Yours and the Cupcakes & Couture gang's! Enjoy it! And I thought my news would be what got the champagne corks popping today!'

'What do you mean?'

'Just had a call, not five minutes ago, from Bianca Farietelli. She loved the hand-sewn silk teddies you sent over. Wants to talk to you about supplying our

Callie-Louise Bridal lingerie via her luxury boutique in Knightsbridge.'

'Oh, my God, I don't think my heart can take any more!' Callie's throat tightened around a lump the size of a golf ball.

'When are you coming back to Pimlico, Callie? It's just that… well, Jules has tickets for *Mamma Mia!* and he's asked if I'd like to go with him and I thought…'

Callie laughed. She knew something was developing between the two of them. She was relieved as it made her next few words much easier.

'Scarlet, how would you feel about becoming my partner? I've decided to keep Gingerberry and I'll be shuttling between London and Yorkshire for the foreseeable future. I need someone I can trust implicitly in the driving seat at Callie-Louise. What do you say?'

'What do I say? I erm… Oh, Callie, yes, yes, yes!'

'Before you make any commitment, I want you to know that I'm thinking of asking Flora to help me out with Gingerberry, so she'll be away from Callie-Louise a fair bit.'

Scarlet laughed. 'You know she'll jump at the chance to spend more time in Yorkshire with a certain handsome former war photographer! You are the most thoughtful, considerate friend I have ever had the pleasure of knowing, Callie. Thank you.'

'See you tomorrow. Let's get this dress of the decade finished!'

CHAPTER TWENTY-SIX

The excitement at Callie-Louise Bridal had reached fever pitch. Even Jules had joined in with the gossip, speculating on what type of headpiece *he* would have designed for Lilac if he'd been commissioned, adamant that he wasn't in the slightest bit jealous of Callie, Scarlet and Flora, not one smidgeon.

The constant frenzy of finalising Lilac's wedding gown, as well as her honeymoon lingerie, kept Callie's inner turmoil at bay. The gown was being collected that afternoon to be transported to the hotel in York and she was hanging on to lucidity by her fingertips. She was exhausted, physically and emotionally. As usual, she was constantly stalked by the spectre of insomnia and only able to drift off to sleep when slumped on the sofa in her apartment above Callie-Louise in the welcoming arms of her old friends Jack and Daniel, and even then she was never granted oblivion for more than five hours each night.

Her skin had taken on a flaky texture. Her lips were dry and cracked. Her diet consisted mainly of sporadic injections of caffeine and the occasional round of toast that Scarlet forced on her when it looked like she was going to faint. If she hadn't had the wedding to distract her, she knew she'd have been looking at her sanity in the rear-view mirror.

Delia and the Cupcakes & Couture gang had done her proud. Under Delia's astute direction they had not only completed every part of Lilac's lingerie order to perfection but had also almost finished the blanket they intended to donate to the Heppleton hospice in memory of Hannah. Callie had promised to drive straight from the wedding ceremony to Allthorpe so they could do this final task as a group over a few bottles of Prosecco and a feast of Tom's wedding cupcakes.

Tom had insisted they accept his generous gift after he'd received the good news that he was to be engaged to deliver a 'Cool Cupcake Cooks' after-school club at St Hilda's starting in September. Enthusiasm for his new venture exuded from his pores and his usually self-deprecating demeanour had gone into hiding.

And Tom wasn't the only one to have undergone a personality change over the last couple of months. If Callie had been surprised to see the transformation in Tom, it was nothing compared to her reaction to Martha's metamorphosis from the shy, blushing caterpillar she had first met to the vibrant, confident butterfly she had turned into. She had invested in a pair of tortoiseshell glasses and taken to wearing her hair piled on the crown of her head, teased into a mini beehive –courtesy of Marietta's ultra-trendy hand.

But it was the phone call she had received that morning from Marcia that had blown her away. She hadn't known whether to indulge in tears of pride or descend into a maelstrom of hilarity.

'The letter arrived this morning, Callie. I can't believe it's real and not a dream! I never thought anyone would be passionate enough about my writing to take me on. Me, Marcia Jane Brown, or should I say, Clementine Johnson?' Marcia had giggled and the sound had lightened Callie's heart. 'It's all thanks to you, Callie. You persuaded me to submit. You had confidence in my writing when I didn't.'

'Well, come on – read it out, then.' Callie had broken off from squinting at the ragged hem of one of the wedding garters Scarlet had rejected and leaned back against her work table as she waited to hear Marcia's most fabulous, but well-deserved news.

'*Dear Miss Brown,*

Re: "The Lustful Lancelot" by Clementine Johnson

Thank you for your recent submission of the full-length manuscript of the above novel. You have a unique voice and your writing style held my attention from the very first line. The plot line gripped me and the passion bursts from the pages as the story progresses. The characters are well rounded and sympathetically drawn and I am confident the novel, despite being your first in the erotic romance genre, will find commercial success.

I would therefore like to offer you a three-book deal with Entraped Erotica Press, the subsequent two perhaps as sequels to your first. Erotica is a new imprint for us, but one which is finding popularity with our readers, and your novels would enhance our current catalogue.

We suggest you ask your agent to contact us so we can further our negotiations and agree an acceptable advance.

Congratulations, Miss Brown. We look forward to a long and fruitful working relationship with Clementine Johnson.

Yours sincerely,

Jasper Smithson

Callie's heart had ballooned at the pleasure and exuberance that had filtered down the telephone line from Marcia that day.

'Callie? Callie? Call for you. It's Theo Drake. Again!' called Flora, waving the office phone at Callie from across the studio.

Scarlet flashed Flora a scorching look. 'Flora, didn't you hear Callie…'

'It's okay, Scarlet, it's not Flora's fault.' Callie sighed as she sat back on her heels and wriggled her aching shoulders. She tucked her grown-out bob behind her ears and turned to face the youngest member of their team. 'Flora, please just tell him that I'm busy with a client.'

'But,' Flora covered the mouthpiece with her palm, 'he begged me to put you on. He says he's calling from Germany. And, well, it's Theo Drake... of The Razorclaws!'

Callie couldn't prevent a wan smile from breaching her lips. When she'd explained to Flora, after avoiding three calls in one day, that she did not want to speak to Theo, Flora's expression had been a picture of confusion.

'But why not? He's gorgeous!' she blurted.

'Yes, he is, Flora. But he wants me to meet him for a drink and I don't have time.'

'But I don't understand. Why can't you speak to him and tell him that yourself?'

Callie had shot a glance at Scarlet who had come to her rescue. She'd gently led Flora away to explain in as few words as possible that Callie did not want to see Theo, nor did she want to speak to him. So, whenever he rang, she was to say, as convincingly as she could, that Callie was busy with a client and couldn't be disturbed. Sadly, Flora would never win any theatrical accolades for lead role in a mystery drama, as each time Theo rang the salon she had stuttered and stammered an increasingly bizarre list of excuses.

After listening to Flora stumble through another one of her epic deliveries and hang up the receiver, Scarlet turned to Callie.

'Why don't you just speak to him, Cal?' she urged. 'You don't have to see him, but the guy sure is keen to speak to you. I thought you said you wanted to be friends?'

'There's no point. I've explored every possible scenario until my brain cells disintegrate and my head is ready to explode. I can't put myself through the torture of seeing Theo enveloped in the arms of some stranger who's managed to wangle her way into his dressing room or hotel room. And how can I go touring with him? Not only do I have a business to run here, which I might add is going to get a hell of a lot busier after Saturday, but there's Gingerberry, too.'

'Delia has managed okay these last few months, and didn't you say that Marcia is helping out part-time, too?'

'Yes, they are both amazing, but I'm not sure the situation will work long-term. Marcia has a publishing contract now. And did I tell you she and Tom have been out on a date? I can't commute between Pimlico and Allthorpe and then disappear off on tour with the band whenever it suits! Delia is going to need more than just a part-time helper if the lingerie side of things takes off after the wedding.'

'Then employ someone to help her full-time. I could maybe do the occasional trip.'

'You are the best right-hand woman a fashion designer could wish for, Scarlet. You've been fantastic. You are also one of my most treasured friends,' Callie said, collecting Scarlet into a hug. 'I know you think I should give Theo a chance, but I also know that if I did agree to meet him, even just for a drink, all the memories would come flooding back and lessen my resolve. I can't allow that, I can't. I've worked too hard and suffered too much pain these last three years to risk a repeat. And whilst we're on the subject, I've made a decision. I want you to set me up on a date with that cousin of yours after the wedding is out of the way. I have to move on.'

Scarlet studied Callie. 'Well, okay, if you're sure.'

'I am.' Callie turned away from her friend's scrutiny, laced as it was with a soupçon of suspicion. She knew she didn't believe her, but she didn't care. 'Okay, no mistakes this time. The courier is due in twenty minutes and I'll sign the paperwork myself.'

It was Friday afternoon. As soon as the gown had been safely dispatched, she was heading over to King's Cross with Scarlet to catch the train up to York. They'd been booked into the same luxury country manor hotel as Lilac and her entourage. She intended to carry out any final tweaks that evening and then grab an early night. They would be needed at six the following morning to dress Lilac.

'You're still adamant you're not going to the reception at Harewood House?'

'Yep, but you have to go, Scarlet. It'll be some party! A hundred and fifty guests, most of them celebrities from the film and music industry. There's even a rumour that Colin Firth will be there with his wife. You can't miss it.'

'Neither can you.'

'I can't go, Scarlet. I don't want to chance bumping into Theo.'

'But you won't. He's performing. He'll be backstage. You can stay upstairs if you really want to. Or hide out in the pantry under the stairs.'

'I've made up my mind.'

'Oh, God, not the classic Callie-Louise chin thrust. That stubborn streak is something you need to work on, Cal. Why can't you just make friends with Theo. Okay, I get why you don't want to get back together with him romantically, but it might make things easier if you agreed to stay friends? Instead of carrying all this hurt and sadness around in your handbag – just offload it, be friends and move on.'

'Like he has?'

'Callie, we've been through this. And Theo's explained it himself. He's a rock singer, in a famous band. There are going to be times when girls throw themselves at him. If you weren't so in love with him, you'd be able to understand this.'

'I'm not in love with him.'

'Oh, please, Callie. Anyone can see that you are.'

Two hours later Callie found herself staring out of the grimy train window at the fields of wheat and yellow rapeseed, punctuated by the occasional squat farmhouse and barn. Just one more day to get through and then she could return to her normal life. She gritted her teeth and prayed that her personal guardian angel had returned to her customary position – after four months' unauthorised sabbatical – to make sure Lilac agreed to Scarlet assisting with her dress before she made her grand entrance down the sweeping staircase at her reception at Harewood House, so she could grab the next train back to the anonymity of London.

That night, as the coppery hue of the sky sank over the horizon like a flickering flame in the nub of a candle, and darkness pressed its velvety veil against the windows of the country manor house, Callie drifted gratefully into the arms of oblivion that sleep offered. As Theo's familiar features swam across a tableau of reminiscences and dreams, she knew for certain that, despite the passage of time, she would always love him and tears dripped down her nose and onto the cotton pillowcase.

But her final thoughts were reserved for sending up a soft prayer that her mum, and Aunt Hannah, would have been proud of what their daughter and niece had achieved.

CHAPTER TWENTY-SEVEN

It was a magnificent day for a wedding. The sky displayed a panorama of uninterrupted cerulean blue. A light breeze tickled along the rooftops carrying with it the scent of summer warmth and excitement. Shafts of multicoloured light spun through the spectacular Rose Window of York Minster, sending a dancing kaleidoscope of colour around the assembled congregation. It was as though the celestial angels had decided to join in the ceremony, too.

A whole battalion of street vendors had lined the city's ancient thoroughfares selling flags, china mugs and printed tea towels. Everyone and their uncle had taken the celebration of Lilac Verbois and Finn Marchant's union to their hearts.

Lilac had been overwhelmed with excitement whilst being dressed that morning by Callie and Scarlet. Her mother had dabbed at the corners of her eyes with a tiny lace handkerchief as she drew her famous daughter in her arms and hugged her tightly. As Callie and Scarlet put the final touches to her fairy-tale gown, Lilac took a sip from a flute of Dom Pérignon and giggled.

'Would you believe I'm nervous? York Minster is a much scarier arena than any film set or theatre stage I've been on. It's even worse than first-night nerves. The butterflies in my stomach are doing a happy dance, though. You know, I adore my dress, Callie. This day is the culmination of all my dreams. I love my career but I love Finn more, and this is going to be the best day of my life when I finally get to hear him say "I will" at the altar of my perfect wedding venue.'

If Lilac was nervous, it was nothing compared to what Tish was feeling. She had been buzzing around like a hyperactive wasp since five-thirty that morning. Her sting was pretty painful, too. But everything was on track, scrupulously organised thanks to the myriad lists she and Nikki had worked on together. She whizzed between suites of the country manor on the outskirts of York, a clipboard clutched to her chest as she directed operations like a debutante film director. So far, every aspect of the morning had been beautifully choreographed.

Callie excused herself from the bridal preparations and returned to the suite reserved for Callie-Louise with a circular box in the signature navy-blue-and-gold stripes of the Jules Gallieri Millinery Emporium, which she presented to Scarlet along with a hug.

'Scarlet, I think now is the right time to give you this.'

'What is it?'

'Open it and see!' Callie smiled.

Scarlet took the box and stared down at it.

'Oo, oo, yes, open it,' clapped Flora.

Scarlet pulled at the gold organza ribbon and twisted the lid off the hat box.

'Oh, my God! Wow!' She reached in both hands and gently lifted out the most exquisite fascinator. 'It's gorgeous, but why…'

'Nothing to do with me,' Callie smirked, exchanging a glance with Flora who had also been in on the secret. 'This has been sent to you with the most sincere wishes of our genius milliner, Jules Gallieri, and his express instructions that you wear it to the wedding.'

Callie had quashed her initial uncharitable thought that the gift might have been a ploy by Jules to get a sample of his work on the TV. When she had seen the look on his face as he handed the box over to her, a suspicion of dampness on his lower lashes, she knew the hat was more than just something beautiful for Scarlet to wear on Lilac's wedding day.

'Thank you. It's the most adorable thing I've ever seen. Help me put it on! Oh, thank you so much.' Scarlet grabbed each girl in turn before standing still to allow Callie to affix the headpiece.

'Don't thank me. This was all Jules's idea and hard work. I'm sure you'll have the chance to thank him personally.'

'Oh, I…' Scarlet's cheeks coloured.

Callie and Flora smiled. 'You look stunning. Be careful not to overshadow the bride!'

'Oh, you know there's no chance of that. Lilac's wedding gown is a true work of art. We are officially the royal trio of seed-pearl princesses!'

There was a knock on the door and Flora trotted across the suite to answer it.

'Oh, hi. Come in.'

Callie heard the surprise in Flora's voice. She twisted round from fixing Scarlet's fascinator, hair pins sticking out from her mouth, to see who had interrupted them.

'Hi, Craig.'

'Just wanted to say "break a leg", if that's the correct saying for a wedding such as this? And would you mind if I get a few shots of you all getting ready to leave?'

'Sure!' cried Callie, gathering up the skirt of the silk summer dress in a delicate aquamarine that she had designed and embroidered herself for the wedding. Jules had also gone to town on the hat he had designed for her. She almost felt like she was the bride! Indeed, if she were really honest, she would have preferred to get married in *her* outfit, rather than the intricate gown Lilac had wanted, stunning piece of artistry though it was.

Callie, Scarlet and Flora grouped together and screamed 'Cheese!' whilst Craig ducked and dived and clicked away until the girls crumbled into hysterical giggles. It was the ideal way to dispel the rising tension. Callie suspected this had probably been the precise purpose of Craig's mission – or maybe not, as she saw his eyes constantly seeking out Flora's and the couple exchanging covert signals like a pair of forbidden lovers.

'Fancy a drink later on when you get a break from all this?'

'Love to.' A grin split Flora's face and her cheeks coloured with pleasure.

'Got those photos I took of you at Harewood House. There are a couple I think you'll love,' he smirked. 'Particularly the one with the naked guy as a backdrop.'

'What naked guy?' spluttered Scarlet.

'Oh, I'll introduce you later, Scar,' Flora giggled, her expression radiant. 'You're going to love him, I promise!'

A snake of limousines, their windows tinted against the sun and prying camera lenses, coiled along the gravelled driveway waiting to transport the bride and her entourage the three miles to York Minster. Callie and Scarlet helped Lilac climb into the first car, along with her mother who was walking her down the aisle in the absence of her father whom, she had assured them, was with her in spirit on her wedding day. That was why the sun was bleaching down from a clear blue sky.

When the first limo had crunched off down the tree-lined avenue, the girls piled into the next one, urging the driver to make sure they arrived at the Minster first so they'd be on hand to straighten out the dress on Lilac's arrival.

The bride's journey down the aisle towards her handsome prince was a smooth glide of pure elegance and style. The floor-length veil could not disguise the glow of joy emanating from Lilac's slender silhouette as she exposed her adoration for her soon-to-be-husband to the watching world. Her wedding gown was exquisite, regal even, under the soaring arches of the church; the perfect length, with a short train in ivory silk, the skirt split by a dart from waist to toe into which swathes of Swarovski crystals and seed pearls had been sewn, shaped like cascading flowers, which, when studied carefully, were miniature blossoms of lilac.

The neckline was demure, respectful of the place of majesty that would bless their union. Hidden beneath the veil was the most magnificent tiara Callie had laid eyes on, and she'd seen her share of celebrity weddings. No diamanté or paste in sight – these were real diamonds, edged in pale lilac amethysts, on loan from Tiffany's. The tiara had its own security detail in addition to the strategically placed personal protection officers for Finn and Lilac.

As the last crystal-clear note of the angelic ballad drifted up to the vaulted ceiling high above the awestruck congregation, Callie stood on her tiptoes to watch Lilac and Finn Marchant beam for the wedding photographer and videographer whilst they signed the register. All of a sudden her mind was invaded by a sense of gratitude that, together, her little team had pulled off the most glorious feat in the fashion world that week, if not that month. Lilac looked every inch the film star she was. There were no creases or wardrobe panics that could have spoiled the day.

Callie smiled as she covertly surveilled the packed congregation, keen to commit every detail to her memory for future extraction over the promised bottle of chilled Prosecco with Nessa and Delia later that day. Everyone exuded an aura of joy and delight at the ceremony they had been honoured to witness in the most grandiose splendour, but mostly of happiness at the sheer bliss that blazed from the happy couple. It was clear to all how much they loved each other and Callie sent up a prayer to the director of their fates that the marriage would be blessed with longevity and good fortune. She added a postscript to her prayer to include her parents and her Aunt Hannah and swallowed down hard on her emotions. It wouldn't do to cry so early on in the proceedings.

As she lowered her eyes from the soaring arches of the ceiling, her heart jolted sharply upwards into her mouth. There, standing a head taller than most of the wedding party, was Theo, looking spectacular in his immaculate grey morning suit and lilac cravat. The shock of seeing him spliced down through her chest, sending shock waves out to her fingertips.

Why hadn't she realised he'd be here? He and Finn had been at uni together and, eight years later, they were still such firm friends that Finn had chosen him as an usher for his wedding. It made perfect sense, but it had still come as a complete shock.

She offered him a smile and he nodded an acknowledgement, his lips twitching to produce those familiar dimples she loved. Wow, he was gorgeous. She held his eyes and a moment of crystal-clear clarity struck. Having just watched Lilac and Finn declare their love to each other, and exchange their emotional vows in the presence of their closest family and friends, she realised she could never imagine standing at the altar of any church, large or small, with anyone else but Theo by her side.

Who was she kidding? She loved the guy, adored him. There had never been anyone else for her. She'd handed her heart to him a long time ago and he'd never given it back. And yet she was grateful for the three years they had spent apart. She had been able to use the time to apply herself single-mindedly to pursuing her dreams, to securing Callie-Louise Bridal's future, to learning who she was and understanding her place in the world. She had neglected her relationship with Theo, underestimated the importance of spending quality time together in order to fan the flames of their partnership – was it any wonder he'd succumbed to the comfort of an embrace from a willing fan after a few bottles of champagne?

She looked away, her thoughts cascading through their joint history. She knew everything about Theo and he knew everything about her. Every childhood memory was in some way tied up with him – and his band The Razorclaws. Theo, Archie, Serge, Rick and Danny – she loved them all – but mostly she loved Theo and she had to tell him.

The church organist chose that moment to launch into an exuberant rendition of the wedding recessional. Callie tipped her head back to prevent her tears from falling, but also to say thank you directly to those who were absent from her life through no fault of her own.

She had to allow her heart to take centre stage for once. It was time to stop running from her feelings and embrace them instead.

CHAPTER TWENTY-EIGHT

'Oh, my God, my feet are killing me,' announced Scarlet, removing her Jimmy Choos and massaging her toes as they strolled round the manicured gardens of Harewood House to grab a breath of fresh air.

The reception was over and, as expected, the speeches had entertained the wedding party for over an hour, with howls of laughter and ahh's of delight as the happy couple's family and friends celebrated their union with crystal flutes of champagne and chorused their congratulations every five minutes.

Tom and a specially selected team of his friends from Betty's had worked miracles with the food, slaving in the kitchens for the last week to produce an exquisite gastronomic feast with a Yorkshire twist that would have impressed the judges of *Masterchef*. Of course there had been Yorkshire puddings to accompany the heart-shaped Chateaubriand, but the guests were a little bemused by the tower of tiny cubes of parkin surrounded by a raspberry jus. However, as predicted by Lilac, the cupcake pyramids were sparkling masterpieces of culinary artistry that put the expensive five-tier wedding cake to the back of the class. It wasn't just the children who were licking the icing and edible glitter from their lips and finger tips.

Callie plonked her aching bones onto a stone bench and allowed her shoulders to sag. 'Did I tell you Tom and Marcia are officially an item?'

'You didn't have to – it's obvious.'

Callie smiled as she recalled her brief visit to the kitchen to offer Tom her congratulations on pulling off the best wedding breakfast she'd ever had. Marcia had, of course, been there organising and directing operations with the assistance of her arch-lever file crammed with laminated recipe cards and lists of instructions and timings.

'Tom's arranged afternoon tea at Betty's as a treat for helping out!' Marcia had said, flushed with pleasure. 'He's promised the best table in the house for me, Mum and Delia. Oooo, I've always wanted to do a proper "afternoon tea". I'm so pleased for him, Callie, and it's all thanks to you. When he got that call from Tish, well, I think he's still coming to terms with the shock, but he's ecstatic – look at him, he's in his element with all his friends around him again. He's thinking of asking one of them to help him out at the bakery so he can go back to Betty's part-time in a development role. He has so many ideas for new products – the creativity is bursting from him! I know he'll be a small cog in a huge wheel there, but it's what he's dreamed of for years! Even his dad approves, he's so proud of him being in charge of the catering for a celebrity wedding. He and all the residents of Heppleton Care Home promised to be glued to the TV today. Tom delivered one of his cupcake pyramids at five this morning.'

'He deserves this opportunity, Marcia,' Callie said. 'He's a talented chef.'

'I've volunteered to lend a hand in the bakery, too. Not on the baking side, of course, but serving behind the counter so Tom can concentrate his afternoons on the experiments and designs. I've photographed every finalised cupcake gem on that pyramid with my iPhone. I intend to print it and file it with the recipe in a binder – that way his assistant can easily replicate the technique.'

Callie smiled – Marcia's dedication to organisation knew no bounds.

'My favourites are the mango and mint julep pyramids and the lavender-infused macaroons topped with a tiny lilac flower made from angelica.' She paused, shot a glance to the other end of the kitchen where Tom was laughing with one of his chef friends looking relaxed and content, and lowered her voice. 'Tom asked me to be with him when the fireworks start. He says he has something important to ask me.'

Happiness infused Callie's heart at the burgeoning spirit and confidence exhibited by Marcia as well as her developing relationship with Tom, who, as far as Callie knew, was her first boyfriend. The first kindling of a new love was a joy to see. She was so pleased for them both.

Callie smiled at Scarlet who was still rubbing her toes, the spectacular fascinator Jules had made for her bobbling precariously on her head. She was relieved that her job here was now done. She had tried to convince Lilac that her assistance was not needed at the reception, but Lilac had insisted she wanted her gown to look fabulous in the photographs Craig was anxious to take in the opulently furnished rooms of the stately home. However, in return, Lilac had agreed that, if she didn't want to stay for the evening reception, she had her blessing to leave after the speeches. Scarlet had looked scandalised at such a suggestion.

'Come on, we'd better get back.' Scarlet linked her arm firmly through Callie's. 'You'll thank me later, but I'm not letting you leave. I can't allow you to miss hearing Theo's performance of the song written for Lilac and Finn's wedding. It's going to be something to tell your grandchildren about when you're in your bath chair!'

Callie knew her objections would be wasted so she plastered a smile on her face and went willingly with

Scarlet to the ballroom. The Razorclaws played to an ecstatic audience already sated by good food and vintage champagne. The roof was nearly raised from its rafters when Finn stepped onto the makeshift stage and joined Theo at the microphone to perform the ballad as a duet. Whilst Finn sang every heartfelt lyric to his new bride, Theo was looking in a different direction as he sang every word straight from his heart.

Immediately after the brief musical interlude, as the temperature rose to sweltering, the whole of the wedding party retired outside to await Lilac and Finn's appearance on the carved stone balcony overlooking the formal gardens of Harewood House. They greeted the crowd of family and friends with waves and shared kisses as a storm of flashbulbs erupted from a coterie of amateur photographers jostling for the gift of *the* photograph that might possibly grace the front pages and glossy magazine covers for months to come.

Lilac had discarded her veil and tiara. Her hair, the colour of liquid caramel, tumbled in loose waves to her shoulders and her eyes sparkled as she giggled with her new husband in front of the cheering crowd. To complete her outfit, she had draped an ice-white, knitted angora bolero jacket around her shoulders, and under the rose-tinted floodlights the tiny crystals sewn into the yarn shimmered and glistened.

'That's your bolero, isn't it?' Scarlet squealed to Callie. 'The one you designed last year and knitted with the Cupcakes & Couture ladies? It looks stunning!' And she flung her arms around Callie for what seemed like the hundredth time that day.

Callie smiled. So, Lilac had chosen to wear it – was that the reason she'd wanted her to stay on after the reception? Scarlet was right. The little jacket did look stunning. It twinkled with sparkles and, against the majestic backdrop of the stately home, it seemed almost to take on the quality of ermine, appropriate attire for the theatrical royalty Lilac so clearly was.

'As soon as the fashion press ferret out the origins of that shrug, Gingerberry will be inundated with orders, you know that, don't you? Liberty's will be expanding their wish list, too,' Scarlet warned.

Callie nodded. As Lilac and Finn disappeared to get ready to leave for their honeymoon in the Maldives, she stared into her future. She was saddened that she would not be resuming the easy camaraderie she had shared these last hectic weeks with Scarlet, Flora and Lizzie when they had paused only to snatch a couple of hours' sleep on the sofa in the office and regular infusions of caffeine.

But Scarlet would still be there, and Flora would be at Gingerberry with Delia, so things wouldn't be too different. She didn't need to base herself at Callie-Louise in London or at Gingerberry when she had such trusted friends to hold the fort. She could design fabulous bridal couture and lingerie anywhere. When she had informed

Scarlet that she was handing over the reins of the Pimlico branch to her, that she intended to split her time between Yorkshire and London, there had been a deluge of tears, but it was the right decision. The Cupcakes & Couture ladies would be an integral part of Gingerberry's secure and stylish future. They would offer hip and up-to-the-minute knitted designs and fabulous luxury lingerie items with weekly crafting sessions thrown in for good measure. Delia, her new partner and co-owner, along with a loved-up Flora, would be available to guide the 'cosiest little haberdashery shop in Yorkshire' to greatness on a daily basis. She would be present for consultation purposes whenever they needed her input.

Allthorpe was her home; it was where she had her roots and where she was surrounded by people who loved her and whom she loved in return.

Except one.

'Hey! Callie, Scarlet, hi. I'm glad you decided to stay!' called Archie, striding down the steps towards them. 'You both look stunning, by the way. Love the… erm, the hat or whatever you call it, Scarlet. Come on, I'm gagging for a cold beer. I think a summer storm must be on its way – it's so muggy. Let's hotfoot it down to the marquee before the hordes descend.' And he linked his arms through the girls' to drag them off towards the overblown tent crouched on the lawn like a squashed meringue.

'It really is a beautiful setting for a wedding celebration, isn't it? I can understand now why Lilac and Finn were adamant in their choice of venue for their Yorkshire wedding. It's God's own country, as they say,' said Callie.

'Yes, that and the fact that Lilac grew up here,' said Archie.

'Nikki, Lilac's PA, said that, too. I'm surprised none of us knew her – she's only a couple years younger than me and Nessa.'

'But Callie, you did know her!'

'What? No, I didn't. I think I'd have remembered if I'd met Lilac Verbois before, Arch.' She smiled as she gratefully accepted an ice-filled Pimm's from an exhausted waiter and took a sip.

'Well, not as Lilac Verbois – that's her professional name. I was chatting to her mother before we performed our serenade to the couple of the day. Lilac was a pupil at St Hilda's, just like you and Nessa…'

'No, Archie, she couldn't have been.'

Archie's eyes crinkled at the corners with the pleasure of being able to deliver this juicy piece of information. 'Remember Lillian Greenwood? The scrawny kid who loved drama – played lead roles in the school pantomime?'

'Ye…e…s.' Callie stared at him, her jaw gaping as it slowly dawned on her why this whole wedding palaver had been so focused on their little corner of heaven in North Yorkshire. Despite her fame and fortune, it was Lilac's heaven, too.

It was home!

CHAPTER TWENTY-NINE

Archie wandered off to find his fellow band mates and Callie and Scarlet perched their buttocks on a worn stone bench overlooking the formal Italianate gardens at the front of Harewood House with the rolling hills of Yorkshire as a Turneresque backdrop. The sky was no longer a clear cerulean blue but had turned into a bruised grey, and a summer downpour threatened at any moment.

'It's been a beautiful day, hasn't it?' murmured Callie, her eyes fixed on the lake to her right.

'It has. Are you still planning to leave, Callie? You really should stay for the fireworks, you know. Lilac and Finn both made it clear you were a special guest.' Scarlet paused, clearly wrestling with the content of her next sentence. She lowered her voice to a whisper. 'I saw Theo sing those lyrics to you. It was the most romantic gesture I've ever seen. Why don't you talk to him, Callie? It's the perfect time to clear the air between you. If you don't do it now, here, when will you get the chance again?'

Callie looked at her friend. It was exactly the same thing Nessa had said to her when she'd called to wish her luck the previous evening. They were right. Everything that had happened over the last three years had taught her that Theo was the only person who made her feel whole. No wonder her dates in the capital had never worked out. How could they when she was in love with someone else?

'You're right.'

'I am?'

'Yes.' Callie stood up and massaged her numb bottom. The bench was cold and hard. 'Come on. Help me find him.'

Scarlet's eyes widened and a smile lit up her features. 'With absolute pleasure.' She hugged Callie to her as a splodge of rain landed on the tip of her nose. She screwed up her face and wiped it away

'Quick!' And they dashed up the steps to the ballroom where the white, linen-covered tables were being cleared away to make room for a dance floor for the evening entertainment.

'Hey, Archie. Where's Theo?'

Archie paused in his task setting up one of the huge amplifiers with Serge and Rick. 'He wanted to get some air before the gig tonight. Said he was going down to the lake.'

'Thanks, Arch.'

The girls sprinted back down the sweeping staircase and made for the front terrace. In the short time they had been inside the house, the rain had escalated into a full-on summer downpour. Needles of rain bounced from the balustrades and the flagstones but the temperature seemed to have climbed even further.

'We'll have to wait until he gets back,' said Scarlet, casting a grimace up to the leaden sky.

'No way. I'm doing this now before I change my mind and chicken out again.'

Callie skipped away from Scarlet, down the steps to the formal gardens and along a meandering path through the woodland. Within minutes she was soaked to her skin but she didn't care. She was on a mission. If she didn't talk to Theo now, she knew the moment they had shared in York Minster would be forgotten and consigned to their past along with everything else. This time she was adamant she wasn't going to allow that to happen.

The lake undulated gently as the raindrops battered its surface. She wiped her dripping fringe from her eyes and squinted towards the tiny wooden boathouse on the shore. A short jetty had been built out into the water and a tethered wooden rowing boat bobbed manically at the end.

And there was Theo, sitting on the jetty with his legs dangling over the side. His back was hunched against the downpour, his head buried deep into the hood of his coat, his hands thrust in the pockets of his jeans and elbows stuck out at right angles. She would have recognised his silhouette in a football stadium.

She removed her shoes and picked her way slowly along the jetty.

'Theo?'

He turned his head and their eyes met, but he looked away, staring at the patterns of concentric circles the rain was making on the lake.

'What are you doing here, Cal?'

'I saw you in church, I… It was a beautiful wedding, don't you think?'

'If you like that sort of thing. You know me, Cal. Never been one for expressions of overblown extravagance. A simple service at the local parish church would do me fine. Don't need all that pomp and ceremony to tell the world you love someone.'

'You're right.'

In fact, for the first time, Callie realised she had never once imagined her wedding day without Theo by her side. Silence expanded around them. Callie glanced over her shoulder. They were alone. Just her and Theo. Together again, sitting beside each other like they'd always been, like they should still be – she realised that now with absolute clarity.

'Why didn't you tell me you came down to London?'

'Saw you'd moved on. Made a success of your fashion business, like I knew you would. I was going to ask you to have a drink but I saw you leave the shop with a guy – a rugby-player type who had his arm slung around your shoulder. I hadn't expected that to hurt so much. I understood what it must have been like for you.'

'That was Andrew, the guy desperate to settle down and produce offspring – the Broody Paediatrician, Scarlet called him.' Callie smiled but Theo didn't.

The rain had lessened but rivulets trickled down her cheeks and dripped from her nose. She knew she must look a mess but she didn't care. She needed to tell Theo how she felt and this was the time she had to do it. If she had to be soaked through to the skin, then so be it. She moved her hand over to his. 'Theo, there's only ever been one person I wanted to settle down with ever since I could dress my Barbie in a home-made wedding gown.'

'What is it with you, Cal? One minute I'm a cheating ogre, the next I'm your soulmate?'

'You've always been my soulmate, Theo, even when we were fighting.'

At last, Theo turned his head to look at her. He shook his head slightly and pushed himself to standing, still maintaining eye contact. 'What do you want, Callie? Do you even know? I can't spend my life second-guessing you.'

'I know what I want. What I've always wanted. What's always been there, buried beneath the hurt and the jealousy of seeing you with your fans, waiting to emerge when the time was right. The time is right. And if you'll have me, I intend to become The Razorclaws' number-one groupie. Whenever you're on tour, I'll be right by your side. I love you, Theo. You are the first boy I kissed and I want you to be the next, and the one after that and the one after that.'

Callie leapt up and faced Theo. She took a step forward, placed her hand on his cheek and moved her lips towards his. Theo curled his arm around her shoulders and dragged her body into his. A perfect fit. Their lips met and Callie gave herself up to a crescendo of emotions: the ecstasy of being in his arms, of being kissed by the one person she was meant to be with. It felt as though she had been waiting her whole life for their paths to converge on that one moment, that one point in time when their destinies aligned.

'Hey!' she shrieked, as Theo broke away from their embrace and lifted her in the air, swinging her round and round and round until she begged him to stop. As he set her down on the jetty, she giggled, the happiest she had been for, oh, three years. She felt grateful, blessed by her guardian angel that at last fate had seen fit to bind them. 'Careful. We might end up in the lake!'

'Can't get any wetter!'

'I think my dress is ruined.'

'You look stunning to me.'

'So do you.'

'I reckon we should get back to the house, don't you? We have a party to attend!' Theo lowered his lips to her ear and whispered, 'I love you, Callie-Louise Henshaw.'

'And I love you, too, Theodore Dalton Drake.'

EPILOGUE

Ten months later

'Nervous, darling?'

'No way. I'm excited.'

'Seb's downstairs. He looks so handsome in his grey morning suit. Nessa's just helping him with his cravat and she'll be right up. I think there might be a spark of something there.' Delia's eyes twinkled.

'You might be right. He did frequent her teenage dreams on more than one occasion.' Callie giggled.

'I think we should start getting you into your dress, Callie,' said Scarlet, who looked stunning in her peppermint-and-gold bridesmaid's dress. There had been no hesitation by Callie on the choice of colour scheme for her wedding, but the shade really did work well with Scarlet and Nessa's almost identical colouring. 'Ah, Nessa, there you are. Come on – don't forget we're walking to the church.'

'It's less than a hundred yards!' said Nessa, bustling into the room in matching peppermint and gold. It was the first time she had worn a dress since toddlerhood and it really suited her. 'You can see St Peter's Church from the window! Doesn't it look amazing? The ivory roses around the lychgate are just perfect. Tish was right – it really is the prettiest little church in the whole of Yorkshire.'

'Okay, off with your robe!' ordered Scarlet.

'Before you do,' said Delia, stepping forward and holding out a package wrapped in tissue paper, her hand trembling slightly, her eyes glistening with emotion, 'I want to give you this – from all the Cupcakes & Couture ladies.'

The three young women settled down on the bed in the bride's temporary boudoir above Gingerberry Yarns. Delia looked on, as proud and tearful as any mother of the bride. Callie placed the gift on her lap and looked at her three best friends in the world.

'Thank you so much,' she whispered. 'For everything.'

'Open it!' cried Scarlet, clapping her hands together with excitement.

Callie slid her finger under the flap and drew out a slither of ivory silk and lace. The garter had been embroidered with peppermint thread and decorated with golden bows, but as Callie looked more closely she saw the words that had been worked into the fabric – *Congratulations on your wedding day – your Cupcakes & Couture ladies*. The letters 'CLH' and 'TDD' had been intertwined in exactly the same logo as the carving Theo had made on the old oak tree in the back garden of Gingerberry Yarns all those years ago.

She held the lingerie in her hands, fingering the stitching, and the strength of her emotions caused their tethers to fray. She stood up and flung her arms around Delia, tears trickling down her cheeks.

'Thank you, it means such a lot…'

'I know, darling, I know.'

Callie pressed a smile through her tears and turned to envelop Scarlet and Nessa in a hug.

'I'm so lucky to have you as my friends. Thank you for everything.'

'Okay. So now we definitely need to get you into that dress,' said Nessa, wiping a stray tear from her own eye.

Scarlet and Nessa held the gown, a sheath of ivory silk, and Callie stepped in, enjoying the feeling of exhilaration as the fabric slithered over her curves. Being six foot tall in her stockinged feet, the dress was the perfect design for her, as well as adhering to her personal taste for simple, yet exquisite, silhouette and drape. She had enjoyed every second she'd spent designing and sewing the gown with the help of Scarlet and Flora.

'Keep still and breathe in.'

'I am,' giggled Callie.

'It's a beautiful dress, Cal, but why in the name of all things bridal did you have to design your wedding dress with so many buttons down the back?'

'If there's anyone who should know the answer to that question, Ness, it's you. Look!' Callie pointed across to something nestled in the folds of her crumpled duvet.

'Oh, my God! You kept it!'

Nessa abandoned the fiddly job of helping Callie into her dress to Scarlet and dived onto Callie's wedding scrap box that lay open on the bed. She riffled through the paraphernalia of magazine snippets, pressed flowers, a scattering of pearls and beads, and pulled out the glossy photograph of the dress Callie had adored from the very first moment she set her eyes on it all those years ago when she had a teenage crush on Theo. 'Wow, every detail is exactly the same. Oh, Callie, I'm so happy for you.'

Nessa reached out to replace the lid and this time tears flowed freely down her cheeks. She ran her fingers over the picture that had been glued on the top of Callie's wedding scrap box for ever.

'Theo was the first person you fell in love with, wasn't he, Callie?'

'And the first boy I kissed.'

'And, unlike me, you've never once changed this photo, have you?'

Callie walked over to Nessa and cast her eyes over the blurry photo of a seventeen-year-old Theo.

'No, I haven't,' she murmured. 'He's always been my soulmate.'

'And you're his, Callie.'

It was true, Theo was her soulmate. He was the first boy she had kissed and, with a slice of luck, he would be the last.

If you loved *If the Dress Fits* then turn the page for an exclusive extract from *The Runaway Bridesmaid*, another sparklingly brilliant romance from Daisy James!

CHAPTER ONE

'What in the name of Christian Dior possessed your sister to choose this vomit-inducing shade for her bridesmaids' dresses?' huffed Lauren, flicking the sides of her sleek auburn bob behind her ears. 'There's not a person on this Earth who can pull off cotton-candy pink successfully!'

'Don't worry,' giggled Rosie as she watched her friend's perfectly outlined cupid's bow upend in a grimace of disgust at Freya's audacity in insisting they wore such a confection of fluff on her wedding day. 'Haven't you heard that pink taffeta is the new black?'

Lauren slipped the dress over her slender body where it ballooned her delicate proportions to twice their size so that she resembled an over-blown meringue. The insipid colour immediately drained her naturally pale complexion, bestowing her with a gaunt, grey appearance. 'Only a lavish application of the extensive range of products from the Clarins beauty counter can even begin to rectify this tragedy of taste! Bring on the fake tan!'

Rosie had to agree with her best friend. From a kaleidoscope of choices in the spectrum of pink – fuchsia, cerise, Barbie – Freya had chosen a saccharine-sweet shade of bubble-gum pink so Rosie and Lauren resembled a pair of nervous flamingos as they loitered on the Juliet balcony of the hotel bedroom suite waiting for the bride to grace them with her presence. Their eyes met and they spluttered into fits of laughter – a welcome sensation that released the helix of tension which had been festering in Rosie's chest all morning. She was grateful for Lauren's support, and their joint humiliation, but – to her distress – her eyes brimmed.

'It's Freya's day, Lauren. Whilst I have otherwise been solely responsible for the organisation of the Bennett-Hamilton wedding circus, all sartorial choices have been made by her, as I hope to repeat regularly throughout the day to anyone who will listen! On the issue of bridesmaid gowns she would brook no suggestions, no guidance, no pleas for elegance over outrage from me. But I have to admit, it *is* one of the ugliest dresses I have ever been ordered to wear, and as you know, I am something of an expert.'

'You are! What number are you up to now?'

'Seven; lucky for some.'

'Maybe next time you'll get to be the bride. And handsome, charismatic Mr Giles Phillips the groom!'

'What planet do you live on, Lauren? Marriage is the last thing on Giles' mind. Or mine for that matter. Don't get me wrong, I'd love to have a serious relationship one day, especially with a guy like Giles, but whilst I'm loving dating him I'm not sure it's anything more than two people enjoying each other's company. We do have a lot in common. Anyway, in the metropolis of Manhattan, all the sane guys are either married to a spouse or their career, or are gay - you have to grab the exception when you can! Now come on, let's get ready to present the lucky residents of Stonington Beach with the most spectacular wedding they have ever had the privilege to attend.'

Lauren gifted Rosie a roll of her emerald eyes. 'What, in this dress? More like an impromptu performance of an eighties musical revival!'

Lauren was right, Rosie thought, they did look ridiculous clad in a froth of pink flounces, more Folies Bergère show girls than twenty-first-century bridesmaids at an elegant Connecticut wedding. They both appeared incongruous next to the elegant A-line splendour of the bride's Augusta Jones-designed wedding gown, with ivory lace, an off-the-shoulder bodice and pleated organza skirt. But, of course, that was the whole point.

Upstaging by the bride was vital.

Nothing was ever enough for her little sister – always scrounging for more no matter whose toes and dreams she squashed to achieve her self-focused goals. With no friends of her own in New York, she had supplanted herself into Rosie's circle of friends, who – unbeknown to Rosie – tolerated her only because she was Rosie's sister. Of course, Freya had struggled to find willing applicants to fill the position of bridesmaid for her forthcoming wedding and had demanded that Rosie 'persuade' Lauren to accede to the honour. With her sharply-drawn, freckled features and graduated auburn bob, Rosie's best friend and colleague could grace any professional photographer's lens and met with Freya's aesthetical demands for her wedding photography.

Lauren had been adamant that, unlike Rosie, she was no doormat and would not deign to bow to Freya's demands. Why on earth would she want to be her bridesmaid, she had argued. She wasn't Rosie – willing to perform the supporting nuptial role at least once every six months for a procession of former school friends and colleagues. Lauren's own spectacular wedding to her college boyfriend, Brett, in the Terrace Room at the Plaza had been the most recent of Rosie's 'best supporting bridesmaid' opportunities a mere four months ago.

However, Lauren had relented when Rosie had pleaded with her to do this for her, if not for her sister, sadness at Freya's predicament clouding her amber-flecked eyes. But Lauren would not allow her friend to forget her sacrifice. She continued with her monologue on Rosie's doormat tendencies and her sister's self-centred, ever-escalating demands.

'Okay, okay, so your mom died when Freya was only eight years old. But she was your mother too, Rosie. How about Freya supporting you for a change, just once thinking of someone else other than herself? Did she rush to your aid last year when Carlos ditched you? Does she even realise that her monopoly on your time may have played an integral part in that? No, instead, she just continued to chase around Europe, floating from one handsome guy to the next gullible girlfriend, or any acquaintance willing to offer her a sofa and a good time. Jacob is the best thing that's ever happened to that girl – like, ever! And she doesn't even appreciate her good fortune. Someone needs to have a serious talk with that little madam. She's about to become a married woman – it's an opportunity for you to make sure she knows how lucky she is. It can't go on, Rosie!' Lauren's face flushed with annoyance.

As she cowered from the arrows of blame slung by her best friend's words of wisdom, Rosie felt like she had been kicked in the head and the solar plexus at once. Then she began to quail in her pearl-and-sequined stilettos as she watched Lauren's eyes, the colour of Irish luck, narrow.

'If you like, I'll do it. I'll tell her how grown-ups are supposed to act. You're too soft on her gallivanting and selfishness. I'm sorry, Rosie, you're a wet blanket when it comes to baby-blue-eyed and supposedly-innocent Freya; butter wouldn't melt in that rosebud mouth. She does not deserve the sacrifices you've made, are still making, for her. She's an adult now – twenty-two for God's sake. She can take care of herself – and if not, Jacob can. It's your turn, Rosie, to make a life for yourself outside Freya's orbit.'

Lauren's mischievous glint returned, but her eyes softened. After all, she put in the same hours at Harlow Fenton as Rosie did. Of anyone, she understood the pressures of keeping all the plates spinning in the air when the vagaries of the world's stock exchanges ate into their family or leisure time.

'Stop taking responsibility, Rosie. It's not healthy. For either of you.'

Rosie gifted Lauren with a watery smile as she moved over to the sash window where white gauze curtains floated like a bride's veil in the light breeze. Pale tendrils of sunshine breached the horizon as she took in the pristine gardens, battling to calm her emotional demons. Serenity would play for the opposing team on this her beloved sister and Jacob's wedding day, and for that she was saddened. Not only were there a myriad of things that could go awry, despite her meticulous attention to detail in the arduous preparations for this auspicious day, but Lauren was right – Freya's demands *had* increased to scatter-gun proportions since her arrival the previous evening for the rehearsal dinner.

That morning as she had dragged herself from the single bed of her childhood, her limbs stiff and her head pulsating, nausea had twisted knots into her stomach. Her baby sister's wedding day! She should be suffused with joy but, with a jolt of guilt as she stepped into the freezing relief of the shower, she recognised that in the place where happiness should be, loneliness lodged. She was ten years older than Freya and she'd had to almost beg Giles to be her date for her sister's wedding.

Rosie made a huge effort to shake off her melancholy and allowed her shoulders to relax. In her chosen wedding dress and with her loose platinum waves rippling down her back, Freya had presented every inch the Princess Bride image she had coveted since her teenage years. And Lauren, her only true ally, was there to bolster Rosie's flagging spirits and don her matching, saccharine-sweet bridesmaid's dress.

Rosie smiled when she thought back to the impish smile of her best friend, so bohemian in her own choice of attire, at the final dress fitting. Lauren eschewed the emulation of the images distributed in the magazines and fashion corridors of Manhattan of the supposedly-perfect female form. She never counted calories nor fell under the spell of the latest designer-inspired craze. Her idea of a perfect girly afternoon was to trawl the thrift shops on Second and Third Streets, delving into the racks of vintage clothing she could up-cycle. She frequently unearthed pieces of jewellery she could dismantle and reuse. Even her engagement and wedding rings had been 'previously loved', much to Brett's delight. His fire fighter's salary would never stretch as far as Tiffany's.

She truly hoped that Freya had met her Prince Charming and that this was the fairy tale wedding she had wished for. She prayed that she had lost her heart to Jacob, a guy fifteen years her senior; or was she settling for a convenient companion with the means to support her in the manner to which she had become accustomed?

A strain of music floated on the air and her eyes picked out the string quartet – originally a five-piece but now minus the cellist who'd reportedly downed a bottle of Jack Daniel's after an exhilarating performance at the Met the previous evening – as they struck up the first chord of a rendition of 'Dangerously in Love' by Beyoncé, Freya's favourite artist.

A wave of exhaustion threatened to buckle Rosie's knees and she collapsed onto the kidney-shaped stool at the dressing table. Insomnia had plagued her for as long as she could remember but it had been especially potent last night, as the tortuous hours stretched before daybreak. Her perpetual lack of sleep ensured the retention of the dark smudges under her gold-flecked eyes. With a sigh, she realised there would be no rest this weekend either, with the ceremony and then partying until the small hours of the morning to the live band Freya had demanded at huge cost.

As she shook her freshly-teased caramel curls from her eyes, she thought of Giles – the handsome, charismatic, *sexy* man in her life. At last, she allowed a smile to play around her lips as she anticipated a whole weekend on his arm, showing him off to her father and Dot and Arnie who had been so supportive of the family after… after…

Thankfully, the continuation of Rosie's reverie was spliced into by a frantic hammering on the bedroom door, followed by the urgent gravelly tones of her father's voice.

'Rosie? Rosie? Have you seen Freya? The hairdresser needs her and it seems she's done one of her disappearing acts again.'

CHAPTER TWO

Rosie caught Lauren's eye-roll as she rushed to open the door to admit her father. Her heart hammered against her ribcage as a spurt of nausea tickled at her throat. Typical Freya! Hadn't she spent every spare moment of the last three months of her life organising Freya's wedding so that it would run with the military precision she was famed for at the office? All Freya had to do was slip into her dress, plaster a smile on her face and turn up on time! So where was she?

'You didn't tell her about Aunt Bernice, did you?' asked her father. As he leant in to kiss her cheek, Rosie caught a whiff of the baby shampoo her father still used, delivering a painful jolt of nostalgia to her nostrils.

'No, Dad. You know we agreed not to tell her until after the wedding.'

'I'll go and find her, Mr Hamilton. She can't have gone far.' Lauren flicked the sides of her bob behind her ears, hitched up her voluminous skirt and strode from the room.

Rosie registered Jack Hamilton's lined, pale face wreathed in concern. His appearance was so suave in his charcoal-grey morning suit and baby-pink cravat – his back erect, his still-thick silver hair and beard neatly trimmed in honour of his youngest daughter's wedding day. But he had a lot on his mind. Not only did he have the responsibility of walking his beloved daughter down the aisle but it was only the third day in twenty-five years that the Hamilton family's hardware store had been closed to the service of Stonington Beach residents and curious tourists bemoaning the disappearance of such Aladdin's caves in their home towns.

She recalled the pang of regret she'd experienced at the previous evening's dress rehearsal when she witnessed her father's slower, more deliberate movements. It had occurred to her that now Freya was to be married, she should maybe consider returning to Stonington Beach to take care of her father and help him in the store which, she'd noticed with a stab of concern, was looking a little shabby around the edges. Jack needed more help than Dot, now herself in her sixties. Would such a step-change relieve her of her constant anxiety about her father's health, the stalking fear that she'd lose him too? Would it alleviate the weight of apprehension that pressed against her chest, maybe even allow her to make some of those human connections she found so elusive in Manhattan?

Gosh, no!

Having taken a year's sabbatical to care for Jack and
Freya after her mother's passing, she had proceeded
to squeeze every last ounce of knowledge from her
studies at college and business school, squirreling away
every morsel of offered wisdom into the recesses of
her mind for future extraction. Why should she even
be contemplating allowing it to drain away into a
small town hardware store? New York City had many
flaws, but she adored its vigour and vanity, its tenacity
and traumas. The only tinge of sorrow that day was
the absence of their beloved mother, but her presence
would be with them all in the hollows of their hearts.

There had been no thanks from her sister for the long
months of grief Rosie had endured in organising this
spectacular occasion from one hundred and thirty miles
away. For giving up numerous weekends to travel out to
Connecticut to taste and select the menus, to advise on
table décor and choice of linen, flower arrangements, wine
lists, whilst Freya was just looking after number one.

A conversation with Dot popped into her mind; Dot
had hugged her goodbye and noticed the deep hollows
of tiredness around Rosie's eyes. 'I hope once this
fiasco of a wedding has finally taken place, it won't
mean your visits down to Stonington Beach will be
any less frequent, darling?' Dot had said. 'Jack adores
having your sharp professional eye run over the store.
No other business in Stonington can boast a high-flying
New York City executive bestowing regular financial

advice upon its eaves and coffers. We love you here, Rosie. Don't be a stranger.'

A second wave of dizziness enveloped Rosie and she slumped down onto the pale blue sateen duvet. Her mind had suddenly seized. Her father managed a tight smile and joined her, resting his hand on her arm. She saw he was studying her as she fiddled with the huge gold hoop earrings Freya had presented both she and Lauren with that morning. Freya had mistaken Lauren's look of abject horror as that of shock at the level of her generosity. Rosie prayed her photograph would never, ever appear in any publication covering the Jacob Bennett, Jr and Freya Hamilton wedding. She would struggle to live down the fashion shame. She felt and looked like a gawky teenager.

'All this will happen for you one day, darling. You're so like your mother, worrying about everything and everyone. You've pulled off a miracle today, organising this wedding for Freya and Jacob.' His eyes sought out hers. 'She's gorgeous, but so are you. You need to take some time for yourself now, darling. That crazy job of yours is squeezing all the sparkle from your eyes. I can see how tired you are, even if your mirror speaks differently to you. You career girls don't understand what you're leaving behind in your blinkered pursuit of corporate acceptance. Manhattan demands insane hours and produces crazy people, their dreams skewed by their ever-increasing obsession with stockpiling the dollars.

'You need to slow down, Rosie. Take some time to smell those flowers you and your mother were named after. Get dating, meet your own Jacob who will love and nurture you. Goodness knows you deserve it.'

He held her to him, his familiar smell mingled with the tang of a forbidden cigar. Rosie didn't trust herself to respond with any opposing argument.

'I wish Mum were here to witness how proud I am of you both today. I've missed her every single day of the last fourteen years. But her love lingers on in the crevices of our hearts. The passage of time has no favourites, Rosie, it treats us all equally. But I knew your mum for thirty years before that disease stole her from her family and she would have wanted all this for you too – a happy life, not a slave to the accumulation of wealth for people who have more than enough to service several lifetimes already.'

Her father knew he'd struck a chord. 'Promise me and your mum that it won't be years before I walk down that aisle again? It was a promise I made to her before she left us that I would see you both settled before I, well… Hey, there are some great guys who come into the store. Want me to fix you up with a date?'

'Dad!'

'Look, Rosie, I'm sorry I can't go to the UK for Bernice's funeral. I would have loved to have seen Devon one last time.' Tears threatened to mist Jack's lashes for the first time on that emotional day. The sadness in her father's eyes sent a shard of panic through Rosie's heart. Was he hiding a health issue? Was there a secret he was protecting her from, another evil incursion by an incurable disease poised to steal away her only parent?

'It's okay, Rosie. I'm just tired. Long hours in the store, you know.' Her father failed to see the irony of this last sentence, having spent the last ten minutes lecturing and berating his daughter against the vices of corporate Manhattan and her solitary lifestyle.

'Rose adored Bernice, you know.' His kind, wise eyes clouded as he grasped Rosie's hand in his, its paper-thin skin stretched and liberally flecked with age spots. 'But she wished her sister had found a partner to spend her life with. Don't end your days like Bernice, Rosie.'

'Are you sure there's no way you can close the store for the week whilst you go to the UK? Maybe the break from the routine will do you good?'

'It's not the store, Rosie.' The look on her father's face caused Rosie's heart to contract and a giant fist squeezing the air from her lungs. 'To be honest, I'm not sure I could manage the trip. It's a long flight, and what with the jet lag and... well. I know how much Bernice meant to you, darling. I'm sure she would understand why we can't attend the funeral, what with the store and Freya on honeymoon and your work commitments. The UK is more than an arduous car ride away.'

With huge effort, Rosie refocused on the present. She glanced down into her lap where her slender fingers were entwined with her father's arthritic ones. Her heart ballooned with love for him and the support he had given her and Freya. She knew he had struggled at times with the gargantuan task of raising two young girls – Rosie was eighteen but Freya had only just turned eight – whilst coping with his own grief. Her unconditional love for him had been one of the reasons she had so swiftly slotted her toes into her mother's shoes to care for Freya – to help to alleviate his suffering in any way she could.

And now Freya was to become a married woman. Rosie adored her sister. Throughout her childhood she had braided her hair, mopped her brow when she was sick, played hostess to her school friends, baked cookies, dressed her up in home-stitched Halloween costumes. She had protected her from every adolescent disaster she could, even forgiven Freya for 'borrowing' her favourite cocktail dress – which she had cut up for a fancy dress outfit.

She truly hoped Freya had found her soul mate. Jacob was a great guy – girls would ditch their grannies for a husband like him. When she had met Jacob, Rosie and Lauren had dragged out their personalised wish lists of essential criteria for potential dates and performed a meticulous comparison with Jacob's plethora of assets: he'd scored favourably with both girls. He offered Freya a life she could only have dreamed of when she'd crawled home destitute from her extravagant exploits in the party capitals of Europe. Having expended every couch-surfing opportunity from the Atlantic to the Adriatic and squeezed every last ounce of enjoyment from her itinerant lifestyle, she'd been forced to return home to Connecticut.

Rosie would do anything to make life easier for Freya. She had endured more than her fair share of pain in her life and didn't deserve to suffer further. And anyway, after her father, her little sister was all she had left of her family. But was she proud of what she had produced? Had she, and her father, over-protected her? Had they been complicit in preventing her from learning how to stand on her own two feet, how to deal with the grenades that life threw in her path?

'Come on Dad. You go down to the garden to reassure Jacob and the rest of the congregation that Freya hasn't run off with the best man and I'll join Lauren in the search.' She witnessed the look of horror gallop across her father's tired features and regretted her flippancy. After all, Freya was a saint in her father's eyes, not the flighty little madam Rosie had been covering for over the last ten years.

'Joking, Dad.' She rose from the bed and placed her hand on his shoulder whilst she stooped to drop a kiss on his cheek. 'Don't worry. Everything is going to be fine.'

But still the butterflies played an active game of tennis in her stomach.

CHAPTER THREE

Jack and Rosie descended the impressive sweeping staircase to be met by a frantic Lauren, hopping from one foot to the other like a toddler in need of a visit to the bathroom.

'No sign of her! It seems Little Miss Superior has melted into thin air, the selfish…' Lauren flicked her eyes from Rosie to Jack and relented on her character assassination of the errant bride-to-be.

'Don't worry, Lauren. Will you escort Dad to the garden for me? Try and placate Jacob and the rest of the guests.' Rosie checked her mother's silver Tiffany watch – her most adored possession. 'Technically, the ceremony is not due to start for another thirty minutes so there's nothing to panic about yet. I'm sure she's just taking a quiet moment to prepare herself for the most important day of her life.'

Rosie heard the expulsion of air from Lauren's lips and saw the smirk around her mouth. She swapped a grin with her friend. Freya adored being the centre of attention, had been milking every opportunity to loiter in the limelight. It was inconceivable that she would hide away for even a second. Rosie had been genuinely concerned that, despite her promises, her sister would be unable to resist a quick visit to Jacob's suite in her bridal gown. Indeed, she suspected that was where she was now.

She shooshed Lauren and her father out of the French doors. Her eyes swept the congregation assembled on the lush, manicured lawn of Stonington Meadows Country Park Hotel, the venue Freya had dreamed of during her childhood forays into planning her perfect wedding celebrations. It had been an incredible surprise to Rosie when Freya had shunned Jacob's offer to pay for their wedding to be held at the Plaza, but then, as Freya explained, everyone had their wedding there. To her right, in neat white picket chairs, every seat was occupied by Jacob's extended family, friends and business connections. Their elegant attire, like the car park, oozed dollars. To her left sprawled a more eclectic gathering of those connected to the bride. Rosie spotted Arnie and Dot, her parents' closest and dearest friends, along with a smattering of Stonington Beach friends invited to share his daughter's special day.

She turned on her heels – a pair of five inch, ivory silk Louboutins that had cost almost a month's salary but which she planned to mount in a glass case to appreciate as a true work of sculptural art after the wedding – and headed up the stairs to the bridal suite.

She knocked and when there was no reply, she pushed open the door. Gosh, her sister could bring chaos to an empty room! Her belongings were strewn on every available surface, she had even opened the drawers of the elegant, kidney-shaped dressing table to drape her discarded hosiery over. A quick sweep of her eyes told Rosie that Freya was not there.

Yet her wedding dress still hung in its plastic carrier on the front of the gaping wardrobe door. Where on earth was she? Wherever she was she must still be in the cream silk kimono Jacob had presented her with the previous evening, her hair in the huge Velcro rollers their hairdresser, Carl, had fussed over that morning.

Rosie dashed over to the window and peered down into the garden. Everyone was there now, and had taken up their positions ready for the imminent arrival of the bride. Even the minister, a local ginger-haired man with a comical comb-over who had christened both Rosie and Freya, was surreptitiously checking his fob watch.

'Oh, God! Trust Freya!' muttered Rosie, her heart drumming at her ribcage and her breath quickening as panic began to swirl through her veins, depriving her lungs of essential oxygen. 'The only thing she had to do was put on her bloody dress and turn up on time!'

Was that too much to ask? Yes, she guessed it was.

She sprinted out of the room and into the corridor, cursing as she wrenched her ankle running in her unfamiliar shoes. As she reached down to rub the pain away, a tinkle of laughter emanated from a door at the end of the corridor which Rosie had assumed was a linen closet next to the glass cube masquerading as an elevator.

She paused, straining her ears, and her heart softened. A smile tugged at the corners of her lips. Freya was most likely snatching a few moments before the craziness of the wedding with the guy who had swept her off her feet. They must have got carried away and forgotten the time. Freya always *had* operated on a different time zone to everyone else. She replaced her smarting foot on the floor and tiptoed towards the door. As she drew nearer, her hand hovering over the ornate brass door knob, a deep-throated groan floated to her ears.

Rosie froze. Why had level-headed, reliable Jacob agreed to bunk off from his duties of herding his relatives for a snatched sojourn of delight with his fiancée, thirty minutes before the ceremony? Oh, God! And here she was about to blunder in without even knocking!

Her face glowed with embarrassment as she cracked open the door and pulled it towards her. She stood immobilised in the doorway, mesmerised by the glistening bronzed back and the hint of incongruously white orb buttocks. She opened her mouth to announce her presence but words refused to form in her scrambled mind or on her lips, which were parting like a gobsmacked goldfish. She began to retrace her steps until her shoulder bumped into the door jamb, forcing out a gasp of pain, not from the collision but from the dawning recognition of the owner of the muscled torso.

'God, Sis, don't you ever knock?'

The man coiling his arms around her sister's body twisted his head towards the interruption and mirrored Rosie's horrified expression.

'Giles!'

ACKNOWLEDGEMENTS

A huge thank you to my family and friends for their love and understanding (and tea and cake) when I'm holed up in my writer's cave. I promise to make it up to you.

And a special thank you to the team at Carina UK, especially my editor, Charlotte, for their support and encouragement as well as the gorgeous book covers! It's a pleasure to work with such lovely people.

Need more Daisy James?

A deliciously enchanting read, *The Runaway Bridesmaid* is set to steal readers' hearts and keep them guessing until the very last page!

Squeezing herself into a frothy, flouncy, bubble-gum pink dress, Rosie Hamilton thinks that being a bridesmaid for her spoilt little sister Freya can't get any worse.

But discovering her boyfriend in a cupboard with the bride, ten minutes before Freya is due to say 'I do', is the icing on the sequinned wedding cake – and Rosie's cue to pack her bags.

Swapping her Louboutins for Wellingtons, Rosie throws her bridesmaid bouquet in the air and flies from bustling New York to sleepy Devon. Now, for the first time in her life, and with the help of her beloved Aunt's diaries, Rosie must put herself first for a change – and decide what *she* really wants…

CARINA™

🐦 **@daisyjamesbooks**

Welcome to the Lonely Hearts Travel Club

Follow Georgia in the *Lonely Hearts Travel Club* series
as she travels the world.

**The new favourite series for fans of *Bridget Jones's
Diary*, the *Shopaholic* series and *Eat, Pray, Love*.**

'Katy writes with humour and heart. The Lonely Hearts
Travel Club is like **Bridget Jones goes backpacking.**'
- Holly Martin, author of *The White Cliff Bay* series

The perfect wedding that never was...

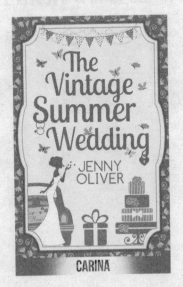

Years ago Anna Whitehall pirouetted out of her cosy home-town village in a whirl of ambition to fulfil her childhood dream of becoming a prima ballerina. Now she's back in Nettleton with fiancé Seb, their wedding and careers postponed indefinitely...

This one summer is showing Anna that your dreams have to grow up with you. And sometimes what you think you wanted is just the opposite of what makes you happy...

Don't miss the brilliant sequel to
The Parisian Christmas Bake Off

Out now in print

CARINA™

0315_C4